Sometii

When Summer Mackenzie and her boyfriend disappear in the fog-shrouded forests of Northern California, it sets off more than one alarm. The sheriff's department is looking for them, the state rangers are on their trail, and even private security companies have gotten involved.

But Summer wasn't an ordinary college student; she was a human born into the immortal Mackenzie clan, a line of powerful vampires from the Great Smoky Mountains. Now Carwyn ap Bryn and Brigid Connor are getting messages from allies across the world, old rivals, and new friends, all wanting to know where Summer is and why hikers along the Lost Coast keep going missing.

If Brigid and Carwyn can't find Summer, tensions between vampire clans might snap, leaving more than just the immortal world bloody.

They might know how to search the wilderness, but the Northern California woods hold more than the average share of mysteries. Secretive immortals, suspicious humans, and ancient myths are all at home in a land where human highways come to a dead end and dense forests meet a rugged coast.

Martyr's Promise is a supernatural mystery in the Elemental Covenant series by Elizabeth Hunter, *USA Today* best-selling author of *A Hidden Fire*, *Suddenly Psychic*, and over forty other works of fantasy fiction.

PRAISE FOR THE ELEMENTAL COVENANT

This story had heart pounding intensity and sweet harmony written in flawless execution.

THIS LITERARY LIFE

It's mysterious, romantic, and full of faith, hope, and love. Carwyn and Brigid are perfect for each other.

NORMA'S NOOK

Is it too cheesy to call this an explosive new series? Because, well... as it turns out, when you have a fire *and* an earth elemental vampire teaming up to solve a mystery, things can get... rocky.

KATHRYN, GOODREADS REVIEWER

MARTYR'S PROMISE

ELEMENTAL COVENANT BOOK TWO

ELIZABETH HUNTER

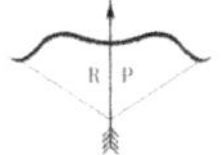

Come, heart, where hill is heaped upon hill:
For there the mystical brotherhood
Of sun and moon and hollow and wood
And river and stream work out their will;

And God stands winding His lonely horn,
And time and the world are ever in flight;
And love is less kind than the gray twilight,
And hope is less dear than the dew of the morn.

WILLIAM BUTLER YEATS, "INTO THE TWILIGHT"

Martyr's Promise
Copyright © 2021
Elizabeth Hunter
ISBN: 978-1941674710

Cover: Damonza
Content Editor: Amy Cissell, Cissell Ink
Line Editor: Anne Victory, Victory Editing
Proofreader: Linda, Victory Editing
Beta reader: Bee M. Whelan

Recurve Press LLC
PO Box 4034
Visalia, California 93278
USA

ONE

Summer Mackenzie watched the waves slowly recede from the ash-grey pebbles tucked against the sweep of the foggy California coast. She turned to her right, keeping an eye on the trail where her boyfriend Dani had detoured to look for a campsite.

Low tide wouldn't be for another six hours, which meant the current leg of their route was impassible until early morning. It would require at least five hours to finish the stretch of trail that took them closest along the beach, and they needed daylight. Summer had learned long ago that you didn't go into the forest at night.

She'd grown up in Appalachia, and even though she'd been away from those ancient rolling hills of North Carolina for three years, she knew better than to disrespect the woods.

Summer heard Dani before she saw him. Her boyfriend of a year might have been an incredible athlete—with the soccer scholarship to prove it—but he wasn't a woodsman.

Dani smiled widely when he saw her, and it still left her a

little breathless. "I found the perfect spot. Come, you should see this."

He wasn't as tall as some of the guys she'd dated, but his shoulders were broad, his hair fell to his shoulders in thick black waves, and his smile could light up the world. He was so handsome sometimes she still did a double take.

Summer was short and, when she was little, often mistaken for a boy with her grubby knees and dirty face. Luckily, her boobs had eventually gotten a little bigger and she wore her red curls long, so the days of someone taking her for a boy were long gone. Even though she still had grubby knees more often than not.

Summer smiled at Dani's enthusiasm. "The perfect spot, huh?"

"Definitely." He held out his hand. "You are going to love this one."

Summer was tempted to leave her pack near the beach, but if Dani had really found a prime camping spot, she didn't want to backtrack, and there was no way they were staying that close to the water; the waves along California's Lost Coast had a mind of their own.

Summer hoisted her bag over her shoulder and followed Dani between two pines. "So what's so special about this spot? There's a clear camping area up on that last bluff that was all leveled off."

He turned, his smile still vibrant. "Trust me. I know you think I don't know anything about camping, but—"

"I have never said that," Summer protested. "I just know you didn't grow up in the woods like me. Your knowledge of soccer—"

"Football."

"Football." She rolled her eyes. "Your football trivia is expert level. I'm just saying that when it comes to what bugs you can eat in a survival situation, I have skills."

Dani grabbed her hand. "Summer, please stay with me so you will never eat bugs again."

She couldn't hide her smile. "So romantic."

"Just follow me, *mi sol*, and you will see."

When Daniel Uriarte first moved from his high-rise in Mexico City to the rainy streets of Seattle, his idea of an outdoor adventure had been relaxing at a beach resort while a waiter brought him a cold beer. Little by little, Summer had worn him down.

She followed Dani as he led her along a slightly worn path leading into the trees, his broad shoulders carrying a bright orange pack as if it weighed nothing.

Since they'd met, Summer had turned Dani from a total city boy into an outdoor enthusiast. They fished, they hiked, and they'd even backpacked a little. He loved boats, and his family had more than one.

Or maybe they were more like yachts?

Ugh. Rich-people vocabulary was confusing.

"How far back is this site?" She looked at the brush that was giving way to denser forest.

"Not too far."

Summer couldn't even imagine the level of wealth that Dani's family enjoyed. In truth, it was starting to become a Thing They Didn't Talk About. They had been dating a year, but she hadn't met Dani's parents, and he hadn't met hers. When any of their mutual friends happened to bring up family stuff, they both changed the subject.

Summer had been raised by a high school math teacher

and a musician in rural North Carolina. Her father had taught her how to hunt and fish—along with her times tables—and her mother had taught her the guitar and how to cook anything out of everything. They were a traditional clan who took pride in hard work, loyalty, and self-sufficiency.

She had no idea how they'd react to their daughter dating the heir of one of the largest tile empires in Mexico. Half the time, she didn't know how to react herself.

Dani walked between another set of trees, stopped, and spread out his arms. "Voilà!" He glanced at Summer, whose mouth was agape. "You see, I knew you would love this."

Love… wasn't the right word. Summer turned in a circle, her eyes scanning the obviously manmade clearing in the middle of the woods.

A nearly perfect circle of tall pines soared into the sky, their tops obscured by a layer of marine fog. As she stood in the center, she looked up and saw the sun disappear behind a cloud.

Dani was crouched in the center of the clearing, kneeling beside the old stone fireplace in the middle. "It's perfect, yes? Some local family must camp here."

No, this was not a family campground.

The dense forest suddenly felt claustrophobic, and Summer felt eyes peering at her through the trees. There was something out there. Something was watching them.

Don't stare into the trees unless they know your face. Her grandmother's whisper tugged at her ear, warning her to leave the clearing.

Summer walked over, grabbed Dani's shoulder, and tugged. "Come on. Let's go back to the trail."

Dani stood and frowned. "What are you talking about?

This is the perfect spot! The area around the campfire is so clear and level. I checked for poison oak." He pointed at the fireplace. "See? There is even some wood left over from the last people who stayed here."

It wasn't even a firepit; it was a full-out dressed-stone stove with grates in the bottom for wood and braces on either side to hang pots over the flames. This wasn't natural—it wasn't even foraged.

This was a lure.

"Dani, just trust me, we shouldn't stay here." Instinct told her that they were being watched. "I think we should head back to the trail, okay?"

Dani looked toward the ocean. "We're not far from it. You can see the ocean from here." He turned toward the coast. "I bet you could even see a fire from the marked trail. And people come back here." He pointed to the trail that had led them into the circle of trees. "See?"

She couldn't explain it, and she loved that he'd found what to any sensible eye seemed like a great spot. "It just... it feels very visible. Everyone can see us."

Dani set his pack down and sat on a piece of log that circled the fireplace. "Summer, everyone we've met on the trail has been so cool. We have to camp until the morning, right? We might as well put our tent in a clear spot with a firepit that someone has already prepared."

Was she just being stubborn? Paranoid? Granted, her family made it hard to discount the mythological, but she was probably overreacting.

Dani stood and held out his arms. "Listen, even if you are right and people can see us, so what? They can see us just as easily from the bluff on that last hill. We're the only human beings out here, we have our bear repellent, and I am tired." His arms dropped. "Please. Can this one thing be easy?"

She looked over her shoulder at the marked trail, then over at the well-worn path through the brush, the forest, and into the clearing. This was obviously a well-used spot on the trail, and the rangers did request that they keep to used camping spots instead of creating their own.

"Okay." She kept her voice small. "But we're pitching our tent right by the fire. I don't want to be near the edge. If something gets into this clearing, I want some advance notice."

THEY'D STOPPED FAR SOONER than they usually did, so they had plenty of time to cook a full meal with the supplies they'd brought along plus some sea lettuce and large limpets Summer foraged on the nearest beach.

After they'd eaten, Dani pulled out a bottle of whiskey and poured a little into both their camping cups. "We're going to sleep well tonight."

"We are." With the tents set up and the coals glowing, Summer was starting to feel as if she'd been paranoid earlier. Sure, they hadn't seen anyone else on the trail since the day before, but it was September and tourist traffic was pretty low.

She leaned back against Dani's chest as he propped himself against a fallen log and stared into the fire. "Did you pack up all the food?"

"Yes." He patted his pack, which held the bear canister they were required to bring. "I'll hang it from one of the trees before we go to bed."

Summer was full from a hot dinner and the whiskey that warmed her throat. She felt herself drifting, and the sounds of the forest at night settled around them. Crickets hummed, and a few night birds started calling. She heard an owl hoot in the distance, and the faint sounds of the sea crashing on the rocks below them lulled her into sleep.

She woke when Dani moved.

"Come on," he said. "Tent time."

She groaned but forced herself up to sitting and rubbed her eyes. She reached for the portable motion sensor that her father had bought for her and set it within range of their tent door; then she went inside to find the small remote and set it.

"Your burglar alarm." Dani smiled as he entered the tent. "Do you think the bears will be scared away?"

"I just like knowing if I need to wake up." She smiled and tucked the remote into a mesh pocket in the tent. If anything tripped it, the remote would beep. Not loud enough to wake Dani, but Summer had always slept light.

"You're worse than Ignacio." Dani stripped off his flannel shirt and shuffled into his sleeping bag, wearing only his pants and a thermal shirt. "There is less wind here than by the beach."

"I know. It might be warmer." Nevertheless, Summer kept her pants and socks on. If a bear—or anything else—attacked the tent, she wanted her shoes on in seconds, not minutes.

Dani rolled toward Summer, put his arm around her waist, and tugged her sleeping bag toward his until she could feel his warm breath near her neck. "Sleep well, Sunshine."

Summer smiled at his affectionate nickname and closed her eyes.

In minutes, she was asleep.

THE BEEPING WAS INSISTENT. Her eyes flew open and her heart was already racing.

"What is that?" Low voices outside the tent.

She sat up, put a hand over Dani's mouth, and nudged his shoulder until his eyes flew open. He frowned and moved to pull her hand away, but the voices spoke again.

"A phone maybe?"

"There's nothing out here that can get a signal." The voices were matter-of-fact. Bored, even.

Summer shook her head and put a finger over her lips as she removed her hand from Dani's mouth. He nodded, understanding the need for silence.

Their tent was a typical backpacking tent, small and compact. Easy to pack and set up, but there was no room to move around without being heard.

Something shook the top of their tent, and Dani sat up.

"Wakey-wakey," the voice said, amusement coloring the words. "Come on out, neighbors."

Summer knew these were no friendly woodsmen. Dani took the canister of bear spray from his pack as Summer removed her hunting knife from its sheath. They slipped out of their sleeping bags. Summer shoved her feet in her hiking boots, and Dani did the same. She eyed her jacket in the corner and took the calculated risk of setting her knife down for a second to put it on. Dani put his on as well.

Don't move. Make them come to you. Waste their energy, not yours. Her father's voice was the one whispering to her now. Her father, who'd been raised by monsters, knew what he was talking about.

A flashlight beam moved around the tent, and Summer concluded that there were two men stalking them. Well… two somethings. Humans were the most obvious, but not the only choice.

Dani whispered, "Summer—"

"Shhhh."

"Oho." A man outside chuckled. "I think the city birds are awake."

"Come on out, little birds." The flashlight moved to the tent opening and didn't move. "Don't make us come in there to get you. That'll just irritate me."

Where were the voices from? Summer tried to decipher an accent, but she couldn't. It was flat—California speech with just a hint of surfer.

Dani's hand gripped Summer's, and he kept the bear spray aimed at the exit of the tent. If he let it off in an enclosed area, they'd be weeping and sick, but hopefully whomever Dani hit with the spray would get the nastier end.

The zipper on the tent started to move. "Come on out now."

Fingers were visible at the entrance now, fat callused fingers with curly black hair on the knuckles.

Dani looked at her with panicked eyes. Summer took a deep breath and tried to breathe through the rush of adrenaline that was starting to course. She held up a hand for him.

Wait.

She motioned to the bear spray and then the tent flap.

Spray them when it opens.

Dani nodded.

Summer pointed her knife at the back of the tent and made a slashing motion. If Dani sprayed the person trying to come into the tent, she'd rip open the back and they could escape away from the sprayed men.

Dani nodded again and took another deep breath.

"You going to be stubborn, are you?" The owner of the voice was losing patience. "Fine, I'm coming in. No funny business; I don't want to hurt you."

Bullshit.

The tent zipper was ripped open, and a bright light glared in their eyes.

"Now!" Summer shouted before she took a deep breath.

Dani leaned forward and let the bear spray stream into the intruder as Summer slashed through the back of the tent, ripping down and away twice to open a flap large enough to let them both out. She scrambled out of the reeking canvas, her eyes already flooded with tears.

Dani had thrown the bear spray canister at the men coming into the tent when they started screaming, and he scrambled out after her.

She clutched her jacket around her and tried to make her steps wide enough that she wouldn't trip over her untied boots.

"Back to the trail." She was coughing and sneezing at once, her body desperate to rid itself of the toxic fumes they'd used to escape. She heard Dani running behind her, wheezing from the bear spray.

Summer used her adrenaline to jump over logs and rocks, heading toward the ocean and the open expanse of coastal bluffs. She could see a light in the camping area on the last bluff they'd passed. If they could just make it there—

"Summer!"

She turned and saw Dani on the ground a few yards

behind her. She ran back to help him up and saw a black-handled knife sticking out of his shoulder.

"Shit!"

"Go." His voice was a painful rasp. "Run!"

She looked up and realized it was too late. Three men were running after them, and none of them were laughing anymore. Summer rose and held her hunting knife in front of her.

The largest one leaned down and grabbed Dani by the leg, pulling him toward them as if he weighed nothing. They were great, hulking shadows in the darkness, three men with broad shoulders and square heads.

Another one of the men yanked the knife out of Dani's shoulder, and he groaned in pain. Summer's knife rose, but she didn't move. The men had Dani; she couldn't leave him.

"Drop the knife please." The largest shadow spoke calmly. He was not crying like the other men, nor did he move the same way. Something about him was... different.

As soon as she felt the ground beneath her move ever so slightly, she knew exactly why this one was different. "I know what you are." She lowered the knife.

Know when to run and when to wait.

She'd never outrun him, never overpower him. Any human attack was a waste of her energy and would only endanger her more. "We're the wrong prey for you."

"Oh?" A slight hint of amusement.

"They'll look for me if I disappear."

The vampire stepped out of the shadows and into the light of the full moon. His fangs gleamed in the darkness as he smiled.

"They all say that."

TWO

Carwyn ap Bryn flexed his hand at the top of the steering wheel as his large converted van wound up the twisting coastal road, heading for a remote research outpost on the edge of the Pacific Ocean. Curling fog raced past their headlights as the road narrowed and traced the Pacific bluffs.

"How much longer?" Brigid asked.

"Maybe an hour or so." He glanced at his wife and vampire mate. "Did you feed already?"

"I did." She nodded toward their small kitchen. "Had myself a pint of the preserved blood in the cooler."

"Good." At over a thousand years old, Carwyn only needed to feed deeply once or twice a month, but Brigid was barely a decade old; her need for human blood was more regular than his.

Brigid looked over her shoulder. "This caravan was a grand idea, old man."

"Every so often I come up with one."

"So you've reached your quota for the year then?"

He reached over and pinched his woman's thigh. "Minx."

"Mountain."

He flexed his shoulders. "And?"

They had spent nearly six months in Southern California, floating from one friend's house to another's and waiting for their van to be customized.

They weren't the typical couple for van life. He, a broadly built earth vampire with flaming red hair and a habit of making himself even more conspicuous by wearing garish Hawaiian shirts, and she, a small, black-haired pixie with a suspicious expression and a penchant for firearms and ripped black clothing.

They didn't exactly blend in at most campgrounds.

Then again, Carwyn had spent over a thousand years figuring out what set humans at ease, and Brigid had been human roughly ten years ago, so blending in was easier for them than it was for others.

To secure the van, they'd built alarms, light-safe shutters, and hiding places into the vehicle along with a false door on the bottom of the caravan where Carwyn could escape in emergencies, tunneling under the ground to safety should danger approach.

Brigid's special requests mostly involved various gun safes built into discreet corners.

She was staring at an old-fashioned road atlas as Carwyn steered the van. "This area all the way up here" —she pointed at a dense green splotch— "this is where we're going?"

"Eventually."

She looked up. "No roads?"

Carwyn smiled. "A few small ones. No highway. They call it the Lost Coast. The road engineers got to that part of the

Pacific Coast when they were building the highway and decided it was too rugged to build the interstate, so they diverted the route inland. Now there are only a few local roads going through that part of the forest to some isolated towns."

While most people considered San Francisco Northern California, the city lay just a little over halfway up the state that stretched along the western North American coast. Above it, the vast and often wild reaches of the Pacific Coast Range stretched into Oregon, blanketed by a network of protected forests, small towns, and river valleys.

"You love that, don't you?" Brigid was a fire vampire, so she preferred cities where electricity was plentiful and her surroundings weren't overly flammable.

Carwyn's amnis belonged to the earth, which meant not only did he draw his energy from the ground, he delighted in wild, untouched places. "Yes, I do love that."

"How dry is it?"

"Not dry. In fact, it's nicely foggy, especially this time of the year."

"Thank the Lord," Brigid said. "Last thing I need is a forest fire on my conscience."

Carwyn smiled. "I believe you're safe in that. I know you prefer the city, but don't you think it's right and fair there are places in the world where Mother Nature has told humans to kindly fuck off?"

Brigid pursed her lips. "Only five percent of the ocean has been explored."

"Now you sound like a water vampire, bragging like that."

The corner of her mouth turned up. "I won't remind Baojia if the subject comes up."

"Please don't."

They were going to "visit" a couple of old friends, though Carwyn already knew their friends harbored ulterior motives for the invitation.

Baojia was a water vampire who'd been born a couple of centuries before in mainland China but had lived most of his immortal life in California. He was currently the security chief for Katya Grigorieva, the water vampire who was in charge of Northern California and most of the Pacific Northwest. Baojia was also married to an old friend of Carwyn's who'd been mortal up until a few years ago. They had two delightfully feral children that Carwyn loved to spoil and then hand back to their parents.

Brigid wasn't keen on most children until they were tall enough that she could look them in the eye, but she was fond of Baojia's mate, Natalie Ellis, so she humored the little ones. Up until her turning, Natalie had been an investigative reporter for a newspaper in San Francisco, but daylight and her new diet were proving to be challenges while maintaining a byline. Natalie was unemployed at the moment, though hoping she'd eventually be able to return.

Brigid and Natalie both had Irish roots, hot tempers, and a passion for helping those who couldn't help themselves, which was why Natalie had called Brigid the week before.

"How long have these two young people been missing?" Carwyn asked.

"I'm not sure. Less than a month."

"Less than a month." Carwyn frowned. "Hopefully far less than that."

"People go missing all the time," Brigid said. "Some people *want* to be lost. Not that I'm worried Natalie would waste our time, but I do wonder what makes this girl special enough to have caught the attention of Katya's security chief."

Carwyn reached for her hand and squeezed her knuckles. "I suppose we'll find out, won't we?"

CARWYN LOOKED at the picture in the file Baojia handed him. With her fair skin, freckles, and dark red curls, the young woman could pass for Carwyn's younger sister or any one of his massive human clan spread across the world.

"Her name is Summer Marianne Mackenzie." Natalie spoke from across the kitchen table, her wispy red hair pulled up into a messy bun. In jogging pants and a T-shirt, she'd dressed for family and not official company. "She's been missing for two weeks."

Carwyn could hear the waves crashing in the distance as he handed the picture of the freckle-faced woman to Brigid.

Natalie and Baojia's converted farmhouse overlooked the ocean but was set back from the cliffs, and the evening fog filled the air with the scent of salt, cypress, and dried kelp. It was a pungent smell but not unwelcome to an earth vampire. Carwyn was naturally suspicious of any place that didn't have a distinctive smell.

"Jaysus." Brigid stared at the girl's picture. "She looks like one of yours, doesn't she?"

Natalie smiled. "I had the same thought. Redheads are getting rarer these days. She could be related to either of us."

He stared at the girl's picture. "Lots of Celtic blood in Appalachia." He let out a long breath and turned to Natalie. "Someone's missing her, I think."

Natalie nodded. "Yeah. Yeah, they are."

Carwyn had always felt brotherly toward Natalie, whom he'd met when she was still a girl in university, and now he felt it even more strongly as the woman had been sired by an earth vampire.

Baojia sat next to his wife and put a hand on her back. "Summer's family has immortal connections. That's why we called you."

"Her father and mother are frantic," Natalie said. "And her extended family is convinced there's foul play involved."

Brigid set the file down and leaned her elbows on the table. "So they called Katya? They must be *somebodies* then."

Baojia nodded. "She's under the aegis of the Mackenzies on the East Coast."

"The Mackenzies?" Carwyn sat up straight. "Logan Mackenzie's brood?"

Baojia nodded.

"Mackenzie?" Brigid turned to him. "Are they related to Cathy?"

"Aye, and I'll be sending a message to her before dawn. She'll murder me otherwise." Cathy Mackenzie was Carwyn's daughter-in-law, mated to a son in Scotland. "We'll help, Baojia. No questions asked. The girl is family."

Brigid put her hand on his arm. "Actually, please ignore that. We need to ask a lot of questions."

"Fine, in an investigative sense, yes." Carwyn added, "Lots of questions."

"I knew we could count on you two." Natalie smiled and put her hands around a bright blue mug.

"What was she doing all the way out west?" Brigid asked.

Natalie sipped her tea. "Summer has been studying

forestry at a university in Seattle for the past three years, so she's not a stranger to the area."

Brigid opened the file again and started taking notes in a notebook she'd pulled from her back pocket. "She's been in Katya's territory for quite a while then."

"Yes." Baojia was mainly in charge of California, but Katya's territory stretched from Seattle down to San Francisco, and any vampire or human under vampire aegis would be required to make their presence known.

Baojia continued. "I checked the records at the office after her family called. I never met her, but Summer has traveled in California a lot, mostly for vacation. She's an experienced hiker, backpacker, and hunter. This trail she took shouldn't have been an issue for her even if she was with a less experienced hiker."

Carwyn asked, "Has she ever had any run-ins with our lot? Does she hang out at vampire places or—?"

"According to her father, she sticks to human companions unless they're family. He trained her to be cautious of vampires. But she always follows protocol when she's here. Alerts my office, keeps us updated if she stays longer than planned. Which is why when Logan Mackenzie reached out to Katya, I took it seriously."

Brigid was taking notes as they talked. "What were her plans for this trip?"

"Summer said she and her boyfriend—no immortal connections—would be hiking the northern leg of the Lost Coast Trail for around a week and then heading back to Washington a couple of days after that."

"And that was two weeks ago?"

"Eleven days now," he said. "They were supposed to reach

Shelter Cove eleven days ago. Had a shuttle all arranged to take them back to their vehicle at the start of the trail and everything. They didn't show."

Carwyn's instincts prickled. "And the shuttle driver didn't report it?"

"She did," Natalie said. "According to her, she called into the King Range station and told the ranger on duty. That's where they would have filed a wilderness permit before they left. You have to make reservations so the trail doesn't get crowded."

"And?"

"They're treating them like lost hikers at this point. They sent search parties out—especially once the boy's family got involved—but it's wild country." Baojia shrugged. "People go missing and are never found. It's not even that unusual."

"She's young," Brigid said. "And you said she's with her boyfriend? Any chance they could have just run off?"

Baojia handed over another, much thicker, file. "Daniel Ramiro Uriarte is the son of Pablo Uriarte and Isabel Delgado; he's also one of the heirs of Uriarte International. They're one of the top building supply conglomerates in Mexico. If you've stayed at a luxury resort in Puerto Vallarta or Tulum—"

Carwyn muttered, "It's on the bucket list."

"—you've likely stayed in a hotel they've built," Baojia continued. "His family is also making a lot of noise. Their head of security, Ignacio Valero, is up in Shelter Cove right now. Has a private plane at his disposal. He's met with the Coast Guard and the search-and-rescue authorities in Humboldt County. Luckily, Daniel's family hasn't offered a reward yet, so we have a little time before the woods are crawling with humans."

Carwyn asked, "Will they offer a reward?"

Baojia nodded. "They're rich. Like, ridiculously wealthy for humans. If the kid doesn't show up within a few days, they're going to offer enough of a reward to have every man and woman in those mountains out in the forest looking for their kid."

Brigid looked up. "And the girl?"

Baojia pressed his lips together. "Let's just say she's not their priority."

"I think they blame Summer for their son going missing," Natalie said. "Just don't bring her up if you need to talk to them."

"Probably not necessary," Brigid muttered. "How long do we have?"

"Until they start blasting the reward money?" Baojia shook his head. "There's no way of knowing. I have a guy in the Coast Guard, but rich people aren't used to taking orders from government agencies, so they're likely to do whatever they want."

"We need to get up there and start asking questions before the reward money is publicized." Brigid slapped the file closed. "How long does it take to get to this Shelter Cove place?"

Baojia leaned on the table. "Along the coast road? Around five or six hours in daylight, likely an hour or so longer at night just to be cautious on the roads. If we take the highway, around four."

"So we take the highway," Brigid said. "We can get there before dawn if we leave now."

Baojia frowned, and Carwyn asked, "What?"

"Summer and Daniel flew into San Francisco, drove up the coast all the way to the mouth of the Mattole River, and parked their car there before they started on the trail."

"So they went up the coast road," Carwyn said. "Took the scenic route." He looked at Brigid. "So if we want to retrace their steps, we should go the long way."

Brigid groaned. "Which means we can't start until tomorrow night."

Carwyn threw his arm around her shoulder. "Come now, Brigid, it won't kill you to rest a little. Plenty of time tomorrow night to interrogate the humans."

"Besides." Natalie flashed her fangs. "If you stay tonight, you can go hunting with me."

Brigid looked at Baojia. "Please tell me she's not going after elephant seals; it's a truly disturbing mental image."

"Deer," Baojia said. "Thank God there are plenty in the hills, because with a newborn, elephant seals are probably not as safe as they should be."

"Deer?" Carwyn felt his night turning decidedly more positive. "I do love a good deer stalk, Nat. I'm in."

"Good." Natalie rose and grabbed Carwyn's hand. "You two boring bloodsuckers can just hang out here and drink vampire juice boxes while Carwyn and I eat fresh."

"Juice boxes?" Carwyn frowned.

"That's what she calls blood bags." Baojia rose. "Brigid, you want some coffee while we go over these maps? I've been looking at missing-person reports from Humboldt and Mendocino Counties too. There might be something there."

"Yeah, definitely." She was already shuffling papers. "I made a note to look back about three years on those."

"I requested five."

"Perfect."

"Boring!" Natalie blew her husband a kiss and headed for the door. "See ya, city slickers."

Baojia turned and shouted, "You grew up in Oakland!"

Carwyn laughed and followed Natalie, craving the smell of ocean air and the taste of fresh blood.

THREE

Brigid waited for Carwyn and Natalie's voices to dissipate before she spoke to Baojia again. "And how is she really?"

"Natalie?" He let out a huffed breath. "Frustrated. She doesn't have a job anymore. And she's always had a job. The kids only keep her so busy. Jake is very... *twelve*." Baojia almost growled it. "Sarah is seven and delightful, but they're busy with school and their friends and sports now. The nannies do a lot of the work during the day, so there's only so much to do at night."

"And she's not working."

He shook his head. "She had to quit full-time writing once she turned. Too many smart, curious people working in close proximity to the new vampire wasn't a good idea."

"Does she have any desire to work for Katya?"

"None." He looked out the window. "This case is actually really good for her. She loves having a problem to solve, and she's thrown herself into this."

"She could assist you."

He winced. "I think the two of us working together is a recipe for disaster. We're not like you and Carwyn."

Brigid raised her eyebrows. "Sorry, were you under the illusion that we always exist in a blissful state of euphoria? We fight all the time."

He shrugged. "I don't know. She needs to find... something, because she's not happy now. She's happy with family life—except when the almost-teenager is being especially rotten—but she needs to be able to work."

"Are the two of you planning on coming with us up to Humboldt?"

"I wasn't," Baojia said. "I need to stay here. But Natalie could. She grew up hiking and camping in that area, and she's spent more time up there since her change. She's pretty familiar with the place." He seemed to warm to the idea. "In fact, that would probably be really good for her."

"Excellent." Brigid smiled. "And then we'll have a local with us."

"You'll have more than one." He stretched his arms up. "Have you met Katya before?"

"Your boss?" Brigid asked. "The frightening teenager?"

Baojia smiled. "She's not that young, but she does play up the innocent kid image when it suits her."

Katya had a reputation for an angelic face and a ruthless appetite for power. She was young, but she'd taken over the Pacific Northwest when she was mere decades immortal.

"Is Katya involved in this?"

"No."

"Are you sure?"

"Very. It's not something she likes to talk about," Baojia

started, "but she's from that area originally. Well, born in Russia, but she came to California as a child, so it's home."

"Why doesn't she want anyone to know where she's from?"

"You know older vampires." He shrugged. "They're possessive about their personal information. I had to nearly pry the truth out of her, and she trusts me about as much as she trusts anyone."

"So not much?"

He smiled. "Only to the extent necessary. You don't become a regional power as young as she did without creating a tough shell."

"True."

"So... Strictly between the four of us, Katya is from the area where the girl went missing, so attacking humans there would not be acceptable. Her father and her sire still live there, and she'd be—"

"Her biological father is her vampire sire too?"

Baojia opened his mouth, then paused. "Uh..."

"If you can't tell me, I understand." Brigid scribbled a quick note in her book. She'd grown up around immortals and knew how tight-lipped they could be about their former human lives. "I know when to stop being nosy, unlike either one of our mates."

Baojia smiled. "If that's not the truth, nothing is. And about Katya? I want to tell you, but I don't know if she'd want me to share it, and the details probably aren't pertinent to solving the case."

"Leave it then." Brigid waved a hand. "I trust you to know what is and isn't important to finding these kids."

"She'll be in the area. Just know that. This time of year,

she's usually at her house on the Russian River, and she has another place she likes up around Ukiah in wine country. I'll drive up to her place with you tomorrow night, then let you two and Natalie go on ahead."

"Are we interrupting her holiday with this?"

"No. The river house is more of a remote office; the winery house is for holidays. She goes to the city if she needs to but stays at the river house for about a month every fall."

Brigid tapped her pen on her lower lip. "Will she be looking over our shoulders?"

"I doubt it; that's not her style. Unless you mess something up, then all bets are off."

"So we're fine." Brigid set her pen down. "We'll find these kids, Baojia. Don't worry about that. Carwyn is like one of those great long-eared dogs."

"A bloodhound?"

"Slightly shorter ears, but yes. And I mean that literally. Give him some personal items from the two humans, get him in the general area, and he'll be able to find them, even in the densest woods. As long as they're touching the ground. He can't do much in the city, but on open ground, it's like nothing I've ever seen before."

"I have every confidence that you're going to find them." Baojia grimaced. "I just hope they're alive when you do."

THEY ABANDONED the van for the night and took one of Baojia and Natalie's guest rooms, which were double-locked and secured from the inside to keep guests safe. The room was dug into the ground under the original farmhouse, and

Natalie and Baojia's bedroom suite was at the other end of the long hallway.

"How was your deer stalk?" Brigid stretched out on the bed, propping her arms and chin on Carwyn's chest. "Was it very exciting?"

"It was lovely," he said. "And Natalie isn't a bad hunter. A bit messy on the final killing bite, but overall—"

"Please stop." She put a hand over his mouth. "I immediately realized I made a horrible mistake even asking."

"You are so lucky you were sired this century," Carwyn said. "You'd have starved in the Middle Ages."

She could feel the slight tug of dawn, but she knew she had at least a half hour of coherent thought left. "I'm perfectly comfortable having less pox and more bagged blood, thank you very much." She smiled. "I don't even like antiques except for you."

He was holding back a smile. "Ah, my gentle rose. What a kind heart you have."

"I tell you who's going to be sorry they crossed this gentle rose is whoever has been taking kids in the forest for the past five years."

Carwyn sat up a little. "Five years?"

She nodded. "Baojia's instincts are good. When we went through the missing-person reports, we started to notice a pattern. The majority of traffic on the Lost Coast Trail is during the summer months, right?"

"Logical," Carwyn said. "Between summer holidays and good weather, May through August is likely the busiest time."

"By far," Brigid continued. "But the trail is passable going into September. There are a few more unexpected storms, wind, that kind of thing. But there are only a quarter of the permits given out in September versus May or July on average."

"And?"

Brigid leaned forward, inches from his face. "So why does September give out a fraction of the permits but produce the majority of missing hikers?"

Carwyn's eyebrows went up. "The majority of the missing hikers on the trail are reported missing around September?"

"Not just along that trail either. It's across both Mendocino and Humboldt Counties. People go missing in September more often than any other time of the year."

"Chance?"

"Over five years?" She shook her head. "It can't be random."

Carwyn stared at the ceiling. "This is a marijuana-growing area, correct?"

"It is. But that's legal now. A grower would have no reason to kidnap a workforce."

"Oh, my love, there are still many, many illegal farms." Carwyn turned his eyes to her. "There are permits and fees. Licenses to sell, perhaps? And then after all that, you'd still have to pay taxes."

Brigid nodded. "All true."

"Locals in this area have been growing marijuana as long as cattle have grazed the hills. There are likely more than a few old-timers and more than a few younger growers who don't like the idea of the government in their business."

"What time of year is marijuana harvested?"

"You're asking me?" Carwyn grinned. "Sure you know if any of that shite worked on us, I'd walk around smelling of it. But it doesn't, so I've no idea, my love."

"We need to find out." Brigid tapped her chin and stared at the wall. "Maybe Natalie knows some of the older growers up there. I imagine there's quite a bit about that area that humans keep to themselves."

Carwyn tweaked the tip of her nose as she started to drift into sleep. "I think, darling girl, your instincts on this may be right on the nose."

THE FOLLOWING NIGHT, Carwyn and Brigid sat at the kitchen table again as Jake and Sarah, Natalie and Baojia's offspring, helped their parents set the table for dinner. It was one of the traditions that Natalie had been keen to continue when she turned.

Since Natalie and Baojia didn't wake until sundown, they had to grab the time they could with their children.

"Sarah?" Natalie turned from stirring something on the stove. "Did you meet your new math teacher today?"

"Yeah." Sarah was a freckle-faced girl with dark brown curls and a piquant expression. "I mean *yes*." She was staring at Brigid, her eyes taking every inch in. Brigid was trying not to squirm.

"Thank you for using proper grammar." Baojia squeezed Sarah's shoulder as he walked past her chair. "What do you think?"

"About grammar?"

He smiled. "About the new math teacher."

Sarah shrugged and kept her eyes fixed on Brigid. "She's okay, I guess. Brigid, are you carrying a gun right now?"

"Sarah!" Natalie turned. "That's none of your business."

"Yes," Brigid answered directly. "When I was human, I was a highly trained markswoman, so I figured I'd stick with that instead of turning to swords like most vampires."

"But a vampire can only be killed by cutting off their head or lighting them on fire." Sarah leaned forward. "Guns don't kill them."

"Sarah!" Natalie's eyes were like saucers. "Where did you—?"

"Who told you all that?" Baojia asked. "Was it Lucien? I swear, we really need to talk to him about age-appropriate—"

"That's an excellent question." Carwyn spoke over all the clamoring voices and shot Natalie and Baojia loaded looks. "As the father of over a dozen children, let me assure you that if they're old enough to ask the question, they're old enough to hear an honest answer."

Baojia raised a single eyebrow.

"Age-appropriate answers, of course." Carwyn turned to Sarah. "What makes vampires immortal?"

"Amnis," Sarah said simply. "It like... connects you to the elements, right? And since the earth lasts forever and water lasts forever and all that, the amnis makes you live forever."

"We don't know exactly how it works," Carwyn said. "But that's as good a guess as others if you ask me. Amnis runs through our bodies in our nervous system. Like blood runs through vessels and arteries, right?"

Sarah nodded. "I learned about that in science class. About the circulation system."

"Good. So the nervous system is similar, but even bigger than the blood-circulation system because we have nerves all over and through our body, right?"

"Yeah." Sarah was getting excited now. "I learned that too.

We have five senses, and that's part of our nerva… nervous system. Like all our skin is part of it even."

"And amnis runs in our nervous system. So the reason vampires kill bad vampires by cutting off their heads—"

Natalie winced.

"—is because that cuts off the brain from the rest of the nervous system,"

Brigid said. "And that breaks the amnis, like cutting a vein or artery cuts the blood system."

"Ohhhh." Sarah's mouth formed a small *o*. "'Cause the brain is like the boss of the nervous system. I get it."

"But if you're a good enough shot," Brigid continued, "you can use a firearm instead. Especially with the right ammunition, a well-placed shot in the neck—"

"Okay, I think that's enough detail." Baojia put a pan on the table. "Who wants macaroni and cheese?"

"Me!" Sarah had completely forgotten morbid curiosity at the promise of noodles and cheese. "Jake, you can't have any yet."

Jake had been sitting sullenly in the corner. "Shut up, Sarah. I know."

"Mom!"

"Jake, don't tell your sister to shut up." Natalie looked at Sarah. "And Sarah, don't tell your brother he's not allowed to eat. That's rude."

Jake looked at Brigid. "So are you, like, working up here or something now? I thought you lived in England."

"Ireland. And we're independent now. We work on more of a contract basis."

"So you're, like, mercenaries or something?"

Carwyn was trying not to laugh. "Mercenaries, darling girl."

Brigid smiled. "We're closer to private investigators. Right now we're helping your dad with something."

"Oh." Jake slumped back in his chair. Apparently private investigators weren't as exciting as mercenaries. "My dad is a mercenary."

Baojia blinked. "Where did you even hear that word?"

"In history class. We were learning about the Hessians during the Revolutionary War."

Sarah reached for her glass of water. "Russians?"

"Hessians, stupid!"

"I'm not stupid. Mom!"

Brigid turned to Carwyn and spoke in Irish. "We're not getting any of these, are we?"

"Why would we when we can simply borrow the ones belonging to our friends and give them back when they get annoying?"

She leaned over and kissed him on the mouth. "I knew I loved you for a reason."

FOUR

Natalie took to the idea of accompanying Brigid and Carwyn like a maternal duck starved of water by two preteen ducklings.

Or something like that. She was practically bouncing in the back of the van. Baojia was driving north along the highway since he had to make calls while he drove, so Natalie had accompanied Brigid and Carwyn.

"Do you think I'll need to burrow?" she asked as they drove north on the Pacific Coast Highway. "I can burrow, you know. During the day? Baojia doesn't like it much, but I find it oddly soothing."

Carwyn watched Natalie in the rearview mirror. "That makes perfect sense; you're an earth vampire. I love a good burrow."

"Unfortunately" —Brigid turned to look at Natalie— "he's married to a vampire who does not. You two, however, are welcome to burrow in the woods. Just don't disturb the coastal redwood groves." She held up a small paperback book. "I've been reading. Their root systems are surprisingly shallow."

"They are," Natalie said. "I never dig there. But there are a lot of spaces in the forest where we can." She looked out the windows. "You can't see as much in the dark, but this coastline is nearly the end of the coast road. We're going to Katya's river house first, right?"

"We are." Carwyn steered the van through a twisting triplet of switchbacks that led them over another bridge and a waterfall he could hear in the distance. "The ocean is close here."

Natalie stared out the window. "Yes. It's why it's the perfect place for us. Baojia is so peaceful near the ocean. It makes a huge difference in his focus. And I'm happy as a clam as long as there are hills and forests."

"And deer."

Natalie grinned. "I never thought I'd enjoy venison as much as I do, but life is unexpected, right?" A shadow flickered over her face. "Thanks, you guys. I really appreciate you letting me tag along for this."

Brigid frowned. "Yer not taggin' along; aren't you our local contact, sure? We're not going to be able to find these two without ya. Speaking of finding the kids, did you get any line on those personal items we requested?"

"I think Katya has someone who discreetly visited their apartments in Seattle—I've learned not to ask questions—so we have some clothes. Luckily, they weren't meticulously clean college students. I imagine she has the clothes at the house."

Katya's Russian River home was just upstream from the bridge.

Carwyn spotted the sign for the turnoff a mile up the highway. "Has anyone from the Mackenzie clan requested passage to come look for her?"

"Yes," Natalie said. "Summer's father, Jamie Mackenzie, and one of their enforcers are already driving cross-country. They'll be two or three more days at most."

"And Daniel's family?" Brigid asked.

"Still conducting their own investigation and not open to collaboration the last time I called. They're still working with law enforcement for now."

Carwyn kept his eyes on the twisting road. "For now?"

"Let's just say that his family is accustomed to working within a system where private security is often more trusted than the police. They are also suspicious that a drug cartel might be involved based on the history of the area."

Brigid said, "The marijuana connection?"

Natalie nodded. "There are plenty of farms that are one hundred percent legal up here. There are also those who never wanted to be part of the capitalist system to begin with." She smiled a little. "Or at least that's what they say."

Brigid was like a tiny bulldog. "Do you have contacts in that group of people?"

Carwyn took the turnoff and headed right, winding along the dark road that tracked up the south side of the Russian River.

"I might." Natalie sounded cagey. "Okay, I do. Or I did. Don't know how many of them are still around, but I did a story on the Emerald Triangle about ten years ago when things were starting to move in the direction of legalization. I wanted to get the perspective of people who'd been living and growing up here for a long time. I kept those numbers."

"Will you call them?" Brigid asked.

"For now, let's see how far we can get on our own," Natalie said. "I'll call them if we have to."

"When is harvest season up here?"

"Roughly September through November, depending on the variety."

Carwyn exchanged a look with Brigid. "That fits."

"Yeah." Brigid looked in the rearview mirror. "For the past five years, a lot of people have gone missing in September."

"I'm not surprised," Natalie said. "Lots of humans come up here, thinking they can make some good money trimming or helping with the harvest, but it doesn't always end well unless you know the right people."

"So it's dangerous if yer not a local." Brigid raised a brow.

"Yeah, even vampires..." Natalie stared out the window and into the night forest. "We might be immortal, but there are still parts of those mountains where I'd be reluctant to go without an invitation." She looked pointedly at Brigid. "People disappear, and they've disappeared for a long time. Some of it is people who want to slip off the grid, but a lot of it is people stumbling into places they shouldn't be."

"We're here." Carwyn spotted the discreet security guards hiding in the trees across from the massive log-constructed house with wrought iron gates and a dense hedge of manzanitas. He rolled down the van window and spoke to one of the guards who stepped forward from the guardhouse.

"Can I help you?"

"Carwyn ap Bryn, Brigid Connor, and Natalie Ellis to see Katya."

The guard hunched down and looked into the back of the van. "Oh hey, Natalie. Didn't see you back there."

She pushed forward between the front seats. "Hey, Luke! Is Raven around tonight?"

"No, she's off. Is the boss with you?"

"He's on his way. I'd guess about half an hour behind us. He got caught on a phone call with Portland."

"Right." Luke stepped back and waved them through. "Head on in. She's expecting you."

A man and a woman pulled back the gates, and Carwyn drove slowly over the threshold and up a graveled driveway that encircled a stone-and-redwood gazebo at the center of the yard.

The house was bathed in warm light from discreet uplighting in the trees to the bright lights guiding guests toward the front door.

"So this is feckin' gorgeous," Brigid said. "I see Katya doesn't skimp on her homes."

"Definitely not," Natalie said. "And I'd say that she actually considers this place her main home. It's the closest to Fort Ross."

Carwyn maneuvered into a parking spot where an attendant was already motioning. "Is that where she came from as a human? Fort Ross?"

"I think that's where her father was from," Natalie said. "I just know that when she has extra time, it's spent here."

Brigid looked at Carwyn. "We're honored then."

Carwyn couldn't take his eyes off the house and the brilliant night sky above them. He could smell the river in the distance and the salty mist of ocean fog over the trees.

"Forget honored," he said. "I'm jealous."

THEY WAITED ONLY fifteen minutes for Baojia to arrive, drinking tea and exchanging pleasantries with their hostess. Katya did look like a teenager, curled up in front of a cozy blaze in the massive stone fireplace that dominated the central room in what Carwyn could now see was a very fancy log cabin.

It reminded him a little bit of the lodge in Cochamó where his daughter Carla hosted guests. The fireplace reached to the roof while a second story ran along either side of the structure. Doorways opened onto twin landings that overlooked the main room of the house.

It was a relaxed atmosphere but not a lazy one. There was a chef in a thoroughly modern kitchen preparing a traditional Russian meal for them while a man and a woman looked at an array of maps spread on a broad dining table.

And by the fireplace, Katya Grigorieva oversaw all of them. Dressed in a pair of well-worn jeans and a wool fisherman's sweater, she was the picture of outdoor chic. Her hair was dark and lay in a long braid down her back, reaching nearly to her waist.

Though she was Russian by birth, Katya had wholly adapted to her modern West Coast territory. She spoke English, Spanish, Russian, and Chinese with equal ease, and one whole wall of her library looked dedicated to the newest tech in the vampire world.

On one monitor, the smiling faces of Summer Mackenzie and Daniel Uriarte were displayed, likely grabbed from some social media channel, which was the easiest way to track humans in the modern world.

On the table by the maps, Carwyn saw bagged clothes along with a cardboard box.

"If there are immortals involved" —Katya started the conversation— "which I'm inclined to believe since the young people still haven't been found, it brings up a host of related issues."

Baojia nodded. "I've been thinking that might be a part of it."

Rules of immortal leadership were clear: if a vampire couldn't control their territory, they weren't any kind of leader, which meant they left themselves open to challenge. Sometimes that challenge would come from an ally or insider, while at others it would be someone simply looking to take advantage of the situation.

Ambition was a powerful drug.

Baojia continued, "The question is, who might be making a move to take over?"

Natalie looked at her husband and winced a little. "I hate bringing it up, honey, but Ernesto has wanted to push north for ages. I don't *think* he'd try to undermine Katya by taking innocent students, but he'd definitely try to undermine Katya. So we can't discount that."

"No, we can't discount Ernesto." Baojia's expression was grim. Ernesto was his sire, but their relationship was... complicated. "I'll try to call my sister tonight. I do want to mention the Sokolovs though," he added. "Last I heard, their people were attempting to push into Alaska."

"Those bastards," Katya muttered. "But Alaska is not Northern California. That would be a very big reach. As much as I dislike them, Sokolov is probably at the bottom of the list." She rose and walked to a small bar cabinet. "Bloodwine, anyone? Alex will be finished with the meal soon."

"I'd love some," Brigid said.

Natalie raised her hand again. "Ditto for me."

"No, thank you," Baojia said, glaring at something in a file.

"Just a beer for me," Carwyn said. "So Ernesto Alvarez is an obvious suspect for practical reasons. I'd say the Sokolovs are a stretch, but they do have a history in human trafficking, and this could have been opportunistic."

"I can accept that as a possibility." Katya poured three glasses of wine and snapped out something in Russian to the chef before she turned back to Natalie, Brigid, and Carwyn. "I'll speak to my security heads farther north and tell them to keep on alert for any signs of incursion."

"Thank you," Carwyn said. "We also have to consider if this abduction is related to Summer's immortal connections or Daniel's family money."

"True." Natalie took the blood-wine Katya handed her. "Both are very real possibilities."

"I can tell you what I know about Summer." Katya handed a glass of wine to Brigid, then took her seat. "Keep in mind, this all comes from reports. Like Baojia, I've never met the girl in person."

The chef brought a tray of soup bowls to the living room and set them on the coffee table.

"I hope you don't mind if we eat while we work." Katya handed out bowls to Carwyn and Brigid. "My time tonight is limited. This is potato-and-leek soup. Alexis is preparing salmon and smoked trout for dinner."

"Thank you, Katya." Carwyn reached for the soup. "Judging from Summer's social media, she doesn't have a typical day person's life."

"She's not a typical day person," Katya said. "According to

Logan, she's family. Her father was adopted into the Mackenzie clan by Logan and his mate. He grew up, got married, had Summer and her younger brother. A very ordinary life save for the fact that the people Summer called Grandmother and Grandfather were Scots-Irish vampires who came to fight in the American Revolution."

"That's the connection to my daughter-in-law," Carwyn said. "These Mackenzies come from the same line. Earth vampires, except for our Cathy, who ended up siring to fire."

Katya shook her head. "Not a pleasant life." She blinked at Brigid's expression. "I am simply being honest. Unlike you, most fire vampires live very isolated lives because of their element."

"No offense taken," Brigid said quietly. "Not every immortal can handle the stress of controlling the most unpredictable element."

Was it a jab? Carwyn hid his smile. Brigid was too clever and too politically smart to make it overt if it was. He quickly changed the subject. "So obviously, with the family connection, I consider this girl part of my extended family. Brigid and I are fully committed to finding the truth no matter what it is."

It was both a warning and a commitment. Carwyn didn't think Katya had any reason to target Summer Mackenzie, especially since the girl had been in her territory and an obvious rule-follower according to Baojia. But it never hurt to remind Katya that no one was off-limits in their investigation.

Katya leaned forward. "Listen, you're not going to get an argument from me. I do want to suggest that it's very possible this is far more mundane than any of us are suggesting though." She glanced at Natalie. "Nat and Baojia know that people go missing up here. This is one of the most productive marijuana-growing areas in the world. There are legal farmers and illegal ones. Legal traders and their black market counterparts."

Baojia added, "People have gone missing for years, and Katya's had to keep a tight rein on immortals in the territory from taking advantage of that situation. Some of the disappearances are accidents; some aren't. But if this is solely a human problem, we're going to need to back off." He glanced at his boss. "Officially, I mean."

Carwyn nodded. "Understood."

Katya continued, "Which means that—for now—you have all the access and help you want. But if we find out the kidnappers are human criminals, you are on your own. Our kind getting involved at that point would just make everything more dangerous."

Carwyn couldn't disagree with the woman, but he could tell by the look on Brigid's face that his mate did not approve. She was a champion for crime victims, human or vampire, and she didn't like the phrase "a human problem."

Nevertheless, she knew too much about immortal politics to say anything.

"So Ernesto," Baojia said, "the Sokolovs, or maybe someone targeting Mackenzie people. These are our main suspects."

"Or humans," Natalie said. "That's always a possibility."

"Indeed." Carwyn already had a plan forming. "Katya, I understand we're sleeping here today?"

"You are welcome." She gestured to the upstairs rooms with an open hand. "All guest quarters are light safe and secured from the inside for your comfort." She glanced over her shoulder. "Or you are welcome to sleep in your... little camper."

Carwyn looked at Brigid. "I think Katya may be mocking our tiny home."

"That's good," Brigid said. "We don't want her getting any ideas about stealing it once she finds out how feckin' fantastic it is."

Katya laughed, and suddenly her face appeared young again. "I see that I'm going to enjoy having you in my territory, Carwyn and Brigid. For now, let's eat."

FIVE

Brigid knelt in the middle of a redwood grove upriver from Katya's home. It was an hour before dawn, and something about the forest had been calling her since they arrived.

She looked up at the brilliant night sky teeming with stars, framed by the tops of the coastal giants. The forest around her was silent, the night birds, small scavengers, and even the insects aware that a predator walked among them.

Brigid circled the grove, fascinated by the dense shoots of redwood that sprang from the base of the trees to form thickets taller than a human.

Growing up in Ireland, Brigid had reveled in tales of the sidhe and the fae folk her aunt loved to share. Sinéad would love these strangely human thickets and probably tell Brigid a story about an old god who became a tree and sent out children from his roots.

No wonder the Native people had tales of giant men roaming the woods. Stories of giants were fitting for a place like this.

But though Brigid came from a land with more than a little love for magic, she was always the practical one. Even after becoming a creature humans would consider supernatural, she gave little credence to myths and legends like that.

Odd for someone who could manipulate fire with her mind.

Still, walking through the forest at night, Brigid understood it. She reached in her pocket and felt for her ever-present lighter. It was in a gold case and engraved with her initials, a ridiculously extravagant gift from her mad husband. When the air was dry, Brigid could use natural static in the air to create flames. Here, however, the air was laden with the ocean mist.

She lit a flame and grabbed it with her amnis. Holding it in her palm, she lifted it as she walked through the forest. The shadows took on a life of their own, racing around her in the still-silent wood.

She smelled a thread of musk in the air, a pungent scent marker from what she guessed was a bear. She detected deer and rabbit and a feline presence that was probably a mountain lion.

More bears.

She turned when she thought one of the thicket men moved. No, just another shadow playing tricks on her.

You'd know, she reassured herself. With her senses and her training, no one would be able to sneak up on her, even in a wild place like this forest. She'd smell them before they even got close.

Like she smelled Natalie and Baojia approaching in that moment.

Brigid turned and walked back to the redwood grove to meet them.

"This place is amazing right?" Natalie was all smiles. "I used to be afraid of the forest at night, but now with my vision the way it is..." She took a deep breath and let it out slowly. "It's my happy place. Except for the poison oak. That shit is annoying even for vampires."

Brigid frowned. "Can we get poison oak rashes? Most poisons don't affect us."

"We don't get rashes that *last*," Baojia said. "But it does linger in our skin for a time while the amnis works it out." He grimaced. "It's over quickly, but while it's clearing our system, it's not a pleasant feeling."

"Ever been bitten by fire ants?" Natalie asked. "It's a little like that."

Brigid didn't know what fire ants were, but she felt like the name told her all she needed to know. "Great," she said. "Good to know." She'd been bitten by a rattlesnake once and thought that had been unpleasant. Fire ants sounded a thousand times worse.

Baojia put his arm around Natalie's shoulders. "Since it's so late, I'm going to stay at Katya's with you guys; I already called the kids' nannies. You three are taking off at sunset?"

"I want to make sure we can get out to Mattole Creek tomorrow night and find camping well before sunrise," Brigid said. "Natalie said she's fine burrowing?" Brigid still wasn't too sure about that one. She preferred walls, alarms, and an ancient husband who could wake during the day. "Are you sure you're going to be comfortable enough, Nat?"

"Oh, it's fine!"

Brigid was still skeptical. She looked at Baojia.

"I know where you're coming from," he said. "But I have come to accept that there's really no safer place for her than underground if she's going to be away from vampire security. I'd rather have her bury herself than risk being discovered by a human."

Brigid nodded. "Fair enough. We also have alarms."

"I just got word from Summer's father. He's driving through the day and says he'll close by tomorrow night. Was wondering if you wanted to wait for him or go on yourself."

"I wanted to take a look at the trail as soon as possible," Brigid said. "But if they want to meet us in Mattole tomorrow night, I'd be happy to see them. I understand Summer's father is an excellent outdoorsman."

"He lives with his family in a very rural part of Appalachia," Natalie said, "so while this landscape might be different for him, I wouldn't worry about him keeping up. He's used to our kind."

Brigid nodded and looked around the dark grove. "I understand why the humans fear it, but I love it here. The fog feels very familiar."

Baojia looked up at the forest giants. "Fear is not an illogical reaction to these mountains, but neither is love."

BRIGID WENT to sleep that morning with the sound of the search-and-rescue dispatcher playing on her vampire-safe tablet in the background. When she woke—Carwyn a warm mountain at her side—she realized their mistake.

"We need to go to Shelter Cove, not Mattole."

Carwyn lifted his head. "That doesn't retrace their steps."

"No, but it gets us closer to where they were taken." She rolled toward him and kissed his mouth quickly. "Hello."

He smiled. "Good evening to you too."

She sat up and opened the map Baojia had given her of the search area, the trail, and the marked campgrounds. "So we know from the ranger reports that Summer and Daniel left from Mattole and headed south, intending catch their shuttle at the end of the trail. The last time anyone spotted them" —her finger found the mark— "was just north of Shipman Creek, which means they were closer to Shelter Cove than Mattole. If we take that route and head north like Search and Rescue did—"

"Then we'll find where they were taken faster." He kissed the top of her head. "Good thinking."

"So we head to Shelter Cove tonight." She nodded. "I'll tell Natalie. She can communicate that to Summer's father so he meets us in the right place."

Carwyn stretched his arms up and out. "Not sure I like the idea of strange humans knowing where we're located during the day even if they are family."

"We can always burrow with Natalie if something seems off." *Ugh*. Burrowing.

"Oh, you'd love that wouldn't you?" He grinned. "Getting in touch with your earthly roots, darling girl?"

"Hardly."

Brigid's sire was an earth vampire. By all logic, she should feel comforted by the ground, rooted to it in an elemental sense.

She didn't. Other than the pressure of the ground against her skin—which *was* soothing when her fire was riled—the earth didn't bring her the same comfort the sea did. What could she say? She liked knowing she could be easily dowsed if her amnis got out of control.

"So Shelter Cove tonight," Carwyn said. "And hopefully we can head up the trail a bit before dawn."

"Or we can wait for the humans."

"Waiting for the humans may sound polite, but it's not my job to babysit them. Right now our focus needs to be finding Summer and Daniel. They've been gone thirteen days. I don't want to even think what they might be going through."

If they're alive.

Neither one of them said it, but Brigid stroked Carwyn's rough jaw and knew her mate was thinking exactly the way she was.

If they were alive. If they'd survived. If they had been taken for a reason and not a killer's insatiable thirst.

"We'll find them," she said gently. "You'll find them, old man. No matter what. I have faith."

"I know I'll find them." Carwyn frowned. "But I need for them to be alive."

"I hope…" Brigid pressed her forehead to his. "I *hope*, Carwyn."

"Let's get out of here," he said. "I want to be on the road."

She felt the dusk outside. "The sun just barely set. Help me pack and we'll be driving away by full dark."

BAOJIA WAVED at them in the rearview mirror as Natalie, Carwyn, and Brigid made their way out of Katya's compound that night. They turned back toward the river road and up the highway, the forest growing denser and denser the farther north and inland they headed.

The landscape transitioned from scrub brush and grasses on the coast to bushes, then cypress and hardwoods as they wound through the hills, then conifers and redwoods as the elevation rose and the forest grew dense.

With the fog shrouding the landscape at night, the silence was even deeper, as if the darkness and the mist had absorbed everything but the van's engine.

Natalie sat in front with Carwyn, giving him directions and explaining more about the history of the land they were driving through—the Native people who continued to make their home there, the Pomo and the Eel River peoples who populated the land for centuries and the Russian farmers who'd come to settle the Northern California coast to support their colonies in Alaska. There were fur traders who'd almost wiped out the adorable sea otter and the *Californios* who later pushed the Russians out to become the dominant power in the north until California was absorbed into the United States.

They drove through old logging towns and passed roadside Bigfoot "museums" where chainsaw sculptures made Brigid do a double take in the fog.

By the time they reached the turnoff for Shelter Cove, Brigid felt like she was in another world. The van's lights were the only illumination as the road grew narrower. Redwoods butted up to the pavement, and oaks and sycamore trees created low tunnels where fog gathered only to race past them in the headlights as they followed the twisting path back toward the coast.

"How far is it from here?" Sitting in the back, Brigid was glad that car sickness had never been a problem for her.

So far.

"Only fourteen or fifteen miles," Natalie said. "But at night it'll take about an hour or so. You have to be really careful about animals, and the road has a lot of switchbacks."

"There will be no street racing here," Carwyn muttered. "And I haven't seen a single other vehicle in over fifteen minutes. I'm guessing people don't go out at night here?"

Natalie pursed her lips. "Around here there are a lot of things that go bump in the night," she said. "I'm guessing that most humans don't want to find out what they are."

"So the plan" —Brigid tried to keep her eyes on the center of the road in front of the van— "is that we're going to find where the two kids were taken, follow them as far as we can, then if we don't have any leads, we'll head into town and ask around." Brigid tapped Natalie on the shoulder. "You said you had a sheriff's deputy you could call?"

"It's been a few years, but I imagine he'll still talk to me. I didn't piss anyone off with the story I wrote about the old-time pot growers, so I'm still welcome." Natalie shrugged. "Which is more than I can say about a lot of the stories I did. Now, the federal government might not like me that much, but I don't really care."

"Did the drug agencies try to get you to spy for them?" Brigid asked. That's a move she would have attempted if she'd been in law enforcement's place.

"Oh yeah. They tried all the threats. Obstruction of justice, hindering a federal investigation." Her face lit up. "One of them even tried to imply that he knew a federal prosecutor who would indict me on RICO charges! Because he said I was an accomplice to the drug cartels even though the cartels that were operating up here probably like me less than the feds do." She shook her head. "It was a bit crazy at times. I have to say, I understand why some law enforcement really hate those guys—and it's almost all guys. At least the big operations were mostly dudes. More women in legal operations."

"Why is that?" Carwyn asked. "The hate, I mean. They were talking about marijuana growers, right? It was legalized only a few years after all this happened."

"It wasn't that the drugs were that bad, though some of the really hardcore agents were true believers in all the marijuana scare-tactic stuff, you know?" Natalie angled herself toward Brigid. "It wasn't even the small-time hippie 'back to the land' types. It was the big operations they hated so much. And it was also their pride. They could never really get control of the area. For all their guns and helicopters and strike forces, the mountains and the growers were never under their control."

"Humans hate that." Brigid looked at the forest around them, and she knew that no matter how closely her mate might be tied to the earth, in this place, he was still an intruder. They all were. As much as she loved the beautiful trees, she didn't feel one with nature in these hills.

Here, *she* was the invasive species.

SIX

The dewy, predawn hours in Shelter Cove revealed a small town that appeared plucked from a New England landscape. Rocky shores jutted into the ocean, and a bright white lighthouse sat prominently on the point. Little streets dead-ended into picnic meadows overlooking the Pacific while mountain homes poked their roofs through the forest facing the sea.

It was a town where everything faced the water, including the cypress and conifers that crawled almost down to the gravelly beaches. To the north was the King Range and to the south the Sinkyone Wilderness, more densely wooded than the Lost Coast Trail and even less accessible.

Carwyn parked in the empty lot near the lighthouse while Brigid went to poke around the beach and Natalie spread a large map on a picnic table.

"I hiked this trail when I was in college," Natalie said, looking at the map. "It's not that hard in most places, and it's pretty even. The beaches and rocks are what's more challenging. You have to understand the tides too." She looked up. "How many days did they say they were taking to do it?"

Carwyn stood over her, looking at the map over her shoulder. "They'd planned for six days."

Natalie shook her head. "Experienced backpackers like them? It wouldn't take them more than four. They must have planned some side hikes." She pointed at several points on the trail. "There are some areas around here that have trails that go farther up into the mountains. We'll have to stay aware because they could have easily taken one of those."

"And if they were taken back in the hills?"

Natalie took a deep breath. "I mean…" She spread her hand over the light green stretch of land on the map. "This is all forest. Forests and creeks and little valleys. Very few roads. Very few people. There's a reason that people hide here. Without a vampire sense of smell, we'd get lost very quickly."

Brigid walked back up the staircase that led down to the water and squinted at the quickly lightening sky. "We need to go. I can feel the sun coming."

They drove away from the coastal overlook and parked in the hills behind a house that Baojia had already confirmed would be empty. While Brigid and Natalie secured the van for day rest, Carwyn poked around the property.

There was a greenhouse between the house and the forest, but when he popped it open, he realized the flourishing marijuana plants were simply a cover for what looked to be an underground complex. An electronic lock was set into the floor and covered with a crate. The entrance to the underground bunker was hidden under an outdoor rug.

Either a doomsday prepper lived here, or a vampire. Carwyn figured there was a fifty/fifty chance of either.

Taking advantage of a hint of signal, he used his voice command software to call Baojia.

"We're here," Carwyn said before Baojia could speak. "Very limited signal. This house, vampire or militiaman?"

Baojia laughed. "Vampire, but he's traveling right now. He's one of Katya's security staff—he works for me. The house gets rented out when he's traveling, so a strange van won't raise any red flags with the neighbors. A human neighbor comes by to take care of the garden, so you don't have to do anything to it."

"The garden?" Carwyn stared at the dozens of marijuana plants. "Yes, I found that already. Very... aromatic."

"Everyone has to have a hobby, Carwyn."

"You speak the truth." He kicked over the rug with his toe and backed out of the greenhouse. Baojia's voice crackled on the other end of the call.

"—called. Headed your— Wanted to check and make sure they—" His voice broke again. "—direction as you."

"You broke up," Carwyn said. "Does Summer's family have this address?"

"Yes."

"Okay. Will they be here before sunset tonight?"

"Also yes."

"Then we'll figure it out from there." He could feel the sun rising. "Okay, sleep well. Brigid and I will take care of Natalie. Don't worry."

"She has no sense of self-preservation. You remember that, right?"

"I do." Thank the Lord the woman had become a vampire. Carwyn didn't know how Baojia had lived with a wife who darted into life-threatening situations, pissed-off drug cartels, and all the rest as a *human*. Brigid, at least, had always been lethal.

He hung up the phone and walked back to the van. Brigid was watching as Natalie knelt on the ground with her hands to the earth and began to hollow out a resting place at the edge of the clearing.

"So if you just shape it like this..." The ground flexed and broke under her hands. "See, it goes pretty fast." In minutes, the earth had produced a tidy little cave hidden by the trees.

Brigid was still making her "are you kidding me?" face. "Do you want some blankets or pillows or... anything?"

"Oh no, I'm completely comfortable like this." She nodded and then sort of rolled into the cave. "I will be wanting a shower when I wake up though."

"Understood."

Natalie waved at him before she pulled the ground over herself like a blanket. In less than a minute, the earth barely looked as if it had been disturbed.

Brigid looked up at him. "You'd do that every night if I was agreeable, wouldn't you?"

"What? No..." It did look cozy though. "Maybe... I mean, I do enjoy a soft mattress, but there is something about a nice, secure..."

"Dirt nap?" Brigid asked.

"That makes it sound frighteningly permanent." He hooked his arm around Brigid's neck and dragged her close. "Come now, Miss Brigid. Let's get you into bed before I have to carry you."

"As long as I don't have to carry *you*, I think we'll survive."

"Now you're just trying to be hurtful."

SUMMER SAT on a fallen log outside the broken-down cabin where she and Dani had been sleeping since they arrived at the farm. She stared up at the stars, but she was too tired to read anything other than what she'd discerned when they first arrived. They weren't all that far from where they were taken, though the drier air told her they were inland from the coast.

She casually scratched her armpit, then wiped the sweat and dead skin under her nails onto the stones that marked the bark path through the farm. She scratched her scalp and did the same thing on the back of the log before she leaned to the left and spit over her shoulder.

"Marking territory?"

Fuck.

Summer made a show of scratching her leg as she stared up at the vampire who ran the show. "I don't know what you're talking about. I'm just worried about poison oak."

"We spray for that on the farm." He stood casually, hands in pockets, looking at her with lazy interest. "Otherwise it takes over. But you noticed that already."

She only gave him a casual shrug. "I just saw it in the guidebooks, you know?"

"You're not the average human, Summer. Stop pretending."

"I'm working twice as hard as everyone here so Dani can get better, okay? What else do you want?"

They'd allowed her that at least. Dani had been grateful to be put on lighter kitchen duty, but Summer was suspicious they would find some way to hurt him more. It seemed too reasonable for them to allow him to heal in relative peace.

In the end, she could see what their captors were aiming for. Dani—a strong, physically challenging male—was docile and under their immediate scrutiny while he was healing from an infection in his shoulder. And Summer was too busy taking care of him and doing Dani's share of the farmwork to plot anything that might lead to escape.

"What do I want from you?" The vampire smiled. "That is a question, isn't it? Once, I might have been more obvious, but I don't think you're that type of girl."

Summer sneered to hide the fear. "If you wanted to rape me, you or your minions would have done it already. We all see the guns."

And they had lots of them. Summer had only seen one vampire though, the man who seemed to enjoy tormenting her with conversation. She didn't know his name and she couldn't place his accent.

"Sexual violence has never appealed to me." He leaned against one of the towering redwoods that marked the edge of the compound and looked up into the trees. "Sex isn't that interesting to begin with, and it's positively dull when I can't make my lover enjoy it."

Summer blinked and forced her face to remain blank. "Sorry, do you want some kind of award for not raping women?"

He laughed. "You do amuse me. You have tremendous self-control for a human, and your brain..." His smile grew. "I can just see the wheels turning."

"Not me. I'm too tired to think."

His accent wasn't native to the United States; it almost

sounded Mexican, but that seemed unlikely when the man's clothing and mannerisms seemed far more European.

Mexico is very diverse.

Dani had told her that many times, so maybe Mexico was the key. Maybe this man had nothing to do with her or her family. Maybe this was all about Dani. That would definitely explain them cutting him slack.

"Has anyone ever told you that you'd make an excellent vampire?" the man asked.

She looked over her shoulder at the cabin, hoping Dani hadn't heard that. "No. Then again, I've never expressed an interest in it because I like sunlight and salad too much."

Fuck him. Fuck all of them, but especially him. Dani needed to get better so they could plot their escape. Her family had probably already sent out the dogs.

And by dogs, she meant her daddy and Uncle Ross.

Her daddy could have a hair trigger, but Uncle Ross was a whole other thing. If Uncle Ross showed up at this place, a lot of people were going to end up headless.

"You know, you guys have to be making money hand over fist with all this weed." She looked over the fields planted between waving groves of pine trees and covered by camouflage cloth. "This is clearly a well-established operation. Why not just hire people to work here instead of kidnapping hikers? It seems like it would be a better business plan."

"That's a good point." The vampire pointed at her. "I should make you a manager."

"Fuck off." She stared over the fields. "They're already looking for me."

"Do you think so?"

"You're fooling yourself if you think they won't be able to

find this place. Even if you kill me, they'll be able to find my body." She looked up. "And then everything you've built here will be destroyed." Summer stood. "I don't like seeing people die. Let me and Dani go; let us go and we'll forget this place exists."

"Oh?" He cocked his head. "You won't try to come back and free all the other workers here?"

Of course I fucking will. "Do I look altruistic, mister? I just want to go home with my boyfriend and pretend this was a dream." *And kill you. I definitely want you dead.*

He was suddenly inches from her face. "I don't believe you." He ran a single finger along her jawline, and she recoiled from his touch. "You remind me of someone I once knew."

"Oh?"

"She's dead."

"Pity." *You sick fuck.* "I'm guessing she never taught you about personal space." Summer shoved him away and walked toward the door of her cabin.

"Summer?"

She stopped at the door, but she didn't turn around. "What?"

"How did you know that herb would help heal your boyfriend?"

She'd been lucky enough to find a stand of wild yarrow growing on the edge of the clearing near the cabin. She'd used some of the flowers to make a tea to break Dani's fever and then made a poultice from the leaves. Within days, the festering wound had started to heal and his shoulder was less painful.

"My mom's, like, a hippie, okay? I just know stuff about

gardening." She didn't wait for any more conversation. She went inside and shut the door behind her, twisting the nail she'd pulled from another part of the cabin to secure it.

It wasn't the most secure lock for the door, but it was subtle and she could pretend like it wasn't there if anyone entered to search the place, which happened every few days.

She sat on the thin pallet where she slept and put her head in her hands.

Daddy. Uncle Ross. Where are you?

She wasn't depressed, but she was worried about Dani, and she was terrified that she'd made the mistake of intriguing a vampire. She knew that the minute that man put a finger on her skin, he could use his amnis to manipulate her mind. He could make her do anything, say anything, think *anything*. Even imagining it made her sick.

"Summer?" Dani's voice wasn't as strong as it usually was, but it was getting better. "He was talking to you again."

She cleared her throat and wiped the threat of tears from her eyes. "I'm okay. How are you feeling?"

"I'm better." He managed to sit up. "The herb tea you made is helping a lot. I'm worried about you."

"I'm fine, handsome." She crawled over and scooted next to him even though half her body was on the bare floor. "I'm strong. I can handle it."

"It's not just the farmwork," he said. "I've been counting people ever since we got here."

She turned to him and put a finger over his lips. "What do you mean?" Her voice was less than a whisper.

Dani matched her volume. "I mean since they brought us, how many other groups have they brought?"

Summer frowned. "Just the brothers." A week after they'd

been taken, two brothers in their late teens showed up. Neither of them spoke English and were relieved when Dani and Summer could speak to them in Spanish.

"Yes. Counting them, there should have been fifteen workers in the cabins."

"Okay, and?"

"But I count the bags we make for lunch. We've only been making twelve."

Summer froze. "Twelve?"

"Twelve. And no other food goes out to the cabins. I'm there all day."

The people who had taken them were smart and suspicious. The kidnapped workers were spread out in the fields and rarely spoke to each other unless they were assigned to the drying room or the kitchen, where they trimmed the buds. That was why food was delivered to their cabins. The bosses didn't even want them speaking to each other when they ate.

Their capture had meant thirteen people were working on the farm.

Then the brothers were taken.

Fifteen. There should have been fifteen.

"Only twelve?" Her breath left her. "That means—"

"That means since we've been here, three people have disappeared."

SEVEN

Carwyn woke a few minutes before sunset and heard a human busying himself outside. The educated guess was the human was Summer's father, Jamie Mackenzie. Nevertheless, Carwyn kept his alert level high.

He felt Brigid stirring beside him and put his finger over his lips, signaling silence as he listened. Brigid nodded and wordlessly moved to sitting. Her head turned to track the human moving outside.

His blood smelled decadent, iron rich and old, a surprisingly unusual scent in the United States these days. Carwyn guessed it was the signal of a human who ate a very traditional diet. If he had to guess, he'd say that the man moving outside their van consumed a lot of wild game.

Moments later, he felt a whisper of amnis as a vampire joined the human.

"Evenin', Ross."

"Evenin', Jamie. Any sign of our friends?"

"Oh, I hear 'em awake, but they're bein' cautious."

"Can't blame 'em for that."

"Nope."

Carwyn raised his eyebrows, and Brigid nodded. She whipped her shirt off and put on a clean tank top before Carwyn could even cop a feel.

His hand was mid boob squeeze when she rolled her eyes. "*Cén aois tú?*" she whispered in Irish.

Yes, he knew he sometimes acted like a fifteen-year-old boy.

"I'm one thousand eighty-seven-years old," he whispered back. "But for over a thousand of those, I wasn't actually allowed to touch breasts, so I don't think those should count."

She couldn't stop the corners of her mouth from turning up. "Yer a menace."

"I know." He leaned down. "Please tell me we can sneak away sometime soon. The bed in this van is not conducive to—"

"Yes." She was flustered. "Fine. Of course. Can we go meet the other half of our search party now please?"

He smiled and pressed his mouth to hers in a quick, firm kiss. "The light of my eternity, Brigid Margaret Constance Connor."

She closed her eyes and sighed. "I will never forgive my aunt for telling you all my names."

He threw open the door to the van. "My only regret is that I didn't ask sooner."

Near the foot of the steps leading up to the wooden porch, two men were sitting, one human and one vampire. A fire burned in a rock pit near their feet.

"Gentlemen." Carwyn nodded. "I'm Carwyn ap Bryn." Brigid came to stand beside him. "And this is Brigid Connor, my mate, life partner, and handler."

The human looked to be in his late forties. He raised an eyebrow, and the firm set of his mouth behind a grey-flecked beard didn't waver. "Handler?"

"He's a gobshite; ignore him." Brigid stepped forward and offered her hand. "Mr. Mackenzie," she said to Jamie Mackenzie. "Sorry to meet you under these circumstances, but I assure you, Carwyn is an expert tracker, and we have clothing from Summer's and Daniel's homes, so we'll be able to start right away."

"A'ight." The human lifted his chin and glanced at Carwyn before he turned his attention back to Brigid. "You know me, and this is Ross Mackenzie. He's... kind of my brother."

Ross leaned forward and stuck his hand toward Brigid. "Jamie's father is my sire. Nice t' meet you, Miz Connor. Your reputation is top-notch. Logan's been talking to Cathy back in Edinburgh, and she speaks highly of the both of you."

They might have different complexions and slightly different hair colors, but other than that, the two men could easily pass for brothers. They both wore the same serious expression, the same heavy facial hair, and the same plaid flannel shirts.

"Natalie is likely still sleeping," Brigid said. "She's the youngest one of us, but she grew up in Northern California and has hiked this trail before. She's the most familiar with the area."

Jamie looked at Ross. "Didn't get a chance to tell you yet, but I ran into that boy's security guard at the little market in town today."

"How'd that go?" Ross asked.

Jamie shrugged. "About as well as I expected. Bastard

accused my girl of being involved in drugs and putting their precious kid in danger. I told him where he could stick his theory and told them to stay out of our way. Told the guy I hoped that his idiot client didn't get my daughter hurt." Jamie looked at Brigid. "That was my first thought, Miz Connor."

"Brigid, please." She pulled over a chair that Carwyn had taken from the back of the van. "What was your first thought?"

"Inexperienced hiker with my daughter." Jamie's voice was a low, quiet rumble in the twilight as he stared at the fire. "Summer has had *real* survival training. Not the shit you see on TV but the real kind. She can take care of herself."

Ross continued. "I can confirm that because I helped teach her." He looked around. "Especially in a place like this, my niece wouldn't have trouble surviving. The weather isn't extreme and there are plenty of resources, plenty of water."

Jamie said, "Our fear is that this boy she's been dating did something stupid and she had to go rescue him." He took a long breath. "But... the longer they're missing, the more I think there's something else going on." He shook his head. "Summer'd have found her way to help by now, with or without Daniel Uriarte, if she'd been able."

Carwyn sat beside Brigid, his arms crossed over his chest. "Ross, have you spoken to Logan about threats against the family? Anything we need to know from rivals? Any in our world you've crossed? They may have seen Summer as a soft target."

Jamie cleared his throat. "This is why I taught her knife fighting so young, Ross. I'm telling you—"

"If it's vampires" —Ross shot his brother a pointed look— "it's no one from our circle of friends or enemies. As soon as

Summer didn't call her mother on the day she was supposed to, we started asking around. Logan has enemies, but none that have connections here on the West Coast."

"That you know of," Brigid said.

Ross nodded. "Point taken. That we know of. Still, it would be real out of character for Logan's rivals to go after a kid. Human parts of the clan are usually pretty off-limits in our neck of the woods."

Brigid leaned forward. "This is off topic, but your accent is deadly and I love it."

Ross frowned. "Thanks, I guess."

"My wife would love yours." Jamie smiled a little. "She's a musician. Plays the harp and lots of Irish-music stuff."

"Hopefully when Summer is home, I'll be able to meet her. She can play the harp for me at the party."

Ross caught his eye, and Carwyn read the Mackenzie loud and clear: there better be a fucking party at the end of this.

A few yards away, Carwyn felt the earth start to open up as Natalie woke.

"She'll be ready after a shower," Brigid said. "So why don't we plan how we're going to attack this?" She took a map from her backpack and opened it. "The reason I asked you two to meet us here is that according to witnesses, Summer and Daniel had already traversed about two-thirds of the trail the last time they were spotted."

Jamie nodded. "We guessed that was why. I agree. We need speed more than anything right now." He looked at Carwyn. "Brigid said you have some clothes of Summer's to use for tracking?"

"Katya immediately sent someone to Summer's and

Daniel's places to get us samples," he said. "We have fresh body odor."

"Good," Ross said. "Summer hasn't been home in months, and she never brought this boy. God knows you're not going to find his family cooperating. They think we're a bunch of backwoods yahoos." Ross reached down and picked up a piece of wood, breaking off a sliver with his thumb to create a toothpick he stuck in the corner of his mouth. "Ignorant pricks."

"I see." He exchanged a look with Brigid. "Well, for now we'd rather keep Daniel's family out of it anyway. As far as we know, they have nothing to do with our world, and we'd prefer to keep it that way."

Natalie walked up to the firepit, covered head to toe in dirt and pine needles, carrying a backpack. "Gentlemen, I'm Natalie." She looked at Brigid. "All I need is a shower and I'll be ready to go."

THEY LEFT the van parked at the house and hiked to the trailhead at Black Sand Beach, heading north under a waxing moon. Brigid had been worried about Jamie Mackenzie keeping up with the vampires, but she shouldn't have been. The man moved over the landscape like a wildcat, keeping up with Natalie and often setting the pace for the rest of them.

Natalie paused at the end of the beach. "We're heading into some areas here where the high tide could be an issue. If Baojia was with us, he'd be able to keep the tide off the path, but we might have to go off trail to avoid the ocean in places."

Brigid spotted a problem immediately. "So the ocean covers the trail at high tide?"

"In places, yes."

She exchanged a look with Carwyn, who must have been thinking the same thing.

"We could lose their scent," he said. "If they left the path in an area that gets covered by the water, we might lose them."

Jamie said, "Just another reason to cut inland when things get too close, right? If they had to cross any of those areas at high tide, they'd have gone away from the ocean."

If they could have. Brigid didn't say anything else. Smooth grey pebbles gave way to grit and dirt under her hiking boots as the path along the coast began to climb toward the bluffs ahead.

The Lost Coast of California was a wild place where forests ran right down to the sea, frigid water churned over craggy outcroppings, and the surf slapped pebbled beaches that rolled and roared with the movement. Fog blanketed the forest, drifting high and swallowing the tops of cypress, oak, and pine.

In the distance, she scented bear and deer along with the myriad small creatures that made the scrubland that hugged the coast their home. In the darkness, Brigid followed Jamie, who walked ahead of her, and Natalie, whose pale skin glowed in the darkness as she led them along the narrow trail.

Natalie's movements were sure and her pace never lagged. They walked in single file at a rapid pace for humans but a deliberate pace for vampires. Natalie led, followed by Jamie Mackenzie, then Brigid, Ross, and Carwyn guarding the rear.

"Nothing of their scents yet." Carwyn had taken two shirts from separate bags at the beginning of the trail, and he kept them at the top of his pack. Brigid knew he'd refresh his senses when they got closer to Summer and Daniel's last known location.

Two hours up the trail, they passed their first camp, but there was no one still awake. Two tents were pitched in a clearing just off the path, and Brigid could hear the peaceful, unhurried breath of humans deep in sleep. There was a remnant of a cooking fire, food stores hung in a bag between two cypress trees, and various clothes were strewn over bushes, probably left out to dry.

Did any of it raise Brigid's suspicions? No. But better safe than sorry.

Brigid put her hand up and went to investigate the camp with Carwyn. Though he looked like a lumbering giant, her mate could use his amnis to dampen any sounds he made crossing the ground. He was silent as a mountain lion when he circled the human tents, venturing into the trees to look for any trace of Summer and Daniel.

Brigid walked back to the trail, shook her head, then turned to wait for Carwyn.

Who came bounding out of the woods with far less stealth, waving at them to run.

Not waiting for clarification, Brigid hissed, "Run!"

Natalie, Jamie, Brigid, and Ross booked it, running up the trail as fast as they could without tripping. She glanced over her shoulder once to see Carwyn leading a bear away from the human tents and back into the forest.

Oh, for fuck's sake. Brigid rolled her eyes. "Again?"

Jamie was watching with wide eyes. "Does he need help?"

"Please," Brigid said. "Look at the chancer. He's having a grand time. He'll lead that girl away from the tents and back into the forest." She started walking. "Let's crack on. He'll catch up when she's gone."

"How do you know it's a girl?" Jamie asked.

Ross muttered, "Looked like a damn *big* girl to me."

"I don't *know*. I'm guessing it's a girl because Carwyn inevitably angers mother bears by trying to coax bear cubs out of trees."

Natalie opened her mouth, then closed it. "Um...," she finally managed. "Why? He does know they're not stuffed animals, doesn't he?"

A hooting laugh rose from the trees along with a string of Welsh curses.

Brigid winced. "I do think he knows that. I'm just not quite sure it's sunk in, you know? They are very cute animals."

Ross nodded. "He's not wrong. Nothin' that aggressive should be that cute. It's Mother Nature trying to fuck with you. Like hippos."

All four of them nodded.

"Good point," Natalie said. "They're the most deadly land animal, but they look like an oversize balloon sculpture."

Jamie muttered, "Ain't that the truth?"

A crashing noise from the darkness of the forest and another string of angry curses, this time in Irish.

"She's really giving him a piece of her mind," Natalie said. "Are you sure he doesn't need—?"

"He's fine." He was never going to learn not to pester bears if Brigid kept firing warning shots to scare them off. "Natalie, how much longer to Shipman Creek?"

"We just passed the Gitchell Creek campground, so we're about halfway there," she said. "But the trail gets a bit twistier up ahead, so maybe another two to three hours."

Carwyn finally reappeared on the trail, sticks caught in his hair and a massive grin on his face. "A proper cuddle with a cub this time, Brigid."

"Yer gonna lose a hand one day and you'll have earned it. They are not toys, Carwyn."

He cocked his head. "But this one came right up to me. It practically climbed my leg, darling girl. What was I supposed to do? Ignore it?"

"Yes." She slapped his shoulder. "Next time ignore it. That cuddle cost us nearly fifteen minutes of you flailing about."

He looked a little chastised, but only a little. "I can say no trace of either Summer or Daniel in that campground, so we're narrowing it down."

Jamie nodded. "Good. Next up, Buck Creek."

EIGHT

For the next stretch of the hike, Natalie took the lead with Carwyn directly behind her. They were depending on his superior sense of smell to find traces of Summer and Daniel even though it had been nearly two weeks since the last time they'd been seen.

"There hasn't been any substantial rain for the past couple of weeks," Natalie said. "That's a huge help. Usually this area gets a lot more, but as you can see from the creeks, it's been a dry year."

"I noticed that." Brigid had been expecting to have to get wet crossing rivers, but so far all the waterways had been low enough for them to cross on rocks or sandbars.

She almost ran into Carwyn when he stopped.

"Carwyn?" Natalie turned. "What is it?"

He was silent and focused, almost in a trance. Brigid grabbed his backpack and dragged it down, reaching for the bagged clothing. She opened Summer's bag and shoved the worn shirt in his face. "Is it Summer?"

He cocked his head but said nothing. "Not Summer."

Brigid reached for the second bag and opened it. She pressed that to Carwyn's face, and the vampire offered nothing more than a short grunt before he began to move.

"He's got Daniel!" Brigid yelled.

Carwyn was already disappearing over a hill with Natalie and Ross on his heels.

Brigid and Jamie followed at a distance, their pace steady. She knew she'd never be able to keep up with the earth vampires over uneven terrain, and Jamie, for all his outdoor expertise, was still human.

"He didn't smell Summer?"

"Don't jump to conclusions," Brigid said. "I don't think that means anything about your girl, Jamie. It just means that Daniel probably sweats more."

He nodded. "Males are usually easier to track."

"Exactly."

The trail they climbed was over a hill and back into the woods, cutting through virgin meadows and scrub brush to reach the edge of the trees.

Brigid could see nothing in the forest, just a black wall of trees butted up to the layer of marine fog. "Carwyn?"

Natalie's voice came out of the darkness. "We're back here, Brig!"

She made her way deeper into the woods, following a narrow animal trail between tall pines and bushy cypress trees. She could hear Carwyn and Natalie ahead of them, but they didn't say a word.

When they finally caught up, Ross and Carwyn were crouched on the ground, their noses inches away from the soil.

Natalie was watching the two men with a grim expression. "Blood," she said. "Carwyn is pretty sure it's Daniel's."

Brigid looked around. "This is nowhere near the trail. Why would they come back here?"

"Good question." Jamie's voice was as grim as Natalie's. "Carwyn, any trace of Summer?"

"There're some faint traces that I think might be her, but I can't even smell Daniel that well—if he hadn't left blood here, we probably wouldn't have found this. The scent profile is degraded."

"I can't smell nothin'," Ross said. "Until Carwyn pointed out the blood, I missed it."

"Probably the marine layer," Natalie said. "Even without rain, there's a lot of moisture." She turned and cocked her head, following something Brigid couldn't see.

"What's that then, Nat?"

"There's a path here," she said, keeping her eyes on the ground. "Worn away."

Brigid followed her until they reached an overgrown stretch of the trail that ran along the ocean. Brigid looked up and then at the sea. "They might have stopped here to wait out the tide. Went inland to make sure they were safe."

"They went pretty far in though." Natalie turned and walked up the path, following the trail through the scrub brush, around Carwyn and Ross, who were still on the ground examining what they thought were bloodstains, and through a pair of trees that seemed to swallow her whole.

"Natalie?" Brigid rushed to follow the vampire into the darkness, only to find herself in the middle of a clearing. "What the hell?"

"Look." Natalie pointed at something in the center. "This is why they came all the way inland. They found this."

The clearing in the middle of nowhere was spooky enough, but the heavy wrought iron and carved stone fireplace in the exact center of the clearing boosted the creep factor far past anything they'd seen so far.

"Who built this?"

"I don't know." Natalie walked in a circle around the fireplace. "It's not made from found materials though. Someone built this to last."

"Backpackers on the trail, do any of them talk about a place like this?" It was the perfect camping spot with a ready-made woodburning stove and a giant room made of trees that would block the sharpest wind from the ocean. The ground beneath her feet was blessedly even and brushed free of limbs, rocks, and debris.

"I never heard of anything like this when I was hiking here," Natalie said. "Then again, that was quite a while ago." She looked around the clearing. "This doesn't make sense. There're no old houses around here. Who's going to build something like this?"

"Agreed. Makes no sense to me either."

Jamie entered the clearing and turned in a circle. "What is this?"

Brigid shook her head. "No idea. Natalie has never heard of it, and there aren't any roads around here. The supplies to build this fireplace would have had to be carried in."

Jamie reached down and picked something up off the ground near the base of one tree. "Summer was here."

"What?" Natalie walked over to him. "Why do you say that? What did you—?"

He held up a broken piece of plastic. "This is from a portable motion sensor I gave her last Christmas."

Brigid's hope plunged. "You're sure?"

"Daniel's blood," Jamie said. "Now this?" He looked around the clearing. "They set up camp here, and someone grabbed 'em. But Summer would have known. She would have had an alert." He turned toward the trail leading to the ocean, where Daniel's blood had been found. "They got away. They were running back to the trail when they shot him. Or threw a knife. Not sure. But they injured him..." He tapped the black piece of plastic in his palm. "Then Summer..."

"She didn't want to leave him," Brigid said. "She might have made it back, but that would have left Daniel alone with whoever attacked them."

Jamie nodded. "She wouldn't have left her partner on his own. Especially not injured."

Carwyn walked into the clearing. "There isn't enough blood for a mortal injury. When they left this place, they were alive."

"But which way did they go?" Natalie adjusted her backpack on her shoulders. "Back out to the trail and you're going to run into all the other hikers, even late in the year like this." She nodded inland. "And this way is nothing but wilderness for miles. There aren't even any trails along here."

"There has to be something," Ross said. "Some track or trail. Maybe enough to get horses or quad bikes down." He pointed at the stone fireplace. "That thing didn't just drop out of the sky."

"I can tell you."

The voice made them all spin around.

Leaning against a tree was the largest man Brigid had

ever seen in real life, even taller than her husband, who was more than a little mountain-like.

This man—this vampire—was tall and barrel-chested, his sandy-colored hair was long and brushed smooth, and a beard fell nearly to his waist.

Natalie was blinking. "Oh my God, it's Bigfoot."

No, but clearly he was a source of some of the myths.

"Who are you?" Carwyn subtly stepped between the giant and the rest of them. "We're searching for two hikers, one of whom is a relative of these men from Clan Mackenzie. We're here under the auspices of Ekaterina Grigorieva, vampire lord of this place."

The corner of the man's mouth turned up in what Brigid thought might be a smile. "I know Katya. I can help you if you like. I have an idea where they might have gone."

"Oh!" Natalie suddenly smiled. "Are you—? I mean..."

"I'm Grigor Petrovich," the giant said. "I'm Katya's father."

SUMMER SAT on the log again, watching the distant brush. She'd been listening and watching for days now, planning her and Dani's escape. Once she realized that humans were disappearing from the camp, she knew she and Dani had no other choice. They didn't have time to wait for a rescue. She'd seen the vampire keeping an eye on Dani as he worked in the kitchen the night before, heard him asking one of the humans who did the cooking how his health was progressing.

The vampire wasn't interested in seeing Dani well; he wanted to know when he'd be recovered enough for... whatever their plan was.

It was hard to tell who'd gone missing—she didn't see every one of the captives on a daily basis—but there was a couple similar to her and Dani who'd been working in one of the drying rooms. Summer had guessed they were also hikers based on their clothes, and they were in their early twenties. She hadn't seen them in days.

She'd been watching their surroundings during daylight and noticed the reflections glinting in the brush beyond the cookhouse. Fishhooks on clear line if she had to guess. Maybe razor blades. She wondered if they had bear traps out here. There could be pit traps too. She hadn't seen any dogs, but that didn't mean there weren't any.

Summer knew what to watch for. Hell, the patriarch of her clan, Logan Mackenzie, had made his money in bootlegging during Prohibition. He was legitimate now, but Summer had grown up on tales of all the booby traps her people had set up around illegal stills.

Dani came out and sat beside her. "What are you planning?"

"Who says I'm planning?"

He tucked a curl of hair behind her ear. "I know your planning face."

"Keep your voice low."

He nodded silently.

"In a couple of nights, there's gonna be a full moon."

"Summer—"

"We need the light. We don't have any flashlights or headlamps. And the ones here... The light isn't going to matter to them one way or another, but we need it. I tried to figure out a way that we could get out during the day, but they watch us too closely. Night is the only time the human guards ease up even a little."

Probably because they were counting on the vampire. Fucking vampire. She was crazy to do this at night, but there wasn't a moment during the day they weren't watched, and so far she'd only seen the one vampire running the camp. She was hoping he might be busy.

"Summer, you can't be serious. I know my family, and I know they'll be—"

"We don't have time." She turned to him. "We'll wait until a couple of hours before dawn when the guards are sleepy." And a vampire would be less likely to leave his lair. "I stole a knife and stashed it, but it's short, not enough to cut through the brush, which means we're going to have to keep close to the trail, and that means booby traps."

Dani looked at her like she was crazy. "Booby traps?"

"I know what to look for, and I should be able to lead us through them if we're careful. My dad and Uncle Ross taught me. But we're out of time."

"And where are we going to go?" He leaned closer to her. "We don't have any idea where we are."

"They're going to expect us to head to the road, but I think the creek is safer. We can follow it down to—"

"To what?" He looked around. "In all your time going from field to field, have you seen or heard anyone, Summer? We are in the wilderness."

"The wild doesn't scare me. These guys do." She swallowed hard. "I can keep us alive in the wild, especially if we're near water. I can keep us alive until we get out of this, but Dani, I need you to trust me."

He looked up at the heavens, but Summer knew he'd follow her. He still felt guilty about leading them to that campsite where they were taken no matter how many times Summer reassured him that she didn't blame him for their captivity.

"Summer, if we do this and they catch us—"

"They'll kill us." She nodded. "Probably. But we have to ask ourselves a real question: Is there any way they're going to let us go? We've seen their faces. They even use their names around us."

"I heard the Russian guy speaking in Spanish to someone and he mentioned a cartel." Dani put his hands in his hair and gripped it hard.

"People go missing every year up here. Lots." She swallowed hard. "Eventually, the rescue teams, they have to give up."

Dani said nothing. His head was hanging and his hands were still gripped in his hair.

Summer's heart split in half. "I'm so sorry I brought you here." She swallowed down the urge to cry. "I thought if we stuck to the trail we'd be fine, you know? It's well-traveled and—"

"And I led us off it," Dani muttered.

"Hey." She pulled his hands out of his hair and wrapped her arms around his neck. "I don't blame you for that if you don't blame me for planning this dumb trip. You wanted to go to Ibiza."

"It's not your fault." He took a deep breath. "It's the fault of these criminals who took us," Dani whispered. "Not us. Not either of us." He kissed her neck and pressed his face into her shoulder. "Summer, the Russian likes you. He's not going to make you disappear, okay? If anyone needs to escape, it's me. Let me try; I don't want you risking—"

"I will not let you go alone." Her arms tightened around his shoulders. "Dani, I love you. And maybe I have a hard time saying stuff like that, but I do. And there is no way I am going to let them take you away from me." She pulled away and met his eyes. "Don't ask me to do it. We're in this together."

He nodded slowly. "Together. I love you too. Did you have to pick this place to tell me?"

"Ibiza would have been a lot more romantic." She sniffed and fought back a smile. "Mackenzie women are ornery. You've been warned."

"I'm counting on your orneriness." He kissed her softly. "And I'm with you. Give me the word and I'll go. Just tell me the plan."

NINE

It was rare for Carwyn to look up to anyone, and he meant that literally. For the time period he'd been born into, he'd been considered a giant, particularly in Wales, which wasn't known for its towering men.

Did Carwyn suspect a Norseman or two had crept into his bloodline? Oh yes.

But Grigor Petrovich was truly massive. Carwyn had no problem understanding how Sasquatch stories were spawned if this man had been running around the Pacific Northwest at night for the past two hundred years.

"How long have you lived here?" Carwyn asked.

"Since Fort Ross was built."

"The Russians didn't live in California for very long. What made you stay?"

"My wife was here," Grigor said simply. "I'd already brought my daughter from Russia. And..." He paused and turned to look at Carwyn. "Much better weather here than in Alaska." He pointed down. "You're standing in poison oak."

"Damn!" Carwyn jumped to the side. "Is this a trail you're taking us to or—"

"I should call Alice." Grigor frowned and threw his head back, making a long, mournful howl that carried through the trees and made the hair on the back of Carwyn's neck stand up.

"Uh-huh," Natalie murmured. "There's no way anyone could mistake that for Bigfoot."

Grigor chuckled, and Carwyn saw Jamie and Ross cross their arms over their chests, their stance and silence evidence of their displeasure.

"Come," Grigor said. "We'll wait for Alice by the stream."

"Why are we waiting at all?" Jamie asked. "Pardon my impatience, Mr. Grigor, but my daughter is missing, and so far, we've just gotten further off track looking for her."

"There's a trail," Grigor said. "But we might need Alice unless you want to get very wet."

Brigid asked, "Is Alice a water vampire?"

"Yes," Grigor said. "Her people have lived here far longer than I have, and these men annoy her."

Brigid shot Carwyn a look. "So you know the men who took Summer and Daniel?"

"I didn't see them take your children," Grigor said. "If I had, I would have stopped them. It's not good for hikers to go missing. That just brings more humans here, and there are already enough humans." He tilted his head ever so slightly. "Alice is coming. We live here because there aren't many people, and the ones who come usually stay on the trails. We can't blame them for enjoying the wilderness. The rangers are the same. Good people."

"These other men?" A woman stepped from the shadows,

dressed in a pair of jeans, a canvas shirt, and sturdy boots. "They're not the good kind."

"Alice." Grigor's face brightened.

The woman had an oval face and light brown skin marked by fine-line tattoos on her chin and cheeks. Her dark hair was tied back in two long braids that fell over her shoulders, and she wore a floppy hat on her head.

Brigid asked, "You're Katya's sire?"

"Yes." She propped one foot on a fallen log and looked at Natalie. "And your husband works for her, yeah? The dangerous dark-haired one."

"Why do you think he's dangerous?" Natalie asked.

"If he wasn't, my daughter wouldn't have hired him." She turned to the two Mackenzies. "I'm Alice. You're not from *our* mountains, but I can tell you're from mountains."

"We're from the East Coast," Ross said. "My niece—Jamie's daughter—went missing a couple of weeks ago. She has curly red hair and fair skin. Lots of freckles, and she's with her boyfriend. He's from Mexico and he's a soccer player."

"You're looking for her?" Alice asked.

"Yes, ma'am."

"And the boy?"

"Sure," Jamie said. "We want to find him too."

Alice smiled a little. "I noticed them on the trail, you know? A beautiful couple. She loves him a lot."

Jamie was losing patience. "That's great, but if you could just—"

"The water doesn't know you here." Alice stepped over a fallen log and headed out of the small clearing where they'd been waiting. "Don't look at it for too long. And don't speak loudly as we're crossing. That goes for all of you but the redheaded girl."

Natalie's eyes went wide. "Why? I'm an earth vampire."

"But the water here knows you," Alice said. "The others? No."

Grigor didn't hesitate a moment before he followed. Jamie and Ross hoisted their packs and were right behind him.

Carwyn and Brigid exchanged a look. Carwyn shrugged and followed Alice.

"Why not?" Brigid asked. "We've still got a couple of hours before dawn."

"She is so cool," Natalie whispered. "That part about the water knowing people? I swear that's real. Baojia says little things like that all the time, then pretends he didn't."

"It does sound a little mystical for him," Brigid said.

"We're vampires," Carwyn said. "Are we really afraid of the mystical?"

BRIGID HIKED over hills and under the ancient bones of redwood groves, some growing in shapes that defied imagination, branching out like candelabra in the darkness. First they followed a trickling stream that led them to a creek that led them to a river.

She looked up at her mate. "Are you getting any hint of their scents?"

Carwyn nodded. "Bits and pieces. The fog and the rain degraded most of the trail, but any place Daniel bled, I get a stronger hit."

"How much blood?"

"Not enough to threaten his life as long as the wound didn't get infected. I'd say it was mostly superficial."

"Or it was wrapped," Jamie said quietly. "Summer knows first aid."

Brigid didn't have a response to that, and Jamie's expression was grim enough that she left him to his thoughts.

Alice stopped on the bank of a wide river with rocky banks. "They would have crossed here. There's a four-wheeler track on the other side."

Mindful of Alice's warning, Brigid only glanced at the dark, rushing water. Maybe it was her imagination, but the stream did seem to have a life of its own.

Alice stepped onto the rocks and spoke quietly as she slowly spread her arms. The water answered her call, rising in a wall as she continued murmuring.

It was hard not to look directly at it; Brigid would never tire of seeing other vampires manipulate their elements. It was like watching another martial artist work; she always learned something even if it was a different practice.

"Cross now," Alice said. "Remember, keep your eyes ahead of you except for the redheaded girl."

Jamie and Ross crossed first, followed by Carwyn and Grigor, with Brigid and Natalie bringing up the rear.

Natalie reached out and ran her fingers along the wall of water Alice held back as they crossed.

"It likes you," Alice said. "Your mate is a water vampire, so your amnis feels safe."

"He is." Natalie smiled. "And I grew up camping in these woods."

Alice's expression softened. "So you're old friends. No wonder."

Brigid didn't say anything as she walked across the streambed, and she didn't touch the water even though she was tempted. As she passed Alice, the older vampire looked at her pointedly.

"You smell of death."

Brigid blinked. "I smell of fire. That's my element."

Alice looked up and around at the dense forest, then back to Brigid. "Like I said. Death."

Warning received. Brigid nodded and continued walking, grateful to reach the far bank. There she could see the tracks from the four-wheelers and a clearing where they turned around.

"This road will eventually lead you to their trailer," Alice said. "But Grigor can get you there without me." She turned to walk back.

"Alice!" Natalie said. "You're not coming with us?"

She frowned. "Why would I?"

Grigor put a hand on Natalie's shoulder. "She doesn't leave the wilderness," he said. "She rarely comes this far. She doesn't like being away from the sea."

"I get it." Natalie stared at the departing woman who disappeared across the stream and into the woods on the far bank.

"I'll take you to their trailer tomorrow night," Grigor said. "But for the day, you can stay at my house."

Carwyn pointed at the stream. "But Alice just left. She doesn't live with you?"

"Oh no." Grigor started down the four-wheeler path but quickly detoured down a smaller track. "Alice has her own place near the river. We don't live together." He turned to look at Carwyn. "We've been mated a very long time. Space is good."

Brigid raised her eyebrows when Carwyn looked at her. She could read his expression in a blink. "Please," she said. "Do you really think I'd trust you not to cause some mischief if I wasn't keeping an eye on you?" She winked at him and followed Grigor.

"Thank goodness," Carwyn said. "I thought my evening-cuddle nights might be numbered."

They walked through another dense wood, this one teeming with wildlife. Numerous deer crossed their path before they darted away. Skunks waddled through the undergrowth, and birds called overhead. It was the most alive the woods had felt since they arrived.

"The animals here are used to me." Grigor answered the unspoken question. "I like having them around."

"What about when you hunt?" Natalie said. "Do you go farther away?"

Grigor frowned and glanced over his shoulder. "I don't hunt the deer."

"Oh? So what do you—? Oh." Natalie pressed her lips together. "Right."

Clearly Summer and Daniel's kidnappers weren't the only ones taking advantage of the hikers on the trail.

"I'm old." The corner of Grigor's mouth crept up. "I don't need to kill the humans. I'd have to kill a deer."

Brigid nudged Carwyn. "You know, when he puts it like that, I'm probably far more ethical than you are."

"Keep telling yourself that," Carwyn muttered. "I smell smoke."

"It's the chimney," Grigor said. "My servant is cooking for us."

Jamie said quietly, "That's fine of you, Mr. Grigor, but we did bring food with us."

"Not as good as my cook's." Grigor pressed through a thick stand of manzanita and disappeared from view. Ross hesitated for only a second before he followed.

Then Jamie.

Then Natalie.

Brigid and Carwyn brought up the rear. As she entered the glade where a moss-covered cabin took up most of the space, she was rendered speechless.

It looked like something out of a fairy story, the old redwood cabin sitting in a circle of larger redwoods like a child among elders. The roof was covered in wood shingles that were overgrown with moss. Light streamed into the clearing, the nearly full moon passing overhead like a solitary sentry.

In front of the cabin in a circle of stone, a figure crouched over a fire, poking at coals and singing a song that sounded like a sea chantey.

"...steady course to the haven" —he sang in a rumbling bass— "hew many—"

"Björn."

The man looked up when Grigor said his name. "Huh," he grunted. "People." Björn looked like he was roughly seventy years old and just as grizzled as Grigor. He stood and straightened shoulders that remained unstooped. "I'll add more meat to the stew."

"We're vampires," Carwyn said. "We don't eat much."

"Speak for yourself." Brigid pushed forward. "That smells amazing."

"Me too." Natalie walked over to the fire and stuck her hand out. "Nice to meet you, Björn."

The old man seemed reluctant to shake, so Natalie pulled her hand back and looked around the glade. "It's beautiful here."

"You people staying the night?" Björn's eyes landed on Jamie. "He's human."

The mountain man nodded. "I'm here looking for my daughter. She went missing a couple of weeks ago with her boyfriend."

"Bigfoot," muttered Björn.

"We know it's not Bigfoot," Brigid said. "Grigor already told us about the humans taking hikers off the trail."

Björn simply shrugged. "Grigor doesn't know everything."

"Come," Grigor said. "I'll show you to rooms, and you can decide if you want to stay here for the day." He spread his arm toward the forest. "You can always dig around, but I'd prefer you don't disturb the redwood roots."

"You go look," Brigid said. "I'll stay with Björn."

Carwyn kissed the top of her head. "Behave."

"It's like you don't even know me at all." She sat on a log across from Grigor's cook and stared at him.

Björn stared back. "I'm not afraid of your kind."

"Good." She stretched out her legs. "Do you have any gum?"

Björn was clearly not expecting that question. "Gum?"

"Chewing gum. I know, terrible habit, but it's better than lighting things on fire. Any flavor will do," Brigid said. "Except cinnamon. Cinnamon's pure shite."

TEN

Fully a half hour later, Brigid was relaxing by the fire, whirling a pocket of flames in a slow, steady circle with Björn staring at her. She'd managed to find some gum in her pack, a precaution she only took when she felt stifled by the control fire forced on her. Between the spearmint in her mouth and the fire tickling her fingertips, she was more relaxed than she had been in days and her mind was starting to clear.

"There has to be something more going on," she told Carwyn when he returned from checking out the cabin.

"What do you mean?" Carwyn sat next to her, and Ross sat across the fire. "Cabin's excellent by the way. Room's secure. Jamie said something about taking a sofa and saving human strength."

"That's good," Ross said. "He pushes himself keeping up with us."

"We're not talking about a serial killer," Brigid said. "People have been stolen, not killed. You don't steal people without a reason."

Ross nodded slowly. "Go on."

"Living captives are a liability," Brigid said. "From a security standpoint, they're the worst possible leverage. You have to keep them healthy but hidden. You have to feed them, shelter them, keep them secure. Daniel was injured, but they kept him. Logically, it would have made far more sense to kill him and leave him to be found. Or kill him and hide the body in a place where it *wouldn't* be found if you cared about subterfuge."

"Captives *are* a lot of work," Carwyn said. "What makes the risk worth it?"

"Money?" Brigid shrugged. "I can't think of anything else right now."

"Whoever took Summer can't be after money," Ross said. "The Mackenzies aren't puttin' on any airs. We're a big clan and a strong one, but we're not rich. Most of our people live pretty simple, and all our humans have day jobs."

"So Daniel?" Carwyn asked. "Daniel's family is extremely wealthy."

"But as far as we know, they haven't received a ransom demand," Brigid said. "So why else would you take a human?"

"Some folks," Björn muttered, "just wrong in the head."

The swift silence that descended told Brigid that the others had the same thought.

"We can't discount a twisted mind." Brigid had been a victim of abuse by her stepfather. She knew that abusers didn't have to have a reason to victimize others. They justified everything in their own sick minds. "But this is an awful lot of trouble to go to to grab victims if you're just looking for a sick thrill."

Carwyn cocked his head. "I hadn't thought about that. It's isolated. It's remote. It takes *work* to grab people from these areas."

"Hell," Ross said. "If ya just wanted to steal a person, you'd have better luck at a Walmart on the interstate."

"Exactly," Brigid said. "If they'd grabbed a random human from a parking lot, they could be on the road and in another state before that person was reported missing."

Ross picked up a stick and pulled out a hunting knife. "Maybe" —he started whittling— "whatever reason they got, they need people who are a little stronger."

Brigid nodded and met Ross's gaze. "I think that's exactly it. They're looking for young, fit people who can survive in adverse conditions. People exactly like Summer."

"Who though?" Carwyn asked. "And why?"

She mulled over their suspects. "Ernesto—"

"Can't see him going to all this trouble," Carwyn said. "And this isn't his style."

"The Sokolovs?" Brigid threw out.

"This is their style, but it's also... complicated."

"True," Brigid said. "Subtlety isn't exactly their wheelhouse. They'd be the ones grabbing people from Walmart."

Ross said, "Me and Jamie are not holdin' out on you. We got our rivals, but we can't think of anyone who'd go after Summer this way."

"So we're back at square one." Brigid looked at the house and saw Natalie walk out on the porch. She marched down the steps, carrying what looked like a tablet or a notebook, and she stomped straight up to Björn.

Björn frowned and looked up from stirring the stew. "Can I help you?"

She opened the notebook and showed something to him. "You drew this?"

Björn nodded. "I do a bit of sketching. I been watching that trailer for a while."

She flipped through a few more pages. "And this man?"

"That un's a vampire like you. Do you know him?"

Natalie snapped the notebook shut. "He can't be."

Brigid stood. "Natalie, what it is?"

She sat on one of the logs that encircled the fire and held the notebook to her chest. "I'm seeing ghosts."

Brigid shot a look toward Carwyn. "What's that mean?"

Natalie flipped the notebook over and started paging through. "So okay. Björn watches the trailer in the woods where we're going tomorrow night…"

"I know how to stay hidden," Björn muttered. "Not a hardship."

"We know all that," Brigid said. "And?"

"There's someone who shouldn't be there." She flipped to the page she'd shown Björn. "This man—this vampire—Baojia and I know him."

The drawing was sketched in black and white, but the man's features looked European, and he had distinct scars on both sides of his mouth.

"His name is Ivan," Natalie said. "He was an enforcer for the vampire cartel that ran northern Mexico, the one who was taking the human girls and testing the elixir on them."

"Fuck," Brigid said. "I remember that. Don't know that I ever saw him though."

"We could never tie him directly to the girls. He used his lieutenants, so they were the ones we took out, and he was too high up in the cartel to push it."

"Elixir is dead," Carwyn said. "There's no reason Ivan would be taking people for that anymore."

"Or there's something else going on." Ross's expression was grim. "Some other drug or experiment. That would explain why they want healthy people."

"If this man was working for the cartel in Mexico," Brigid said, "why would he be up here? How could he even be operating without Baojia knowing he was around?"

"Good question," Grigor said from the porch. "Tomorrow night we must find these people, extract the truth from them, and find the humans they've taken."

"As soon as I can get signal again, I'm calling Baojia," Natalie said. "If Ivan is in Northern California, I guarantee it's not with Katya's permission."

BRIGID WAS SURPRISED to find she actually missed their van. An hour before dawn, she was secured in one of Grigor's rooms, which was really just a slightly nicer cave dug into the hill with a floor lined in cheap carpet and a shared bathroom down the hall. The walls were only lightly plastered, and she could feel the chill of ocean fog drenching the air.

Carwyn would be thrilled.

The bed, on the positive side, was enormous, fitting the giant vampire who had become their unexpected host. Natalie had taken the other bedroom while Ross was more than happy to dig his own cave in an area that wouldn't disturb the redwood roots. Jamie was sacked out and snoring in the den, and Brigid had no idea where Grigor was, but she was beginning to suspect Katya's father really was a Sasquatch.

She was looking through her notebook when Carwyn returned from the shower.

"Brilliantly refreshing," he said. "While I do give five stars for the size of the bed, the bath facilities may knock the review down a peg or two."

The corner of her mouth turned up. "Am I to assume that 'brilliantly refreshing' means the water has a slight chill?"

"Oh yes," Carwyn said, his Welsh accent getting stronger the closer he got to sleep. "Ice-cold might be closer to reality."

She looked up from her notebook. "Did you expect Bigfoot to have a water heater?"

He glanced at the kerosene lamps that lit their room. "Actually, this is far more civilized than I gave Bigfoot credit for. Perhaps five stars are in order."

She tossed her notebook to the side and opened her arms. "Come here, ya fine one. I can warm you up."

His eyebrows shot up and he dove into bed, tossing aside the towel that had been wrapped around his hips. "Tell me what you had in mind."

Brigid was laughing before he managed to tug her shirt off. "You're such a beast."

"We're in the forest." He was already working on her pants. "That seems appropriate, doesn't it?"

"You're just excited about having a real bed to play in." She closed her eyes, put her arms around his neck, and spread her hands wide, drawing heat to her palms and warming his skin, which was icy from the shower.

She slid her palms over the broad span of his shoulders as his mouth found a particular spot behind her ear that

Carwyn knew she loved. Her legs, now blessedly free of pants, rose and wrapped around his hips.

Anywhere their bodies touched, heat bloomed. Mouth to neck. Hand to shoulder. Thigh to hip.

Brigid arched her back when Carwyn found her small breast with his mouth and tasted it with the patience of a starving man. One hand gripped her wrist over her head, holding her down, as the other teased between her legs, threatening to drive her insane with sensual hunger.

"Yes," she whispered. "There."

"Like this?" He moved his hand, teasing her.

She pounded her fist on his shoulder. "Don't you dare!" She'd almost been at climax.

Carwyn's laugh was pure evil. "I'm still cold in several key places, darling Brigid. I can't have you losing your fire too soon."

Brigid narrowed her eyes, wrested her wrist from his grasp, and spread both hands on his backside. Then she heated her hands so hot and so fast he yelped and burst into laughter, trying to wriggle away.

"Mercy, Brigid!" He was choking on laughter. "Damn you, woman."

She let his butt go with a warning pinch. "Don't tease a vampire about her orgasm. Especially when she's in a real bed for the first time in over a week."

"Oh, love." He scooted up to her and pressed kisses along her jaw. "I'm sorry. You're right, I deserved a burned arse."

"I didn't actually burn you, did I?" She sat up and tried to look, but he flipped her forward and onto her knees, then quickly scooted under her and spread her legs.

"There now, let's try this angle, shall we?" He pulled her hips down over his mouth and feasted.

Brigid nearly fell on her face. "Oh fuck *me*."

He lifted her up a second so he could speak. "That is definitely the idea."

"It's a good one." Her eyes rolled back. "A very good one."

In a few short minutes, Brigid was screaming his name and gasping for release. She pounded on the bed, a headache already threatening.

It was a peculiar quirk that none of her female friends had ever mentioned or complained about, but when Brigid came very hard, it was as if all the blood in her immortal body rushed south and she came away with a blinding headache. It was the only time she ever felt that particularly human pain anymore.

Carwyn flipped her over and scooted up, wiping a hand across his mouth. "Headache good?"

"Dear God." She covered her eyes, a wave of sharp pain rolling over her temples. "Give it a second and it'll pass."

"I'd love to know if this happens to other vampires, but as you're my first long-term sexual partner in roughly a thousand years, I can't really offer any insight."

"Right. Not something they cover at the Vatican Office of Immortal Clergy then." Her husband had been a Catholic priest for most of his vampire life. Sometimes the learning curve was thrown off for both of them.

The wave of pain in her temples passed, and Brigid was left with a euphoric high, her amnis dancing in her body like effervescent bubbles in a glass of champagne.

"*Jaysus.*" She reached for him. "That was on another level. You really are a beast."

"Grrrr." He pretended to bite her hip. His fangs were out, scraping the skin and raising light red marks.

Brigid's own fangs dropped. She wanted his teeth in her. She wanted all of him in her. "Come here."

"Feeling better?" He got on all fours and crawled up her body, caging her with his massive arms and legs.

"Feeling..." She reached down and closed her hand over him. "...a need."

He lowered himself, met her mouth in a luxurious kiss, and whispered, "We can't have that."

She kept her eyes locked on his as he slid into her, the intimate connection of their eyes as vital as the link between their bodies.

"I adore you," she whispered.

His expression melted into softness, even as he moved his hard body in hers. "My life." He kissed her forehead. "My wife."

She pressed her face to his chest and buried herself in his scent and the rhythm of his body with hers. Before he came, he flipped them over, letting her straddle him as he reached for his climax.

"Teeth." His jaw was clenched. "Give them to me."

She leaned forward, put her arms around his shoulders, and sank her fangs deep into his neck.

Carwyn roared, and the ground shook around them as he came.

ELEVEN

It would have been too obvious to strike the trailer at dusk. Carwyn wanted the humans to be either sleeping or sleepy. If there were vampires at the trailer, it wouldn't matter when they attacked. But the humans they could wait for. It was roughly three in the morning when they crept close to the clearing.

The trailer was actually two trailers attached to each other with a ramshackle shed at one end. Tracks leading to the shed told Carwyn that's where the vehicles were stored. He couldn't see anything else of interest in the small clearing. Just the trailers, the shed, and an old windmill attached to what looked like a water pump.

"The same as you remember it?" Carwyn asked Grigor.

The giant had melted into the forest, barely visible in his dark clothes and mud-smeared face and beard. "I don't see any changes."

Björn mumbled, "The truck is gone."

"The truck?"

The older man nodded. "There was a new truck parked

here the other night. King cab with darkened windows. Covered bed. It was expensive."

"I didn't see the truck," Grigor said. "But if Björn says it was here, it was here."

"Okay, tell us more about that later." Brigid crouched down next to Carwyn and looked from behind a tree. "For now, let's focus on the trailer. I'm scenting four humans and one vampire."

"I don't think the vampire is here," Björn said. "I think he drives the truck."

"I can smell him, but the scent might not be fresh," Natalie said. "There are a lot of competing scents in the area, but something about his stands out. It's... dry."

"Is Ivan an earth vampire?" Carwyn asked.

"I believe so." Natalie kept her eyes on the old white structures. "These trailers are a lie."

"What do you mean?" Brigid said.

"I mean they're new, but they're aged so they don't look new." She pointed to the base. "Do you see any rust? None. Things rust in months up here, if not faster." She pointed to the roof. "No moss. They dirtied up the siding, did a little damage to the panels, and smeared some paint. But these trailers are new. No more than a few years maximum."

Grigor nodded. "That fits. I don't pay much attention to humans, but Björn, does that seem correct to you?"

"I think I found this place about two years ago, but it could have been longer." He shrugged. "Don't keep track of time so well."

"So we have new trailers showing up just around the time that the rate of hikers going missing on the trail spikes up,"

Carwyn said. "Do you see any of them here though? Any hikers?"

"No," Björn said. "Never. Just the guys. I thought they were growing pot out here, but I couldn't find any fields. And I looked way all around the place. If they're pot growers, that would make sense being all secret-like."

"I suppose." Brigid didn't take her eyes off the trailers. The moon was full over the clearing, and she didn't hear a soul stirring.

Now was the time to act.

SUMMER SHOOK DANI'S ARM. "It's time."

Without a word, the man rolled up to sitting, rubbed his eyes, and started packing the small knapsack he'd tied together with a pillowcase and some rope. He stuffed some food and some of the yarrow weed in the bag, then threw it over his shoulders.

One of the things their kidnappers did was take their socks every night and give them fresh ones in the morning. It served two purposes. Their feet stayed healthy with fresh socks, and captives were less likely to leave if they didn't have socks for their hiking boots.

It couldn't matter. They'd wrapped their feet as well as they could with scraps of cloth they'd torn from their clothes and the blankets in their small cabin. Then they stuffed their feet in their boots and forced them on.

Was it comfortable? No. But Summer knew it would be more comfortable than nothing once they got running through the forest.

"I didn't see the Russian tonight," Dani said.

"That means nothing." Summer was hoping that Dani was right and the vampire had other errands to run since the shiny black pickup was nowhere to be found, but she wasn't betting on anything. "Do you remember the plan?"

Dani started wrapping the strips of blanket around his face to protect his skin. "Let you lead. Only step where you step until you signal that it is clear."

"Yes." She was betting on booby traps leading toward the road and a few leading to the creek, but once they were in the creek itself, they'd probably be safe. "We're going to follow the water downstream. If you follow water downstream far enough, you're going to find people."

"Follow the water downstream." Dani nodded. "And keep our eyes down."

"There are probably fishhooks or razor blades hanging in the forest," she said. "That's what the masks are for." The last thing they needed was a fishhook in the eye. "And if we get separated?"

"Follow the water downstream," Dani said. "I got it."

Summer looked out a crack between the cabin walls and saw moon shadows from the brilliant night sky. "Okay, we need to go. Follow me."

Summer moved to the back of the cabin and shifted the two boards she'd loosened over the previous few days. She let them fall down, then shimmied out the opening before she loosened another one so Dani could get through.

"You got it?"

Dani wriggled his body through the narrow gap, the backpack trailing over his head. Then he righted himself and gave her a thumbs-up.

Summer began the careful trail behind the cabins, headed to the creek path where she'd worked one day, helping one of their human captors fix the pipes that watered the plants at that top of the hill. It was barely more than an animal track leading down to a creek with a wide shallow pool and falls below it, but Summer figured that worked to their advantage.

Climbing over the falls would be tricky, and she was counting on their captors thinking any escapees would choose the faster escape route of the road.

She grabbed a walking stick she'd stashed near the drying house and used it to feel the path in front of her. As they left the rough clearing where their cabins and the marijuana fields were, the forest became darker, denser, and more oppressive.

She could hear chittering in the woods and knew there were more animals here than the deer that occasionally wandered into their camp. This was mountain lion country. Bear country. And while neither of those two predators would choose her and Dani as a first meal, if they were hungry, all bets were off.

She poked her stick at the ground and walked carefully, keeping her eye out for the guard who patrolled the cabin area at night. Summer was betting on him passing out with the six-pack she knew he stashed behind a redwood tree.

He was counting on all their captives being exhausted from the day's work and sleeping. Summer was counting on his laziness.

She poked the ground in front of her as she walked, steering them around two pit traps. She waved a pine branch overhead, careful not to walk into the lines of fishhooks ten feet away from the clearing. It was a haphazard effort that they ducked around, easily finding their way back to the path after detouring around some brush to avoid them.

"Are we clear?" Dani whispered.

"We'll be clear when we get downstream," Summer said. "Don't get casual." She didn't mention the slice one of the branches had taken out of her arm. There had been a few razor blades attached to branches.

She was poking at the path and alternately waving the branch overhead, their progress necessarily slow, when she felt it against her ankle. "Fuck."

"What it is?"

"Tripwire." Her mind raced. A tripwire, even if she eased her ankle back, could be rigged to set off an explosive, an alarm... damn near anything. "Dani, I'm going to ease my ankle off it, but stand back. There could be an explosive or something."

"An *explosive*?"

"I told you to stand back!"

The minute she eased pressure off the wire, she heard a gunshot go off in the trees.

"Dammit!" It was an old sort of alarm that bootleggers often used, a way of warning people away and alerting the compound all in one go. "Now we gotta move."

She picked up the pace, and Dani kept close behind her even as they heard voices shouting in the distance.

Though Summer and Dani had been walking for what felt like hours, moving slowly and avoiding the booby traps, their progress had been slow. Summer could just barely hear the waterfall in the distance.

"Summer?"

"Keep going." She kept her eyes on the path, kept moving forward, kept pushing toward the creek.

Once they reached the creek, the booby traps would be history and they could move faster. Once they reached the creek, they'd have a chance.

BRIGID MOVED THROUGH THE SHADOWS, her body a blur that Carwyn could barely see in the darkness. She rushed the front of the trailer with Natalie and Ross on her heels as Carwyn, Jamie, and Grigor moved around to the back. Björn sat waiting at the edge of the clearing with a shotgun and a clear line of sight.

Moving around the back, Carwyn saw a door about five feet off the ground, a back entrance that had never had steps built up to it. He glanced at Grigor and himself, then at the door.

Grigor nodded. "This is a good idea."

Carwyn heard the door to the front of the trailer burst open and a shot rang out.

"Brigid!" Carwyn bashed the door in, splintering the bottom half in one swift punch.

"Alarm," Jamie said. "They had a shotgun rigged to the door."

While it was nearly impossible that a shotgun blast, even a direct one, would kill a vampire, Carwyn was still furious. He tore away the remnants of the door and pulled himself up into the trailer with one heave, only to be faced with a trembling human pointing a gun at his face.

The man snarled, "Wait a goddamn min—"

Carwyn roared and punched a fist into the man's face as the handgun fired into his shoulder. It burned through his flesh, and his fangs ran down. Carwyn bared his teeth and batted the human to the side, throwing him into a wall where the man crashed, then crumpled to the ground.

He turned to the left and saw Brigid moving swiftly in the darkness, fighting against an agile human with knives.

Jamie launched himself into the trailer, immediately heading into the dark back rooms, hunting knife ready for action.

And Ross...

Carwyn blinked as he saw the quiet mountain vampire rip off a human's head with one swift twist. Blood was dripping down the man's jaw and neck. Ross saw Carwyn and Grigor watching him.

He lifted a hunting knife. "I gave this to Summer for her birthday. Bastard tried to cut me with it." Ross flipped the knife over in his fingers and shoved it into his pocket, blade-down, before he followed his brother to search the back rooms.

The invasion of the trailers took only a few swift minutes, but when they were finished, four humans were lined up against one wall, their hands tied behind them, and three were dead on the floor, blood leaking from their broken bodies.

Ross came out of the back hallway, wiping his chin and neck with a black bandanna, his face grim. "We didn't find any hikers, but there's a woman here."

Brigid stepped forward while Natalie and Carwyn watched the human captives. "Where? Who is she?"

Ross dropped his voice. "I have a feeling she's a sex

worker, but I know she ain't here of her own choice if you catch my meaning. Not with a face as beat up as hers is. Jamie's talkin' to her now, but she's real skittish. Might be better if you or Natalie join him." He looked over at the mess of bodies on the floor. "And she sure don't need to be seeing any of this."

Natalie and Brigid exchanged a look; then Brigid walked back down the hallway while Grigor and Carwyn dragged the bodies into the room where the rest of the humans were tied up.

Carwyn sidled over to Natalie. "I heard the shotgun."

She rubbed her chest. "We weren't quite fast enough. Bastard got both of us in the shoulders, but it was scattered. I'll be picking bird shot out of my boob before I go to sleep."

"Now that's an experience I imagine you didn't get when you were a print journalist."

She nodded. "That is a very accurate statement."

THE CREEK WAS in sight when Summer began to feel the first hint of relief. She turned to Dani just in time to see one of the guards running toward them, brandishing a club.

Her eyes went wide. "Dani, duck!"

She pulled him down, but not fast enough. The blow to his head glanced off, and he fell to the ground.

The slope near the creek was a tumble of rocks and branches, the winter rain not yet flushing the waterway to its banks. Summer and Dani stumbled and tumbled toward the water, the guard with the club nearly on top of them.

"I found them!" he shouted. "Tell Ivan I found 'em!"

No—this couldn't happen. They were almost there. They were almost to safety. "Dani, get up!"

The guard was on them again, beating Dani in the abdomen as her boyfriend grabbed for the club.

"Summer, run!" he yelled.

No, she couldn't leave him. She raised her walking stick and brought it down on the guard's head. She jabbed his shoulder and tried to trip him with the stick, but he wouldn't go down.

"Hey, Ricky!" Another guard had found them.

Dani turned to the guard and hurled her stick like a javelin in his direction. "No!"

"What the fuck?" The other guard ducked away from the stick but didn't change direction. "Hey!" He sent out a sharp whistle. "Ricky found 'em by the creek!"

Summer picked up another small log to try to knock the man off Dani, but her boyfriend was on the ground, rolling toward the water and clutching his belly while his head bled over the rocks.

"Dani!" Summer was sobbing. "Get up! Get up please!" She reached for his hand, but the guard brought the club down, breaking her hand and bloodying Dani more.

Her boyfriend looked up and spoke through bloody lips. "Summer, run."

She looked at the guard who'd been beating Dani. He was running toward the creek bed, crawling over the rocks to reach his partner.

"Summer, I love you. Get out of here!" Dani's mouth was bloody and his face was smashed. He was moving his arms, but his legs were frighteningly still. "I can't... you know I can't."

She shook her head. "Don't ask me to leave you."

"Get help." He blinked hard and shoved her away. "If we have any chance—"

"Ivan's coming!" one of the guards said. "I just called; he's on his way back."

Summer's head shot up and her eyes went wide. Ivan. The Russian. The vampire.

Dani gripped her hand with the last of his strength. "*Summer, run.*"

TWELVE

"I'm not the police." Brigid sat against the wall of the trailer, her elbows propped on her knees. "I don't give two shites about your work. I want to make you safe, and I'd like to take care of these bastards so they don't hurt anyone else."

"It wasn't all of them," the woman said quietly. "There were a few who left me alone."

And maybe karma left them alive.

Brigid didn't say it. Talking to victims of assault never got easier for her, but it was something she forced herself to do. She had a responsibility to be there for them. To stand up and listen when they spoke. If they could live it, if they could survive, then she could listen. For them and for the girl she'd been. The girl no one had seen until the monsters called.

So Brigid sat on the floor of a dirty trailer in the middle of the forest and listened to Renee tell her what had happened, smoking a cigarette with the woman after she hadn't picked one up in ten years.

"It was a pretty standard job," Renee began. The guy

hired her in Redway and paid in advance. He seemed nice enough, but she should have listened to her gut when he said he wanted to head to his trailer instead of the hotel she suggested.

That had been three weeks ago.

"Renee, I don't want to put any pressure on you, so only answer if you want to." Brigid leaned against the wall, propping her forearms up on her knees while Renee drank a soda Natalie had found in the refrigerator and smoked her cigarette.

The woman was probably in her early thirties but looked a decade older. "What do you need to know?"

"Jamie, the man who found you, he's out here in California, looking for his daughter. She was up on the coast trail hiking with her boyfriend," Brigid said. "She had long curly red hair and a Southern accent. Pretty distinctive. Have you heard any—"

"Yeah." Renee looked out the window and sniffed. "They'd take people pretty often. Maybe... once a week or so? They'd pick people from the hiking trails. They said..." She frowned. "I'm trying to remember. The Russian guy—he never touched me, but he was the scariest—he told these guys to pick people who could 'handle it.'"

"Handle it?" Brigid asked. "Handle what? Did he say?"

Renee shook her head. "Nah. I tried to stay away from him. He was, like, the scariest guy I ever met."

Brigid frowned. "Why?"

The woman looked confused. "I... I dunno. There was just something about him."

Instinct. Brigid nodded. The woman had good instincts. She knew a predator when she saw one. "Summer went missing about two weeks ago. That would have been a week or so after Jerry took you."

She bobbed her head. "Yeah, I think I heard them. She was real sweet sounding." A light went on behind Renee's eyes. "Yeah, she had a country accent like him. Like the guy who found me. And the guy they took with her, he sounded Mexican. I mean... like a Spanish accent, you know?"

"Did you hear them speaking?"

"Just a little. But the other guys? They all sounded like... regular. Like from around here. Except for the Russian if you count Ivan. So it was easy to hear they had new people."

"I understand. What happened to them?"

"Uh, the Mexican guy, he was hurt or something. They kept arguing about what to do with him, but the girl was saying he'd be fine. You could tell they were pissed at her, but she was just like..." Renee smiled a little. "She was like a pit bull. So the guys argued about it, but then Ivan came in and said he wanted both of them."

"Then what?"

"Nothing." Renee took another drag. "They left. That happened a lot. Ivan would come and take people with him. He usually brought the pot for the guys to sell—at least I'm pretty sure that's what they were doing—and then he'd leave again with any people the guys grabbed."

"And?"

Renee shook her head. "And nothing. If Ivan takes people, you never see them again."

Damn. The knot in Brigid's stomach tightened. "Okay. Thank you, Renee. Can I get your number so I can check on you in a couple of days?"

"Sure, I guess." She took a drag on her cigarette. "Thanks for the smoke. I quit, you know. Like a year ago."

"I quit ten years ago," Brigid said. "Don't tell my aunt. Sometimes you just need one, am I right?"

The woman was staring at the opposite wall. "Yeah."

"Who can we call for you?" Brigid asked softly. "If you want to go to the police, we can."

"No. No cops. The sheriff's deputies up here hate me. Park rangers aren't much better." She leaned her head back against the wall. "I guess my sister. She's up in Shively."

"You gonna be okay if we send Jamie with you? We've got to clean up here and get back to our place before anyone comes looking."

Renee's face went pale. "I heard the shots. And the fighting. Is it bad?"

Brigid shook her head. "You don't have to worry about that anymore. Nothing you're gonna see. I just need to know if Jamie is okay to drive you. I'd trust him to carry my sister or I wouldn't even suggest it."

Renee nodded. "Yeah, that's okay I guess. I can tell him where to go."

"We're a ways away from our vehicles," Brigid said. That was an understatement. "Is there an extra truck around here?"

"Yeah, there's the quads in the shed, but there's an old truck back behind that if you look. I didn't notice it at first 'cause it's kind of covered up with brush, but it works, 'cause that's how Jerry picked me up."

"Thanks." She patted Renee's knee. "Give me a minute to talk to the boys and I'll be right back."

Brigid walked out, told Jamie about the truck, and gave

him the news about Renee's sister in Shively. He nodded; then he and Ross went out to get the vehicle running while Brigid looked for Carwyn and Natalie.

The Mackenzies had thrown carpets or dragged furniture over the worst of the bloodstains in the front room where Carwyn had broken the door. She could take Renee out that way to avoid the remnants of violence.

"Natalie?"

The redhead pulled open a set of accordion doors that separated the front room from the den. "Looking at the carnage?"

"This place is a mess." Brigid peered at the bodies in the corner.

"Yeah," Natalie said. "Luckily, there's enough pot in the kitchen that the anonymous tip we can call in will make sure they all stay in prison for a good long time. I haven't seen a hint of a permit around here, so you know they weren't following the law. The guns alone will send them away."

"Can't do that." Brigid shook her head. "No police on this one."

Natalie stared at her. "What are you saying?"

"The police find this place, they'll probably get the woman's fingerprints. I don't want her mixed up in this. She's already said she doesn't want the police called on what they did to her." She nodded to the four gagged and tied men. "She confirmed that these are the men who took Summer and Dani along with any number of hikers from the trail. They obviously know about vampires because they've been working with Ivan." She turned to Grigor. "I say we take them to Katya. Let her decide what to do with them."

Grigor nodded. "Sure. We can take them to Katya. Or we

can let the mountain vampire kill them. He would do it quickly."

The tied-up men watching them went deathly pale.

"That's right," Natalie said. "I bet Ross would enjoy it too. Work a little tension out of his system."

"We may need information from them, so I don't want to kill them yet." She kicked the foot of one gagged man. "Oh, darling husband?"

Carwyn glanced at her. "My love."

"Get these four on the trail back to the forest. Björn can watch them with Jamie today. We'll sort out what we want to do with them tonight. But we need to get going; we're running out of night."

Carwyn saluted. "Your wish, our command." He nodded down the hall. "Take care of the young woman. We can head back with Björn, and Grigor can wait for you and Ross."

"Sounds like a plan."

SUMMER RAN along the rocks that lined the creek, tears pouring down her face. She could hear the men shouting and kicking at Dani behind her, but she forced herself to keep running.

Follow the water.

Find people.

Get help.

If she could find help, she could find her way back.

Summer, run!

She ran, and she didn't look back. She jogged through the

shallow stream, her boots becoming soaked with freezing water. Her legs were heavy and her throat burned.

Follow the water.

Run, Summer.

Keep going.

She grew hopeful when the sky began to lighten. Daytime brought people and made the monsters hide. In the distance, she saw a bridge over the creek. A junction where the water met the road? The best of both worlds.

As she approached, she crawled up the riverbank, watching over her shoulder for any hint of the guards. She had no idea where she was, but she'd been running for at least an hour.

When she saw a truck approaching from the south, she crawled up the side. Coming from the south was opposite of where the farm was. She stood in the center of the road and waved her arms.

Help.

Help me. Help Dani.

"Help." Tears poured down her grubby cheeks; her face was so hot she thought she might be running a fever. "Please."

The truck slowed down, and Summer fell to her knees. It would be a farmer or a tourist. Anyone was better than—

"Well, well."

Her eyes shot up when she heard Ivan's voice. "No!"

He smiled and cocked his head. "You are a resourceful girl."

Summer sprang to her feet and ran, but Ivan was immortal. She was in his grasp before she could even let out a proper scream.

"*No!*" She pounded on the arm that wrapped around her waist and held her. It was as effective as beating on a rock. "No, no, no, nooooo!"

"What a mess you've made." He dragged her at his side, kicking and screaming. Then he threw her into the back of the truck, slammed the cover down, and she heard a lock click.

All the things she knew about breaking out of a car trunk were useless in the back of a pickup. She kicked up at the cover with all the force she could muster, but it wasn't enough. When they arrived back at the farm, she heard Ivan get out of the truck and knew it was hopeless.

"Hey, boss. You find her?"

"I had to loop back around the river, but yes."

"What do you want to do with her?"

There was a long silence.

"For now, just leave her in the truck. Where's the other one?"

Another silence that made Summer's heart stop.

"Yeah, Ricky kind of lost his temper with that one. The kid beat up his hand real bad, and he has that club..."

"What are you saying? Did the buffoon kill him? That one was *valuable*."

"Yeah... He's gone."

Pain ripped through Summer's chest, leaving her unable to breathe. Unable to move. Unable to even cry.

No, no, no, no, no!

"I'm real sorry, Ivan."

"A lot of idiots you are!" Ivan muttered curses in Russian. "Do you think I'm keeping them for a hobby?" Ivan's voice was acid. "For some... collection? You fucking idiot!" The sound of a slap cracked the air. "*Don't* let this one die. Check on her every few hours and make sure she doesn't overheat."

"Yes, boss."

Summer curled into herself, forgetting the blisters on her feet and the bruises over her body. Everything in her felt cold. Dani was dead.

Dani. My beautiful Dani.

I shouldn't have left you.

I never should have left.

"Summer?" Ivan's voice was patronizing when he patted his hand on the truck cover. "I'm very sorry about your boyfriend, but this was your fault for trying to escape. Behave today while I'm gone."

Dani.

She had nothing left. Nothing left to fight for. Nothing left to live for.

Dani, Dani, Dani.

"Summer, do you hear me? Be good today."

I'm going to kill you, Ivan.

Summer closed her eyes and rolled over, praying for the oblivion of sleep.

I promise, Dani. I promise.

I will *kill him.*

THIRTEEN

Carwyn watched Brigid as she slept, mentally mapping the geography of his mate's face. Her pointed chin and pixie features would have been sweet if she were the smiling type. Her dark brown hair was cut short, sticking out at odd angles from sleeping. Pillow lines crossed her face, and a slight frown turned down the corners of her mouth.

She was a tiny, taciturn, avenging fairy godmother to the victims lucky enough to have her heart. Carwyn knew that Brigid would call the woman they'd found in the trailer the night before. She'd call and she'd follow up. She wouldn't just find the name of a shelter in her area, she'd track down a social worker or community member as stubborn as she was and give that person Renee's address and phone number.

Denying Brigid Connor's determination to help you wasn't really an option once she had you in her sights.

He brushed a hand over the crown of her head, smoothing back the cowlick that stuck out. She shifted, and her lips pushed forward into a pout. He resisted the urge to kiss her awake since she'd nearly collapsed in Grigor's living room that morning before dawn.

He could feel her amnis waking, the slow shimmer of vibration in her blood that enlivened her body and animated her features.

Brigid's eyes blinked awake and immediately found his. "Where are we?"

"Grigor's house in the King Range National Conservation area in Northern California. Katya's territory."

She closed her eyes, then opened them slowly. He could see her collecting the disparate pieces from her memory. "Did Jamie get Renee to her sister's?"

"I believe so. I heard him coming in around nine in the morning. He spoke to Björn before he passed out, but he's awake again."

"The humans?"

"I'm not saying that Ross and Grigor buried them somewhere, but I'm not... *not* saying that either. I'm sure they have air."

"I'm sure they've pissed their pants as well." She sat up and rubbed her eyes. "They were taking the kidnapped humans somewhere, and from the amount of marijuana they had in that trailer, I'm going to guess it's a farm. Now that we know who the vampire is behind it, we need to—"

"Eat first." He shoved a bag of preserved blood in her face. "You're pushing yourself."

Brigid looked slightly sheepish, and Carwyn pulled the blood away.

"Or have you been hunting on your own?" The corner of his mouth turned up. She was adorable when she was guilty, and it didn't happen often. Other than swearing in front of her aunt, not much made Brigid Connor feel ashamed.

"Not hunting exactly, but I decided the men we took could spare some of their blood. Considering how much they've likely spilled."

"Fair point." He flipped the bagged blood in his fingers. "So none of this for you, eh?"

Brigid narrowed her eyes. "I keep seeing signs to 'eat local.' So I did."

He chuckled and pulled her in for a fast kiss. "Very conscientious of you, wife. What was next on the agenda?"

"I want to question the men before we take them to Katya. That trip's going to eat up an entire night, which I don't want to do, but I think you and I should take the men back in the van and leave Natalie up here with Ross and Jamie if she's comfortable with that. They have a vehicle and they can drive into town, ask around, and maybe Natalie can meet with the police officer she was speaking about."

"No police up here," Carwyn said. "Too rural. It'll all be county sheriffs and deputies."

Brigid shook her head. "Feckin' American law enforcement. It's about as organized as my granny's yarn drawer."

"You don't have a granny."

"Details." She got out of bed and dug around in her backpack before she pulled off her shirt, yanking on another before Carwyn could even say a proper hello to her breasts.

So inconsiderate.

"Are you ready to go?" she asked. "I have a feeling this is going to be a very long night."

IT TOOK NEARLY HALF the night to return to the house in Shelter Cove with the four humans in tow, then another four hours driving the "fast route" to Katya's house along the Russian River.

Baojia had only been home with the kids two nights before the call from Natalie came that they'd found humans who were working with his old rival. He was pacing when they arrived.

By the time the men were standing in front of Katya and Baojia, they looked less like a criminal gang and more like the residents of a drunk tank after a holiday weekend.

"You killed three of them?" Katya asked.

"One shot Natalie, and I—we—picked out the birdshot, and two got in the way of Ross Mackenzie."

Katya examined the men like bugs on a microscope slide. "Understandable." She pointed at one. "You took a girl two weeks ago. Southern accent. Curly red hair."

The man went pale. "She's the one who said someone'd come looking for her."

Katya raised an eyebrow. "You should have listened to her."

Baojia was standing at Katya's shoulder with his arms behind his back. "Who do you work for?"

The men looked from one to the other, all but one shaking their heads.

"Hey." The man who didn't shake his head rolled his eyes. "Fuckheads, they're vamps like Ivan. You think they're going to take no for an answer?" The man looked directly at Baojia. "My name is Henry Cliff. I've worked for Ivan about three years."

"Did you know he was in this territory without the

permission of the vampire in charge of the Pacific Northwest?"

"Dude, I didn't even know there *was* a vampire in charge of the Pacific Northwest. My brother and I were out of work, he offered us jobs, we took them. We figured he was weird, but whatever, you know? We didn't hurt anyone."

Katya's eyebrows shot up. "Kidnapping people isn't hurting them?"

"When we hand people over to Ivan, they're healthy. That's all I know."

Brigid definitely wanted to stab him. "What did Ivan want you to do? Did he mention the Lost Coast Trail specifically?" She glanced at Katya. "I hope you don't mind my asking."

"Of course not." She motioned toward the men. "Ask anything you like. I'll make sure they answer."

One of the men looked like he was ready to throw up.

"Ivan didn't mention the trail," the palest man said. "That was our idea 'cause… you know, most of the people on that trail are from away. Ivan just said we should grab hikers because they were pretty healthy, you know? They'd be good workers."

"He makes 'em work on his pot farm or something," Henry said. "He's not killing 'em. If he was killing 'em, he wouldn't care who we grabbed."

Katya was rubbing her temple. "I'm never going to hear the end of this."

Baojia glanced down. "You had no way of knowing. They spread out the abductions enough—"

"Two years my parents have been telling me there's a stranger in the area, and I brushed them off," Katya muttered.

"You think my mother is ever going to let me forget that?" She glanced at Brigid. "You met Alice?"

"Yes. She seems… stern."

"She was an excellent stepmother and wonderful sire, but she has a very…" Katya took a deep breath. "…*very* long memory."

Henry was nodding. "I know what you mean. My old man—"

"Human, be quiet." Katya held up a hand, and two guards approached the four humans. "Alexander, will you—?"

"Wait!" Another one of the humans decided he knew how to talk. "We know more stuff. Like…" He looked at his fellow captives. "Like where Ivan…?"

The rise of his voice and his panicked eyes told Brigid that the men had no idea where Ivan took the kidnapped hikers. They did a job every couple of weeks. Ivan gave them money and marijuana to sell for cash.

The brilliance of his plan was the banality.

"Take them away." Katya waved her hand, and three more vampires appeared to take custody of the humans. "We need to get trackers in the area." She looked at Brigid and Carwyn. "I am in your debt for exposing this vampire trespassing in my territory."

"It was Natalie who caught the ID," Carwyn said. "We can't claim credit. She spotted Ivan as soon as she saw Björn's sketches."

"Björn." Katya smiled. "I tried and tried to sire him, but he wasn't having it. No desire for immortal life." She steepled her fingers and looked at the fire. "He would have made an excellent vampire when he was young."

Baojia moved to sit in the armchair adjacent to Katya when the humans had been taken from the room.

"What will you do with them?" Brigid asked.

"We have places to put them for now." Baojia looked at Katya.

She said, "I'll wait until Ivan is apprehended before I decide their fate."

"If one of the live ones is named Jerry," Brigid said quietly, "he's a sexual predator. Don't let him leave here alive."

Katya raised a single eyebrow. "Understood."

Baojia leaned forward. "I've already told Katya this, but you should know: I checked with my sister and called the Mexican cartel in Ensenada about Ivan. As of two and a half years ago, he's a rogue. This is the first anyone has heard of him popping up since the Mexicans kicked him out of their organization."

Katya muttered, "Likely story."

Baojia smiled a little. "Katya is convinced that Ernesto allowed Ivan to head into her territory to destabilize her so he could press north."

"He's been trying to get me out of California for centuries," Katya said. "He's such a snob."

"Is it because you're Russian?" Brigid asked. "I know the Spanish—"

"It's not that I'm Russian, it's that I'm young." She kicked her feet up on the coffee table. "Ernesto has always been very big on immortals paying their dues, so to speak. I started with a very strong takeover of a vampire he'd once been friendly with; then I secured San Francisco and pushed north. I did not stop. I did not negotiate. Ernesto thought I was an upstart; I think he was jealous of my drive."

Brigid glanced at Baojia, who was nodding.

"He thinks Katya's a kid," the water vampire said. "He doesn't even make a secret of it."

"He's a shortsighted old man. Think about how he treated Baojia." Katya turned to her lieutenant. "He kept you on security detail in San Diego for years when he should have been giving you more responsibility, not less." Katya shook her head. "He's a fool."

"I do think Paula is telling the truth though," Baojia said. "I know her pretty well and we videoconferenced." He looked at Brigid. "She's not that good a liar, and she's sure Ernesto has no idea Ivan is up here. Though she admitted that if he'd known, he still probably wouldn't have told Katya because the man's Russian."

"And Ernesto is an asshole," Katya muttered. "Like Ivan, actually. They'd make a good team. The Mexicans were smart to get rid of him, but I'm still not convinced about Ernesto."

Carwyn asked, "Are you sure Ensenada cut him loose? Their main business is narcotics; he's growing marijuana."

"The Ensenada cartel has actually been branching out a lot." Baojia looked at Brigid. "High-end tequila."

"Really?"

"Surprisingly good markup."

"I don't think we're looking to invest," Brigid said. "But I'll remember that."

"I knew Ivan when I was in San Diego," Baojia continued. "Drug networks are what he knows. They cut him off after he pissed off the wrong people too many times. I didn't get the details, but it was pretty clear that if he heads anywhere near their territory, his head is theirs."

Katya took a deep breath. "So I have a rogue in my territory undermining my people, taking humans, and violating human and vampire law." She turned to Baojia. "Take the people you need, head north, and deal with him. Hopefully by the time you get there, Natalie will have narrowed down the search area. Take care of it, Baojia. I don't want to hear Ivan's name again."

"Understood."

One of the servants approached with a tablet, heading for Katya. "Ma'am, there's a call for Baojia. I believe it's his wife."

Katya waved the secretary closer.

Baojia reached for the tablet in the thick vampire-proof case. "Natalie?"

"Are you with everyone?"

He set the tablet on the table, and Carwyn and Brigid crowded into the frame behind Baojia so Natalie could see them.

"What's going on?" Brigid said. "We're going to have to stay here tonight; we don't have enough time to get back before dawn. What did you find out?"

Natalie was sitting in a dimly lit room with Ross sitting beside her. "I was able to touch base with that deputy like I hoped. He's been working night patrols along the highway from Redway headed up to Eureka, so he knows the area we're talking about and he knew all about Summer and Daniel because the Uriarte family's security has been working with the sheriff's department."

"The men we took don't know much," Carwyn said. "But we're pretty certain that Ivan has an illegal farm up somewhere in the mountains. We have no idea where yet."

Natalie's face was grim. "We may have just gotten a real big clue. A couple of fishermen found Daniel Uriarte."

Brigid felt her stomach drop. "His body?"

Natalie shook her head. "He's alive. Barely. Hypothermia and he's very badly beaten, but he's alive. They have him in the hospital in Santa Rosa. Last I heard, he was in a medically induced coma."

"We'll go by tomorrow night," Baojia said. "See what we can find."

Brigid looked at Ross, whose face was a stoic void. "We're not giving up," she said. "We're not giving up on Summer. We're going to find your niece."

FOURTEEN

Brigid stood in the hospital hallway with a nurse, trying to get information about Daniel Uriarte's condition.

"I'm sorry," the nurse said. "I sympathize with your problem, but I can't tell you anything about my patient."

"I'm a licensed private investigator." Brigid pulled out her wallet and showed the nurse her forged credentials. "I understand the sheriff has been working with Mr. Uriarte's private security. Are you telling me that Miss Mackenzie doesn't deserve the same cooperation?"

"I'm not telling you that. I'm telling you that if you want information, you need to speak to the sheriffs too." She held up her hands. "I can't tell you anything."

The nurse walked away, her blue-and-purple scrubs softly brushing together in the nearly silent hallway. Brigid leaned against a wall, contemplating her options.

Carwyn came to lean against the wall next to her. "No luck?"

"None." She glanced at the hallway. "There are two private security guards on him. I could take them both."

Carwyn turned his head, glanced at the men, then looked back at Brigid. "You could. I think his mother is sitting with him though. So there is likely more security in the room."

"I could use amnis on the mother," Brigid said. "Use that to get her to spill what they know."

Carwyn reached around and rubbed the tight knot between Brigid's shoulders. "That's a definite idea."

"But?" She definitely heard the implied "but."

"But why do any of those things when there's a deputy in the cafeteria right now," Carwyn leaned down and whispered. "He just ordered a hot dinner."

Which likely meant he was there for an extended break. Without another word, Brigid pushed off the wall and headed down to the basement, where a sign pointed to a cafeteria named Tio's.

Brigid spotted the sheriff's deputy immediately by the dull brown uniform and the hat. There were few places left in the world where anyone could wear a felt Stetson cowboy hat unironically, but rural Northern California appeared to be one of them.

"Deputy Ramirez?" Carwyn asked. "We got your name from the department. My partner and I were hoping you might have a minute—"

"You're not from the newspapers or anything, are you?" The man had light brown skin, dark hair, and greenish-brown eyes. He appeared young compared to most of the law enforcement officers Brigid had seen in the area so far.

"No." Brigid sat across from the man, who was demolishing a plate of what looked like meatloaf. "My husband and I are private investigators. We're representing Miss Mackenzie's family, and we were hoping you might be able to share some information about Mr. Uriarte's condition or any details about where he was found."

The young deputy shook his head. "I'd say you needed to talk to that Valero guy, but I know he's not real friendly."

Carwyn smiled a little. "To be fair, it's not his job to be friendly; it's his job to find the Uriarte's son. Just like it's our job to find Miss Mackenzie."

Deputy Ramirez rubbed his chin, which was thick with the day's growth. "So you're from North Carolina or something?"

Brigid smiled. "We're actually from Southern California, but my husband is a friend of the girl's grandfather, so we volunteered to come north to do what we could. The Mackenzies don't have the kind of money the Uriartes do. We're just trying to help."

The young deputy nodded. "Gotcha. I gotta say, that guy's family? They are *loaded*. They've had, like, their own private army out looking along the trail, shadowing the search-and-rescue guys, but it was completely useless in the end."

"Why's that?" Carwyn asked.

"The area the fishermen who found Daniel? It's over forty miles from where those kids must have started out."

"Forty miles?" Brigid asked. "So there's no way—"

"No way those two made it all the way over to that part of the forest without finding help." Deputy Ramirez shook his head. "They'd have crossed over the highway, several main roads, and the state park. No way. Especially with everything Miss Mackenzie's family has told us about her outdoor experience."

"So you're saying that someone took them from where

they went missing and dumped them somewhere else?" Carwyn asked.

The deputy looked distinctly uncomfortable. "I hate to tell you this, but we found no trace of Summer anywhere near the scene. The fishermen took us back over there—"

"Over where?" Brigid asked. "Where was Daniel actually found?"

"Just off the Eel River on one of the creeks that runs into it. Locals call it Rocky Creek, which is kinda ironic because it's one of the best fishing spots. Nice clear water in that area."

"So it's out of the way," Carwyn said.

Ramirez nodded. "Definitely. Whoever took Daniel back there must have known where to go. That's not a place where tourists wander off, you know?"

"Can you show us exactly?" Brigid pulled out a map. "We're willing to go out on our own, but we need to know where he was found. It's possible we may spot something—knowing Summer and all—that you might have missed."

Ramirez pursed his lips, but he didn't say no. "Okay, just letting you know: if you get lost, no one better expect us to look for you. We're already stretched thin enough as it is."

"Understood." Brigid glanced at Carwyn. "We're pretty savvy in the woods. If you can point us in the direction, we'll find it."

He nodded. "I can give you the names of the guys that found him too. If that'll help."

"It definitely will."

"Deputy Ramirez," Carwyn began, "I don't suppose you know if Daniel said anything when he was first brought in to the hospital? Did anyone ask him about Summer?"

"Yes and no," Ramirez said. "I don't think the kid got a

word in edgeways once his security got here. We tried asking him about Summer, but the doctors and nurses gave us hell."

"And there was no sign of her at the creek?"

Brigid reached for Carwyn's hand. "My love, he already said there wasn't." She glanced at the human across from them. "Thank you, Deputy Ramirez. If you'll give us your mobile phone number, we'd be happy to call you if we find any sign of Summer."

"That'll be great." Ramirez looked relieved. "Yeah, just any information you can find, please pass it on."

Brigid was guessing he'd been everyone's punching bag for a few weeks, and when a department was getting pressure from multiple sides to solve a mystery, being in the middle was far from fun.

"You'll have it," Brigid said. "We'll help in any way we can."

BAOJIA STARED at the two men from the back seat of the van. Brigid, Natalie, and Jamie were standing a little distance from the front door as the two fishermen who'd found Daniel Uriarte spoke from just inside. Carwyn and Ross sat in the front of the van, holding Baojia back from hovering over his wife.

It was nearly midnight, but Brigid had called ahead and the two men agreed to meet them and share where they'd found Daniel as long as Brigid and Natalie promised they wouldn't use that spot for fishing.

It was one of their easier negotiations.

The father and son lived on the edge of one of the tiny

mountain enclaves at the border of the state forest. Old logging equipment in the front yard gave witness to a more prosperous past life, and an array of antlers decorated the back of an ancient workbench by the woodpile.

"Why aren't they using amnis?" Baojia grumbled after the meeting had stretched into the second hour.

"Because Natalie said she may want to use them for an extended quote or interview or something." Carwyn watched his wife and friends work their own, more human, magic. "If the fishermen can't remember them, that makes it more complicated."

Baojia looked off into the trees that grew dense through the town. "What is this place?"

"Doubt it has a name," Ross said. "It's more of a wide spot in the road than a town.

"I imagine they call it something, but it won't be on a map." Carwyn looked at the forest behind them, knowing that Baojia's men were spread out through the trees like deadly shadows. At the first sign of danger, they'd swoop in and anything threatening Natalie would be crushed beyond recognition.

Fortunately, when she turned after shaking the fisherman's hand, she was smiling.

"Good." Ross nodded toward his brother. "They got something. I can tell by Jamie's expression."

"Really?" Carwyn resisted the urge to ask how. As far as he'd been able to tell, Mackenzie men—mortal and immortal alike—had two expressions: stoic and faintly bemused. If it weren't for Ross's immortal pallor, Carwyn doubted he'd be able to tell one from the other.

Brigid, Natalie, and Jamie opened the van door and jumped inside while Baojia went to speak to his men.

"Okay, so the guys gave us really detailed directions, but we are not going to find the way on maps." Brigid spread out the map and pointed at highlighted trails someone had penciled in. "Once we turn off the main road, we're depending on the Stewarts. Old Mister Stewart said there's a dirt track the van can get over with no problem because it hasn't been raining much. Then when we get to the stand of old-growth redwoods, there's space to park. From there, it's about a mile hike in to the creek."

Ross frowned. "They seriously couldn't find a more convenient spot to fish trout?"

Natalie smiled. "We didn't ask them that."

Baojia walked back to the van and scanned the map. "My guys are waiting to follow the van." He put his hand at the small of Natalie's back. "Are we going to have time to find this place before dawn?"

"We've got at least four hours, so I think we will," Natalie said. "But we'll probably have to camp in the woods once we reach the mouth of the creek."

"There is another access road," Brigid said. "But I don't know if we want to try to hide out there. It's a spot farther up the creek where the road actually crosses with a one-lane bridge, but the young man said they don't go that way, as they prefer not to be seen by anyone passing through the area."

"Do you think they're criminals?" Carwyn asked.

"The Stewarts?" Natalie said. "No. They're just fishermen protective of their favorite spot. However, they mentioned that some residents back there—they didn't say who—get 'real annoyed' if trucks are going around there when it's dark.

They didn't say morning or evening, they just mentioned *dark*."

"Interesting," Baojia muttered. "It could be normal humans moving drugs they don't want to register."

"Or it could be vampires," Brigid said. "Either is a possibility. We're all assuming that Ivan's farm is there, but this could be a coincidence."

"Coincidence or not," Carwyn said, "it's the best lead we have. I say we go search Rocky Creek."

"There was one more lead," Jamie said. "But it doesn't make much sense. The old man said that before Daniel passed out, he kept repeating something that sounded like 'seagull aqua.'" He looked at Carwyn and Baojia. "Any of y'all know what that might mean?"

"If Daniel was injured and pretty out of it, he was probably speaking Spanish." Baojia crossed his arms over his chest. "Seagull aqua?"

"Aqua was probably *agua*," Natalie said. "That's pretty obvious, but seagull?"

"Seagull?" Baojia asked. "Or *sigue* maybe?" He looked at Carwyn. "Maybe he was trying to tell them where Summer was. *Sigue el agua?*"

"Follow the water?" Carwyn said. "That—"

"That's it!" Jamie nearly shouted. "Summer was with him." He stared at Ross. "Follow the water. Summer woulda told him that."

"Follow the water." Ross nodded before he glanced around the van. "It's a rhyme. 'Over the heel and 'round the carn, follow the water from trickle to burn.' It's a rhyme we teach the kids when they're little in case they get lost in the mountains."

Jamie said, "It's to teach them that if you find water, stick close to it and follow it downstream because small streams usually lead to bigger ones."

Ross furrowed his dark eyebrows. "Summer doesn't know these mountains, but the same rule applies. She'd have followed the water downstream until she reached help. And if Daniel and her got separated, she'd a' told him to do the same thing."

"So we need to find this Rocky Creek and start searching there," Carwyn said. "If we do that, hopefully we'll find Summer."

Ross and Jamie were silent; Carwyn could scent their desperation staining the close air of the van. "We'll find her, lads. We know where to start now."

"My men and I will follow you," Baojia said. "Let's not waste any time. If Summer is still up there, it's been over twenty-four hours since Daniel escaped."

FIFTEEN

Summer was finished. The vampire's men pulled her out of the truck just before sunset and sprayed her down with a hose before they put her in a brand-new cabin with sealed floorboards and walls, an empty bucket in the corner, and a lock on the door. She lay on the ground, staring at a wall made of sealed boards, and thought about Dani.

She didn't care what happened to her anymore. Dani had been right. They should have stayed at the camp. They'd tried to escape and nothing had happened to her, but Dani was dead.

Summer, run!

She couldn't stop hearing his voice. Couldn't stop seeing his face. Hearing the fists pounding against his body as she ran away.

She ran away.

How could she ever face her family again? Mackenzies didn't abandon people they loved. Mackenzies didn't run from danger. They defended the wounded. Helped the injured. It was a code of honor she had breached when she abandoned Dani to the Russian's men. She could never show her face to her father or her uncle again.

This was her fault.

The door creaked open after the sun had hidden itself behind the mountains, and Summer knew that the vampire called Ivan had decided to pay her a visit.

"Summer Mackenzie."

She hated the sound of her name in his mouth.

"I thought you should know your family did come looking for you."

She blinked, but she didn't move.

"I'm sure you think that they'll find you here, but they won't. We're miles and miles away from the trailer they raided. Very far from where you were taken."

Something touched her neck. It was Ivan's cold fingers on her skin. He picked up a curl and smoothed it down. "Such a wild woman you are, Summer Mackenzie."

She resisted the urge to cringe, the urge to flee, the urge to react in any way. She stared at the wall with her back to Ivan and the door.

"A wild, untamed thing." Ivan's finger ran over her shoulder and down her arm, but still Summer didn't flinch. "I do so enjoy you."

In the distance, Summer heard a truck start up and a woman cry out. Then a door slammed and she heard nothing else.

"I suspect your pretty man noticed that people were going missing." Ivan must have been feeling conversational. "So you decided to escape." He patted her hip. "Don't worry. That won't be you. We only get rid of the ones who are worn out by the work. You are nice and strong."

"What do you do with the weak ones?"

"Oh, you decided to talk." He leaned closer, and his finger touched her hair again. "Lovely. What do we do with them? You know, you're the first person I can share this with, Summer. The first person who understands our world."

Was he giving them to vampires? Summer knew there were vampires who kept broods of people to drink from, like humans kept milk cows, but most vampires she knew either drank from paid employees, hunted animals, or went into the city to vampire clubs if they were real old like her Grandpa Logan.

"I don't understand that much," Summer said. "I'm not like you." *In so many ways.*

"But you know what we eat." There were his fingers again, crawling along her neck, combing through her hair, and pulling so hard when he reached a tangle that her eyes began to tear up. "You know we like a bit of fun. We're predators, my dear. Blood always tastes better with a healthy chase to season it."

Her stomach turned, but Summer didn't throw up and she didn't flinch. "So you're running hunts with humans?" It was a practice her grandfather had told her about, but Summer didn't know it still happened. Human hunts were supposed to have died out over the centuries. Only sociopaths would still hunt people when there were far more civilized options available to modern immortals.

"Not... precisely. See, how would that be a challenge? We're predators, but we're rational too. What fun is a hunt if the prey is weak?"

You sick, sick bastard. Summer continued to stare at the

wall even though she felt like throwing up. "So you give them weapons or what?"

"In a sense," Ivan said. "What I do is... even the playing field a bit. Try to keep it more challenging for everyone."

"So it's a fair fight?" *Yeah right.* Summer had seen her father spar with her uncle. Her father might have been a fierce and skilled man, but there was no contest between him and her immortal relatives.

Ivan chuckled. "It's as fair as I can make it." He petted her shoulder. "You don't need to worry about that business though. I find you far too interesting to waste."

"Goody for me." *I'm going to kill you. I'm going to drive a knife through your heart, put a bullet in your neck, and chop your head off with an ax.* Imagining all the ways she planned kill Ivan was the only thing that allowed Summer a fraction of peace.

She wondered if he knew she wanted to end his life. After all, Ivan wasn't an idiot. He likely knew how much she hated him; he just didn't care.

She could be patient; she could plan. She wasn't fooling herself over her deficiencies as a human because one of the first things she was taught as a child was how to recognize mortal vulnerabilities and work around them.

Summer lay on her side, wide awake and glaring at the walls of her wooden prison, ignoring the monster who petted her like a toy poodle. He would get nothing from her. Not a reaction; not a tear.

And when she was ready, he would die.

THE DIRT TRACK that led off the main road near a bend in the Eel River was little more than a horse path, but they were able to navigate it with a little luck, and there were only a few places where Carwyn had to get out and move the van onto less muddy ground.

Brigid sat in the passenger's seat while Carwyn drove over the bumpy track. Natalie, Jamie, and Ross were sitting in back, and Baojia's vehicle followed them.

Jamie spoke up from the seat right behind Brigid. "I suppose this would be completely impassible if it were raining harder."

Brigid smiled. "This isn't rain."

"This is mist," Natalie said.

Ross muttered, "Looks like rain to me."

Brigid turned to look at him. "Mist isn't rain. Trust me—coming from an Irishwoman—this is mist."

"This area reminds me of North Wales," Carwyn said. "Different trees but the same feeling."

"Young," Ross muttered.

Brigid frowned. "What's that?" Was he implying something about her age? What the fuck?

"The mountains here." Ross stared into the darkness as they drove along a ridge. "They feel young."

Carwyn smiled at the man. "Yes. I know what you mean."

Brigid tried not to roll her eyes. *Earth vampires.*

"I'm just glad everything is damp," she added. "The last thing I want to worry about is accidentally setting off an uncontrolled burn." In California, with its dense, overgrown forests, that was something Brigid worried about almost everywhere she went. Luckily, the coastal north was far less flammable than other places.

The fog hung low over the forest as dry brush, oak trees, and manzanita along the river gave way to underbrush heavy with ferns, tumbled granite rocks, and soaring pines. They had turned away from the path that followed the main tributary and were climbing up the side of a steep hill, switching back and forth as they drove toward Rocky Creek.

The mountain peak above them was lost in the dark, heavy cloud cover, but even if the sky had been clear, Brigid suspected the woods were too dense to allow much light to filter down.

She reached for the map. "Carwyn, you might be getting to the redwoods." She'd spotted massive leaning giants in the distance. "Be ready to stop." She glanced behind them to see the truck carrying seven vampire soldiers and Baojia was still close. "Do you think Katya's men—?"

"Baojia's men." Carwyn raised an eyebrow. "He'll have trained them."

"Are they all water vampires like Katya and Baojia?"

"I suspect they'll be a mix. I'm pretty sure at least two of them are human, though they do a hell of a job blending in. They'll have some earth vampires with them for defense or quick escape."

When it came to disappearing quickly, nothing beat a skilled earth vampire who could literally make the ground open up and swallow you.

"So you won't have to dig their shelters," Brigid said. "Good."

"I can help if they need it," Ross muttered. "Ain't no thing when they're lookin' for our girl."

"Remember this." Brigid turned to the two Mackenzies. "Baojia isn't just a friend in all this; he's Katya's enforcer. His priority will be to eliminate Ivan and any other immortals or humans who are collaborating with him. That means that finding Summer is on us."

Ross and Jamie turned to Natalie to get her reaction to Brigid's words.

"There's no divided loyalties," Natalie said. "I do my job; my husband does his. Look at it this way: We'll be able to look for Summer better knowing they're dealing with Ivan and his crew."

"What if we need to get information from Ivan?"

"Then you better ask him quick." Natalie's face was grim. "My husband and this vampire have a long history. Baojia is pretty keen to end it."

"We're here," Carwyn announced.

Having driven the van in a complete circle and finding no outlet, he parked under a bushy redwood tree that had sprung new shoots from the base. They tangled and clumped together, knitting themselves into a monstrous apparition in the darkness, nearly twice as tall as the average human.

"You know," Brigid said. "It's not hard to understand why Bigfoot legends started here."

Carwyn shut off the van and pocketed the keys as the vampire and human passengers began to unload. "I don't know what you mean." He frowned. "Are you talking about Grigor?"

"That definitely helps." Brigid wandered around the van, taking in the darkness, the dense fog overhead, and the soft scampering in the distance. "I mean all of it though. A forest so old and alive you can nearly feel it breathing." She walked along the circle of the grove. "Earth so rich anything you plant just springs to life." Brigid kicked a clump of earth dug up by some animal burrowing. "Everything around here feels like it's watching you."

Natalie looked into the trees. "If we stumble onto someone's illegal farm, the forest very well could be watching you. Some of the growers up here plant cameras near their fields." She looked at Ross and Jamie. "You guys know about all the tricks moonshiners have pulled over the years?"

Ross frowned at Natalie. "Uh, you might be surprised to know a few of my brothers and me *were* those moonshiners. So yeah, we know what to look for." He looked at Jamie. "You reckon they have bear traps out here?"

"Hopefully not."

"Any well-worn path," Natalie started, "look for fishhooks. If you have a hat, wear one even though the sun is down." She tugged on a baseball cap with a long brim. "Look down. There could be pit traps, and yes, also animal traps, the old kind."

Brigid continued, "Be aware of your surroundings. Mountain lions aren't aggressive unless they have cubs; but they're fast and they're silent. Rattlesnakes will warn you, but they also strike faster." She was forgetting something. What was she forgetting? "Oh!" She smiled. "Good old trip wires are also pretty common. That's why Carwyn will be going first along the trail."

He frowned. "What? Why me?"

"Well, you're quite sturdy, aren't you?" She patted his shoulder. "You aren't afraid, are you?"

She was teasing him. The real reason Carwyn would go first along the trail was to scent for Summer. He had the keenest nose in the lot of them, even Summer's own relatives.

She tossed him the backpack with the sealed clothes. "Once we get to Rocky Creek, you'll need this."

"Find Rocky Creek," Carwyn said. "Then we'll have to make camp. We aren't going to get enough time to go upstream tonight."

Brigid looked into the woods, securing her backpack before she stared up into the stars.

Keep going, Summer. Stay alive.

We're coming for you.

SIXTEEN

They spent the day in dugout shelters around the mouth of Rocky Creek. Carwyn and Brigid were the last to hide, taking their time to make sure that all the rest of the hunting party was well concealed and nothing was visible from the surface.

They'd reached the mouth of the creek with an hour of darkness to spare, which gave them just enough time to excavate shelters, store weapons, and generally make themselves invisible to any humans passing by.

Brigid lay in the small refuge Carwyn had dug, tucked against the vampire with the biggest heart she'd ever known. "You're thinking about Summer, aren't you?"

"She's not asleep right now," he said. "Or I doubt it. I doubt sleep is very comforting to her."

"Do you think she's still at the farm?"

"Yes. That's why we're heading upstream."

"Why?"

"Because I think if she were free, she'd have found help by now. It's been two full nights and two days since Daniel was found. If she'd made it out, she'd have gotten back to town in that time."

Brigid curled closer into his chest. "I was nothing like that when I was human."

"What do you mean? You are one of the most competent women I've ever known. And I've known quite a few."

She smiled. "I could find my way in Dublin, tell you where to find criminal elements and where the safe neck of the woods were. I knew the city, but surviving in the wild?" She shook her head. "I'd have been bear breakfast out here as a human."

"You'd have learned if that's what your native environment was," Carwyn said. "Summer's family told her that wilderness survival was important, so she learned it."

"My family taught me that knowing ancient languages was important, but I didn't learn those, Carwyn. Your argument might have a few holes."

His arms came around her and snugged her to his chest. "You'd make it. If you had to? You'd figure it out. I have no doubt at all."

"Why?"

"Because you're a survivor, Brigid Connor. That's what you do."

When he held her close, pressed her skin to the roughness of his clothes or the fine curling hairs along his skin, she felt the fire that lived in her retreat. Carwyn somehow knew when she was most on edge, and he used that knowledge to defuse her. Many nights she felt like she was walking the edge of explosion.

Not unlike the giant ticking time bomb Ivan presented.

She felt sleep starting to reach for her, but she fought it. "Ivan. If Baojia kills him—"

"He's rogue. No one would blame him. Even Ivan's sire would struggle to find a justification to avenge him."

"But that could happen? Does anyone know who his sire is?"

"No idea at all. And as I said, when it comes to the unwritten rules of vampire politics, Ivan is already dead. Operating in foreign territory without the permission of the vampire in charge isn't *done*, Brigid. Not without consequences. The mere fact that he's here and doing anything challenges Katya's leadership. She has to see him dead, or she'll be seen as weak. And you don't become the ruler of a territory like Katya's without being ruthless."

Brigid pictured the smooth, pale complexion and wide eyes of Katya Grigorieva. The vampire wore fuzzy slippers to meetings and schoolgirl braids in her hair. The idea that her facade hid a ruthless predator was hard to imagine, but not impossible. After all, Brigid had seen both humans and immortals at their worst; she had no illusions that a pleasing facade couldn't hide the worst monster imaginable.

"Go to sleep." Carwyn ran his finger through Brigid's cap of hair. He teased her nape and played with the longer feathers around her temples. "I'll wake you at dusk. We're going to have a long night ahead of us. Even if we find Ivan's farm, we're going to need time to surveil it, see what the best approach should be."

"He's already killed enough humans." Brigid's eyes began to droop as sunrise tugged at the sky. "Not any more. Not a single..."

She was out.

SHE WOKE to gentle hands stroking over her neck and a hard body pressed against her.

Someone was hungry.

Brigid turned to him, knowing her mate by his scent, his touch, and the amnis they shared. If she were blind, she would know him. If she lost her sense of hearing, she should know him. Nothing in the world would allow her to mistake any other for the man who possessed her heart.

In the darkness of the earth around them, Brigid wrapped her arms around his shoulders and he moved over her, spreading her legs as he entered her.

Their union was silent and slow, their bodies cradled by the earth he commanded. The cave he'd created was warm from Brigid's heat, her amnis burning with a low intensity that Carwyn's absorbed. Their bodies flowed together in one heated tangle of arms and legs, and when Brigid came, the sigh she released was the single sound that echoed in the darkness.

Carwyn came moments after, his body tensing before he climaxed with a soft groan.

He pulled her limp body over his chest. "What a wondrous creature you are."

She closed her eyes, her body and blood alive with energy, tied to this mountain of a vampire who was her anchor in the world. "I love you so much."

He stroked his fingers through her hair. "Words are not enough."

She cocked her head up to look at him, but there wasn't even a hint of light for her vampire vision to latch on to.

"Words are all we have though." She pressed her ear to his chest. "I wonder what your heart used to sound like."

His immortal heart beat, but not as often as a human heart. No one in a thousand years had heard Carwyn's human heart, and Brigid was oddly sad about that.

"If you put your ear up to a cow, you'll probably get a decent facsimile," he murmured.

"Yer *such* an odd man. I love you, but you are so odd."

"You know what I found myself wondering the other day?"

"About cows?" Brigid closed her eyes and settled into his embrace. These quiet, rambling conversations were one of her favorite things about being married to Carwyn, and they usually ended with one or both of them dissolving into laughter.

"I was wondering" —his thumb brushed along the edge of her eyebrow— "what you would look like with wrinkles."

She snorted. "Isn't that one of the benefits of having to drink blood every night for the rest of my life? I don't have to worry about those."

"I was just wondering." His smile was in his voice. "I think you'd be adorable with little wrinkles along your eyes." He tapped her nose. "What do they call them? Crow's-feet?"

"Even the name is horrid!" She turned over and propped her chin on his chest. "Men get wrinkles and the whole world sees them as distinguished and proper. You get to be 'silver foxes.' Women get crow's-feet. What does that even mean? I cannot believe the witch connotations are accidental."

"Oh no, I'm quite sure they're not." His thumb ran along her jawline. "What can I say? I daydream about growing very old with you and having great-grandchildren running around, making us laugh and telling us stories about whatever mad thing the humans will have invented by then."

He was a creature of family who had done everything he could to re-create in the vampire world the human family he'd lost. He'd sired a dozen children and seen their clans, both human and vampire, grow and flourish. He'd watched over them like a protective father.

And then he'd met her.

"I think we need to visit Cochamó soon." Brigid rubbed the back of her fingers along Carwyn's rough jaw. "You need to be with Isabel and Gus for a while. Be around all their people. Watch the nippers and hear some stories."

Isabel was one of Carwyn's oldest daughters, and she and her mate had their own children, both human and vampire. They lived in an isolated valley in South America where they ranched and farmed. It was a place of music and dancing. A place where a family dinner meant roughly a hundred people coming over.

His hand gripped the back of her neck. "You always get uncomfortable at Isabel and Gus's."

"And when I do, I spend some time on my own and then I'm fine." She scooted up and kissed him. "You always take care of me, Carwyn. Let me take care of you too. Once we find Summer, stop Ivan, make sure everything is good here, let's go to Cochamó."

"Are you sure?"

"Very sure. I'll even voluntarily get in a boat if we can't borrow Giovanni's plane."

He hugged her tightly. "It's a grand idea, Brigid. Thank you."

ONE BY ONE as the sun sank beneath the horizon, the vampires emerged from the earth, shaking off dust and washing their faces in the river. They broke out bottles of blood-wine to feed their appetites, and a few of Baojia's men ran off when they heard a deer in the forest.

It was a dirty, ragged bunch of warriors, and they pleased Carwyn's nose immensely. The city smell had been overwhelmed by the scent of earth, forest, roots, and rot. The evening fog curled around the water vampires, drawn to their amnis, and the ground rippled happily when Carwyn dug his hands into it, filling the hole he'd dug for shelter and restoring the land to what it had been.

Baojia had brought one wind vampire with him, a nimble woman with dark curling hair cut short around her head. She wore black, as all his soldiers did, and her skin was a deep, rich brown; when she took to the air, she moved like a shadow.

"Daxa transferred to San Francisco two years ago from Bangladesh." Baojia stood next to Carwyn, staring at the disappearing shadow. "Lucky for me. She's young, just looking to stretch out from her sire's organization. Get some experience working for someone else."

"Her sire have connections with Katya?"

Baojia nodded. "Old friends. Trading partners."

"She's open to new talent." Carwyn looked at Baojia. "Your boss. That's good to know."

Baojia nodded. "Coming from an organization that was all about blood ties, seniority, and connections, it's been a real shift for me. A good one."

"What's the plan for tonight?" Carwyn asked.

Baojia's soldiers were quickly erasing any trace of their presence from the riverbank, and Natalie, Jamie, and Ross were standing by Rocky Creek, ready to go.

"You lead the way," Baojia said. "Daxa is flying overhead, looking for any air cover and scoping things out. If she sees anything, she'll report back. I told her we'd be keeping to the creek."

"Correct." Carwyn waved Brigid over. "Are we ready?"

Brigid looked over her shoulder. "Have you seen Ross and Jamie? Jamie's been ready all day."

The corner of Baojia's mouth turned up. "Let him know that he'll be able to join Lin and Brady tomorrow morning if he likes. They're the human couple on the team, and they keep up. They were scouting around today while we were in the ground."

Brigid nodded. "I'll tell him. Let's hope we can make good enough time that we'll have a bead on the farm before dawn."

Baojia nodded toward the stream, looking at Carwyn. "We're ready when you are."

Carwyn walked to the creek and took out the sweatshirt Summer had been wearing in Seattle. He inhaled deeply, thinking of the young woman's picture and holding it in his mind with the intricate scent of apples, salt, and vanilla, trying to find the thread that was Summer within all the artificial scents of the modern world.

He could sense it, but it wasn't clear yet. "Follow the water." He began walking up the center of the creek, companions falling behind him as he took in the smell of the land around him.

Pine and cedar, salt and earthy moss. The forest was lush

with life, but Summer's scent was too diffuse to point in a specific direction.

Follow the water.

Carwyn kept walking, his pace slow and steady. He didn't want to miss a single thread that might lead him in the correct direction.

An hour up the creek, Carwyn spotted an unusually high table sitting on the edge of the creek. "What is it?" he asked Natalie.

"That? Oh, it's probably a fishing platform," Natalie said. "In the spring when the water is really high, that's gonna be your safest way to fish in the creek. Getting anywhere near the water is really dangerous."

"But it's not now?" Carwyn looked down at the center of the stream where the water came nearly up to his knees.

"No, this is nothing. See the marks on the side?" Natalie asked. "Those are to measure high water. The past few years have been dry, but that's a change. Usually, creeks this size are twice as big, even getting into the end of the dry season like now."

Carwyn kept his eyes ahead, noting the twisting stream and exposed rocks. Every now and then, he got a strong hit of Daniel's scent and knew that the young man had fallen down this creek like the fishermen thought, bumping along the rocks and snags along the bank until he was found.

"Daniel came this way," Carwyn said. "I can smell his blood."

SEVENTEEN

Brigid watched Carwyn work, watched him move deliberately at the front of their company, his bare feet dug into the soil and his hands reaching down every so often to feel the earth, as if the scent of Summer Mackenzie might live in the ground itself.

"What's he doing?" Ross leaned over and spoke to her.

"I don't know," Brigid said. "You're an earth vampire, aren't you?"

"I can't smell things through the ground though, can I?"

"Are you over a thousand years old?" Brigid asked.

Ross's eyes went wide. "No, ma'am, I am not." He looked at Carwyn with more consideration. "Has he ever done anything—?"

"Yes." She glanced at Ross. "He's found people, and he's lost people. He lost a son. They kept him on concrete. Carwyn couldn't find him in time."

The pain of Ioan's loss still haunted Brigid many nights. When she'd been a child, Ioan and his mate Deirdre had been her protectors. She'd thought they were invincible.

Ioan's death had left wounds in Brigid and Carwyn's lives that still hadn't healed.

She saw Carwyn lift his head, turn, then turn again. He frowned and then sprang up to the edge of the creek bank a moment before a mountain lion leaped from the trees.

"Oh fuck!" Brigid yelled, drawing her weapon. "Baojia!"

"I see it." The soldier's voice came from the other side of the creek, where he was already positioned to shoot. "Carwyn, move out of the—"

"No!" Carwyn yelled. "We're in her territory."

He batted the lion back as if it were a house cat, crouching down and spreading his arms wide, giving himself the appearance of a predator far larger than he actually was. "Come now, my lovely. We're just passing through."

Even human predators like vampires could be shocked by their animal counterparts. Brigid had seen a massive Russian vampire freeze like a Popsicle in the face of a grizzly bear.

She kept her muzzle trained on the mountain lion. "Carwyn, what do you want to do?"

He waved at Brigid. "Everyone up! Put the gun away, darling girl. Move to the other side of the creek and give her a wide berth. Be calm, but move quickly."

The animal screamed into the night, snarling with curled lips as Carwyn circled it, trying to keep its attention. Brigid backed away and slowly climbed to the opposite bank, but she kept her eyes on Carwyn.

"See that waterfall in the distance?" He kept his voice even. "Everyone head toward that and just keep moving. Ignore us."

"Carwyn, I have a sight on her." Baojia was on the opposite bank, a rifle pointed at the mountain lion.

"Look at her," Carwyn said. "And put the gun down. She's got babies nearby. That's the only reason she's being this aggressive. Get out of here and she'll leave us alone."

Brigid was the first to lead the team up the creek, nudging Natalie, Ross, and Jamie up the rocky waterway as Baojia and his team moved up behind them.

All the while, Carwyn distracted the cat from them, circling her and moving in hypnotic fashion as her high-pitched snarls turned into growly vocalizations that nearly sounded like pathetic complaints.

"There we are," Carwyn said soothingly. "See? They're all leaving. Bad vampires. I imagine we smell all wrong, don't we, love?"

Brigid backed away, but she still kept her gun trained on the animal. She had plenty of respect for nature, but there were many mountain lions in the world and there was precisely one Carwyn. She'd sooner fly a helicopter to the moon than let a single scratch come to his head.

"Brigid, darling?"

"Yes?"

Carwyn didn't take his eyes off the lion. "Put the .45 away, my love. I know what it sounds like when you holster it; please put it away."

Brigid smoothly slid her 1911 revolver in her waist holster while palming a 9mm compact from an inside pocket of her jacket. "Okay. She's not backing away."

"I'll be the one to do that." The minute he took a step back, the lion screamed again. "Oh yes," Carwyn said soothingly. "You're very deadly."

"Stop playing with the big cat," Brigid said through gritted teeth. "It is not a pet, you madman."

"I'm not saying it is," he said. "But you can't say that her reasons aren't justified."

The farther he stepped back, the lower her snarls became until the only signs of aggression that Brigid saw were curled lips and long fangs.

"See?" Carwyn said, nearly caught up with the rest of the group. "She's just a protective mother."

When Carwyn reached her side, Brigid finally put the 9mm away, keeping her eyes on the snarling cat. After a few tail-twitching moments, the mountain lion slinked away into the underbrush and Brigid heard a collective sigh rise from the group.

"Well, that was fun." Carwyn pushed back toward the front of the group.

They kept moving deliberately, walking along the top of the creek until well past the mountain lion's range. Near the base of a waterfall, Carwyn climbed back into the river.

"Carwyn?"

He froze just as he passed a large outcropping of rocks that reached into the creek, then fell to his knees and put his face to the ground.

"Carwyn, what is it?" Brigid knelt next to him and saw traces of blood in the soil. "Daniel?"

"Yes."

Ross knelt next to Carwyn and breathed in deeply. "I smell it too." He looked up at the crashing water falling over the granite rocks. "That's a sixty-degree angle at least."

"He must have been banged up on the rocks," Carwyn said. "Managed to get to this bank and rest for a while."

"Daniel fell all the way down?" Natalie said. "That waterfall has to be twelve feet at least. And he was already beaten up."

They made their way back up the side of the creek, but it took some time for the human members of the team. The rocks were unstable, and Jamie fell twice, nearly twisting his ankle between two boulders.

Past the crest of the waterfall, the creek continued on a gentle uphill slope, disappearing into the trees as it branched off to the left.

"I've got her now," Carwyn said. "This way." He moved more swiftly, clambering over the rocks and keeping to the center of the creek.

Brigid didn't understand why they were walking through the water if Carwyn had her scent. "Why aren't we following her trail?"

"I want to make sure she didn't cross the river to try to lose vampires and detour through the forest on the other side."

Jamie noticed a spot where a tumble of rocks was disturbed. "Look at that. That exposed dirt is fresh. Looks like Daniel tried to climb up here maybe."

"Blood on the rocks." Brigid could see the drops now. "He was beaten badly to still be bleeding like this."

Jamie turned his face downstream. "Whoever beat him up musta figured he was dead and left him." A touch of wonder colored his voice. "He managed to get into the waterway and follow it all the way down without drowning."

Ross put a hand on his brother's shoulder. "He's tough. She wouldn't have been with him if he wasn't."

Baojia's face was grim. "The current would have done a

lot of the work, but it would have banged him up even more. It's a miracle that kid's alive."

Brigid ignored them and kept her eyes on Carwyn. It wasn't that she didn't care about Daniel, but the boy was safe in Santa Rosa and Carwyn had Summer's trail.

Carwyn was walking forward, leaving the group behind him. "We're close. I don't want to lose her scent."

A hush settled over the group and they began to hike again, the earth vampires clambering along the rocks with no effort while the others struggled to keep any more rocks from shifting.

Brigid heard a bird trill overhead.

Baojia put a hand over his mouth and answered the soft call. A moment later, Daxa the wind vampire landed on a smooth slab of granite that overlooked the waterway.

"Farm," she whispered and pointed over her shoulder. "Made up of about fifteen scattered fields, all covered with camouflage netting. There are cabins around the largest area. Something that smells like a communal bath and kitchen area in that section too."

"Here!" Carwyn knelt down, his face in the rocks before he looked up and his eyes narrowed. "She ran from that direction." He pointed upstream toward a dense wall of forest.

"Yes," Daxa said. "The farm is right in the middle of those trees. Maybe two kilometers away? There's a path that leads down to the river and several others that lead in circles. It's designed to get people lost."

"She was here." Carwyn turned in circles. "I was… Everything overlapped. I smell her there" —he pointed at the forest— "but she was here."

Baojia nodded. "Anyone else?"

"Humans," Carwyn said. "Multiple humans."

"Guards maybe?"

Daxa nodded. "Does anyone have paper?"

Jamie reached for his backpack and slung it to the ground, grabbing a large map he'd picked up in Redway. "You can draw on this one."

"Okay." Daxa knelt down and drew with quick, precise strokes in black marker. "Here's where we are, and here's the bridge you just passed..."

Carwyn was still lost in tracking Summer's scent, and Brigid followed Carwyn. He backtracked to the creek bed beyond the bridge and knelt down.

"What are you seeing?" Brigid said.

"She was in the water," he said. "She'd run ahead maybe? Or followed Daniel? The scents overlap; maybe he followed her? But she crawled up here." He looked at the bridge. "Maybe thinking this road would lead to a town nearby."

"I think this road goes quite a ways before it hits anything important."

"But she wouldn't have known that. She would have thought..." He stood and crawled up the bank, paused at the road, then followed his nose across the bridge and down the asphalt a little bit. "Her scent ends here. Abruptly."

Brigid surveyed the scene. A girl running down a creek, knowing what kind of predators she was dealing with. She'd try to throw off scent and get some space. Then she climbs up from the creek at the bridge. Why?

"Do you think there was a car passing?" Brigid asked. "Why else would she have left the water? She knew how vampires track; the water was a safer bet."

"She could have been injured, decided the road was a better option than the waterfall."

Brigid came to stand by Carwyn. "If a car picked her up, she could be safe already."

He frowned. "Who's to say that whoever picked her up was friendly?" He glanced at Ross and Jamie, who had followed them. "You heard what the fishermen said last night. They don't use this road because the locals don't want outsiders up here."

Summer was an outsider. To anyone looking to protect an illicit farm, she'd have been a liability, kidnapped girl or not.

She took Carwyn by the shoulders. "Do you still smell her? Is her scent alive? Recent?"

"Yes. She's not far." He pointed at the trees. "Summer is somewhere in those woods."

"Then let's keep going to the farm." Brigid looked at Ross. "As of right now, it's still our best lead."

They joined the others, who were looking at the rough sketch Daxa had drawn. Brigid could tell that Jamie and Ross were about ready to storm the farm and to hell with any consequences. Brigid wasn't so sure that was the wrong idea. Then again, Ross and Jamie had one goal, and Baojia had another. They wanted their daughter and niece; Baojia needed to catch Ivan.

"We have humans with us." Ross nodded toward his brother. "Why don't we let them take the farm during the day? No vampires; less risk."

"But more guards," Baojia said. "And we need to get Ivan."

"We need to fucking get my niece out of there," Ross growled. "I don't give a fuck about your—"

"Both goals are important." Brigid stepped between the

glaring men. “Ross, for Summer’s long-term safety, it would be better if Ivan was eliminated, correct?”

Jamie and Ross exchanged a look.

“I can keep my daughter safe,” Jamie said.

“And keep her a prisoner on Mackenzie land?” Brigid asked softly. “Is that really the kind of life she’d want?” She looked at Baojia. “I understand that the minute Summer is rescued, Ivan knows he’s a target and we’ll have to move fast, but we don’t know what condition any of these humans are in. Daxa said there are multiple cabins; we can assume more humans are being kept in them. We don’t know their status; some might not be able to wait. These are innocent people, and we need to remove them from danger as soon as possible.”

“I agree,” Baojia said. “But catching Ivan means saving future victims too. He’s a rogue right now; fair game to anyone. The minute he senses that he’s a target, he’ll abandon everything, scamper off, and find protection from someone powerful. He has the money and the connections to do it.”

“So we need to plan this carefully,” Carwyn said. “It might be possible to get Summer out—clearly she already tried to escape once—while leaving the other humans there. Just until we can catch Ivan.”

Brigid racked her brain, trying to figure out how they could rescue all the kidnapped humans while still leaving Ivan clueless that he’d been found out.

She had nothing.

Baojia was right, and Brigid understood where he was coming from. When he and Natalie had confronted Ivan before, the Russian had been under the protection of a powerful vampire cartel, so killing him would have had major consequences and possibly thrown off the balance of power in Southern California and Northern Mexico. Baojia'd had to let the predator loose.

But that had left Ivan free to continue victimizing people, killing unknown numbers under the nose of human and vampire authorities.

Now they had a chance to stop a serial predator, but only with careful planning. Planning that didn't take into account the desperate, instinctive need of a father to save his daughter.

There. Brigid smiled. "Got it."

Carwyn turned to her. "Got what?"

That was it. Make it about a father rescuing a daughter. Make it *personal*.

"We can get Summer out tomorrow," Brigid said. "And we can get Ivan. I have an idea."

EIGHTEEN

Summer was working under the eyes of two armed guards, one of whom watched the field where she was hoeing weeds and one who was assigned only to her. She'd forced herself to leave the cabin the day before, knowing that while Ivan might relish the time she spent staring aimlessly at the wall, she was disgusted with herself for giving in to grief so completely.

The guards, sensing she was a favorite of their boss, had offered her kitchen duty, but she refused. One, it was lighter work and she didn't want to get soft. And two, being in the kitchen offered zero opportunity for escape. In the fields, she had a chance.

She hadn't wavered in her determination to kill Ivan, but she'd shifted her focus. She needed to escape before she could kill him. She had no tools in camp other than the hoe they'd given her. And while imagining the dull edge mashing its way through Ivan's skull was satisfying, it wasn't very practical. A hoe was not a real weapon. She wanted an ax. It was one of her Uncle Ross's favorite weapons, and she had pretty good aim. Or a knife. Killing Ivan would mean cutting his spine, and she'd practiced that on pig carcasses with her father.

She let her mind wander, imagining what Ivan's head would look like split cleanly in two by a throwing ax. *Regenerate* that, *fuckhead.* A smile touched her lips.

"Keep working." A rifle butt nudged her shoulder. "You don't work, you don't eat."

Summer dug the hoe into the ground again, fighting back the poison oak that snaked from the forest into the marijuana fields. She needed to eat to stay strong. She needed to stay strong so she could escape.

She hacked at the red-tinged vine with care so as not to let any leaves or stems fly. The plant was insidious and itchy as hell. She knew enough about poison oak to take the coveralls the guards offered even though they made her sweat.

They can track sweat.

She knew her father would be coming for her, knew her uncle could track her. They might come for her at any time—her father during the day, Uncle Ross at night—so washing her scent away hadn't been a big priority. Not since Dani...

She closed her eyes and pushed the thought back.

I'm going to kill him, Dani.

Summer worked steadily through the morning and into the heated, hazy part of the afternoon. Though the air in California was dry, the air in the middle of a marijuana field was heavy and humid, the sickly sweet aroma of ripening marijuana clinging to her skin, the pollen coating her nose and airway. In the distance the forest was quiet, save for the lone call of a mourning dove.

She would give her last bottle of water to jump into the

swimming hole behind her grandfather's house. The hole was shaded, so even in the deepest heat of summer, it stayed cool.

"Summer."

She blinked and looked around, confused and surprised to see the guard on the ground, a dart sticking out of his neck. What the...?

"Summer!" A voice hissed from the trees and her eyes went wide. "Keep your eyes down."

She'd recognize her father's voice anywhere. She kept her eyes on her work and returned a mourning dove call to her father, hoping the guard watching at the end of the field wouldn't notice.

"I've got my eyes on you," her dad said. "Uncle Ross is here. We have a whole bunch of friends to get you out, okay?"

She nodded slightly, blinking back tears. Even though she couldn't see him, just the sound of her father's voice felt like coming home.

"Blink once for yes, twice for no. Are you hurt?"

She blinked twice.

"Okay, pumpkin. That's a big relief. Are you in any immediate danger? Is anyone hurting you?"

She blinked twice.

"Thank God. We saw signs that you escaped once. Can you get out at night again?"

She didn't think so. She blinked twice again.

"I hear you. Do you know how many other people are here? How many kidnapped people?"

She didn't know for sure. She blinked twice.

"You have an idea?"

She blinked once.

"Over ten?"

She blinked once.

"Over twenty?"

She blinked twice.

"Okay, honey. And how many guards have you seen? Over ten?"

She blinked twice.

"Okay, over eight?"

She kept her hands on the handle of her hoe but held out nine fingers. That was as many as she'd been able to identify at least. That wasn't counting Ivan.

"Good girl. How many vampires?"

She held out one finger.

Just one. Just Ivan.

"That's it?"

She blinked once.

"Okay, baby girl. It's kind of hard to explain, but we gotta be sure to get that one vampire before he scampers. Is he always here at night?"

She blinked twice.

"Okay. You have any idea if he'll be here tonight?"

Two more blinks.

"Okay." Her dad let out a long breath. "Okay. You keep your head down, Summer. Keep your head down, and when it's time, we're getting you out of here."

She blinked once.

"Either me or one of my friends is gonna be watching you all day, okay? If you are in immediate danger, you give us a dove call again, y'hear?"

She blinked once.

"I'm so proud of you, pumpkin. I'm gonna hug you real soon, okay? Then we're gonna call your mama."

She was blinking, but it was to keep the tears from showing across the field.

"You grab that dart out of that guard now, honey. He'll be waking up soon enough, and we don't want any questions."

Summer reached out, grabbed the small dart out of her guard's neck, and tossed it into the next row just in time for the guard to start groaning. Picking up her water bottle, she crouched next to him and patted his cheek.

"Hey." She reached out and tapped him carefully. "Dude, I think you collapsed or something."

The man frowned, then sat bolt upright and reached for his gun. "What the hell?"

"I don't know." Summer shrugged. "You just passed out. Have you been drinking enough?"

The man looked at the gun, then at Summer, then over his shoulder to the woods.

"I'm not gonna try to escape again." Summer sighed. "I know we're in the middle of nowhere, okay?"

The guard narrowed his eyes. "Did Johnny see me?"

"Who?"

"The guard at the end of the field. The one keeping an eye on the other two girls. Did he—?"

"I don't think so." Summer held out her water. "You want some water?"

Something passed over the man's face. "Fucking hell, don't be nice to me, okay?"

Summer shrugged again. "What else am I gonna do?"

"Not that." He stood and picked up the rifle. "Get back to work."

NIGHT HAD FALLEN, and Jamie Mackenzie was staring at the fog-shrouded tree line of the farm with an intensity that told Brigid they had one shot at doing this right. One shot at subterfuge before Jamie and Ross Mackenzie ran rampant over that farm, tearing off heads and taking revenge on whatever human or vampire might have harmed Summer.

"Okay, we've confirmed that the guards are spread out," Brigid said. "Daxa says even more at night. I'm honestly surprised Summer wasn't successful in her escape, based on what we've seen so far."

"Booby traps," Jamie muttered. "The three of us probably neutralized at least a dozen today while we were keeping an eye on the farm from the trees. I suspect they hit one of those and it alerted the guards."

"How many do you think are left?" Brigid asked.

Jamie shook his head. "We eliminated all of them we could. Ross is up there now, keeping an eye on our girl. If he comes across any others, I'm sure he'll get rid of them, but there's no way of really knowing."

Baojia said, "Daxa is keeping an eye on the farm from overhead, but I doubt she'd be able to spot any booby traps on the ground."

"Then we just keep going with the plan we made last night," Brigid said. "And a tripped booby trap or two isn't going to harm that—in fact, it might make the scenario look better. Our best bet is to make it look like Summer—and possibly a few other victims—have gotten away," Brigid said. "If the guards do what I think they'll do, they'll call Ivan. When Ivan comes, we grab him."

"What if Ivan doesn't come after the farm is compromised?" Baojia said. "Then we've just tipped our hand, and he knows that we know about the farm."

"Why would he abandon the farm now? He already knows that Summer and Daniel escaped," Carwyn said. "Daniel even got away and Ivan didn't abandon the farm, so we're guessing that he's not worried that humans will be able to find him here even if they get out."

"He probably figured that Daniel escaped but never made it back to civilization," Natalie said quietly. "Will he assume that about Summer?"

"There's no reason to think that he knows Summer is different from any other human," Brigid said. "He probably doesn't even realize she knows he's a vampire."

Baojia stood from his crouch by the map and addressed his soldiers. "Once Summer is out and the guards are following her, we penetrate the perimeter, break into teams, and search the cabins. If there are any humans obviously in need of medical care or actively being harmed, we get them out. If they appear unharmed, then we have to leave them for now. As soon as we assess the cabins and remove any humans who cannot wait, we pull back and wait beyond the tree line for Ivan."

"But we get Summer out tonight," Jamie said. "That's not negotiable."

"Agreed," Carwyn said. "We're getting her out tonight."

As long as we also get Ivan. Brigid hoped they'd truly received the memo. There were multiple objectives to this mission, and only careful timing would achieve the goal.

"We've got ten hours of night left," Brigid said. "Let's not waste it."

CARWYN LEFT Brigid and Baojia in the trees to watch the compound as he and Natalie moved silently though the forest, skirting along the edge of the farm. They passed one guard, evading him easily, and found Ross crouched behind a large redwood, his eyes trained on the most secure cabin in the compound.

"That's where they're keeping her?" Natalie asked. "How are we supposed to make it look—?"

"Doesn't matter how," Ross said. "They won't be asking questions right away. They'll ask later, but at first they're just gonna be looking to get her back. Hopefully by the time they stop to ask questions, Ivan will be dead."

Carwyn craned his neck to look into the clearing. "The light is shining right on her door."

"Give me a word and I'll tear through the back of that building," Ross said.

"No, if there's video—"

"I don't give a shit." Ross turned to him, his eyes ice-cold. "My niece has been waiting long enough."

"Ross." Natalie put a hand on his shoulder. "Of the three of us, which looks most human?"

Ross looked between Carwyn and Natalie. "You, Red, but only by a fraction. Either of us could pass. Carwyn? Forget it."

"But I probably look the most harmless," Natalie said. "Let me sneak around. If they get me on video, so what?"

"Ivan knows what you look like," Carwyn said. "He won't have forgotten. You could blow the whole op if they send him video before he gets back."

"Then me," Ross said. "I'm going in, and I'll take her

across the farm and into the trees. Same route she took last time. That'll make the most sense to them." He glanced at his watch. "Where's Jamie?"

"With Baojia and Brigid."

"I'll signal him when we're headed their way." Without another word, Ross was a blur. Carwyn heard a low growl coming from the vampire's throat and then he was gone.

SUMMER WAS STARING at the doorway, waiting for it to happen. She'd sensed her Uncle Ross as soon as darkness fell and knew he'd be coming for her. She just hoped he had an ax with him.

She was poised to run; they'd taken her socks, of course, but she'd wrapped her feet with strips of cloth she'd torn from her pant pockets. She squatted in the cabin, already having stretched her legs to warm them up.

The night air was cold, but she didn't feel it.

When the first bang came against the door, she stood back. With two strong kicks, the door collapsed in and her uncle's unmistakable silhouette stood in the doorway, security lights glaring behind him. In the distance, someone fired a shotgun.

"Let's go." Ross held his hand out, Summer took it, and they ran.

He pulled her to the edge of the first field. "They won't be able to sight us in here."

"We headed to the creek?"

A sharp nod. An engine fired in the distance, and the guard began to yell.

"There's a guard along the creek now," Summer said. "They posted him—"

"He'll be taken care of." Ross's voice was sure.

Summer shut her mouth and ran. She tripped a few times running through the rows of marijuana, but a childhood of running through cornfields taller than her daddy had taught her how to move quickly and quietly through furrows.

A shot rang out, and she ducked instinctively.

"They're way off," Ross muttered. "These assholes can't shoot for shit, honey." Still, his grip tightened on her hand. "Keep going."

She was exhausted by the time they broke through the edge of the field and made for the trees. There was still a dirt road to cross, and she could see the headlights of a quad bike coming toward them. More shots rang out in the night.

"She's getting away!"

"That's Ivan's favorite. You better fucking—"

"I'm going as fast as I can!"

More shots rang out.

"Don't shoot her, you fucking idiot! He wants her in one piece!"

Summer kept her head down and ran faster.

"That's my girl," Ross muttered.

They made it into the trees, but Summer didn't pause. If her Uncle Ross had led her this way, he would have cleared the booby traps from the path.

He moved like a shadow through the redwoods, and Summer followed his steps, running as quickly as she could as the tumbled slope gave way to tangled brush along a gravel-strewn path and then the rocky banks of the creek.

She saw vampires moving in the darkness, closing the space behind them, but Summer still didn't stop.

"Ignore them," Ross said. "They're goin' after the Russian."

Summer pulled his arm. "They're waiting for Ivan?" Her eyes went wide.

Ross turned and pulled her into a hard hug. "Don't you worry about him. That bloodsucker is their problem, and—"

"Ivan's not here."

Ross frowned. "We know that. We've been watching, but if he finds out you've flown the coop again—"

"He's not going to come back." Summer's chest was tight and her knees felt like buckling. "Not tonight. He told me last night. He was going up to the hunt."

Within seconds, Summer was surrounded by a bevy of vampires she didn't recognize, a fierce-looking Asian man, a hard-eyed woman with frighteningly pale skin, and a friendly-looking redhead who sidled up to the Asian vampire.

It was the fierce man who spoke. "What do you mean, the hunt?"

NINETEEN

Summer's words slapped Brigid like a dash of icy water. "Ivan is hosting hunts again?"

"That's why he's kidnapping hikers." Summer was trembling and pale. She looked inches away from collapsing, but her voice was strong. "He told me after he captured me again. We tried to escape before because we realized that people were disappearing, but then Ivan told me—"

"Summer!" Jamie ran toward his daughter and enveloped her in a fierce embrace. He immediately dragged her away from Brigid, Baojia, and Natalie, ushering her toward the creek as Ross brought up the rear.

The vampire turned and looked at Brigid. "Do what yer gonna do. We're seein' to our girl."

Brigid turned to Carwyn, who had come to stand behind her. "What do we do? If Ivan's not going to come tonight, that blows my entire plan out of the water."

It was rare for Brigid to see her husband turn cold and hot in the same moment. He was one of the most warm-hearted immortals she'd ever met, but in that instant, she saw the icy rage behind his blue eyes.

"These men were keeping humans captive and feeding them to Ivan for his hunts." Carwyn turned his face to the humans approaching with guns and quad bikes, swarming the woods and looking for Summer. "We're taking them all out."

Baojia said, "Carwyn, we have to—"

"No." Carwyn's jaw was set. "We will get Ivan, but this farm is being cleared *tonight*."

With that, Brigid saw her husband bare his teeth and rush toward the oncoming lights. Baojia, with a low curse, followed him, Natalie at his side.

"Sweep the camp," Baojia shouted to his people. "Gather the humans in the kitchen."

Brigid saw the moment that the guards realized vampires were coming after them. The quads turned and headed back to the camp and the guns fell silent.

"Get out of here!" one yelled. "Get to the trucks!"

One bike split off and made for the road, only to have a shadow sweep down from the sky. Daxa plucked the human from the back of the bike and tossed him toward the waterfall where he tumbled over as the bike veered over the bridge and flipped end on end.

"Baojia!" Brigid yelled, watching Natalie sink her teeth into the neck of a guard, twisting his head until the pop was audible. "Where are your humans?"

Baojia turned and nodded his head toward the farm. "I had them positioned near the cabins. They're point on getting the humans out."

But there were only two of them, and the dozen cabins

were scattered over the farm. "If they try to eliminate witnesses..."

"Fuck!" He bared his fangs. "Daxa! The cabins! Pick off any guards you see heading toward them." He whistled, and two black-clad soldiers were at his side. "Go with Brigid. Getting the humans is the priority. Try not to reveal yourself."

"Yes, boss."

"On it."

Brigid ran toward her husband. Carwyn was already charging through the forest and into the clearing where most of the cabins had been built. He ran like a galloping bear, jumping over brush and leaping over fallen trees.

Brigid didn't have his power, and she was perilously close to losing control of her fire, which would be disastrous in the middle of the woods even if they were foggy and moss covered.

"Follow Carwyn!" She pointed at his disappearing figure and made sure the two soldiers were following his lead before she veered back and headed toward the sound of water.

Better safe than sorry.

She dunked herself in the flowing water of the creek, feeling the sizzle of cold against her heated skin. Water bubbled around her fingertips, and a faint fog rose around her. She dunked her entire body in the creek, submerging her head and raising it just in time to hear the gun cock over her.

"I know what you are," a voice said. "And the gun's pointed at your neck. Don't fucking move."

CARWYN HAD LOST all sense of strategy or politics. All he could think of was humans being taken, beaten, and hunted. The bruises all over Daniel Uriarte's body and the tortured look in Summer's eyes. God in heaven knew what else they'd find when they rescued the humans from those little rickety cabins around the farm.

He reached the first cabin and paused, trying to contain his rage. "Don't scare them more, old man."

Carwyn knew he could look like a beast when he was enraged. It was something he'd learned how to temper, even as a human. He'd always wear a smile, pitch his voice to a soothing low timbre, and slump his shoulders just a little. Anything to put the vulnerable at ease.

He had to concentrate when he heard muffled crying coming from inside. He took a deep breath and clamped down on the bite of anger. "We're here to get you out," he said softly. "Can you open the door?"

Hesitation coming from the other side. Carwyn looked over his shoulder to see two of Baojia's soldiers at the cabin in the distance, the female soldier with her hand against the wall, probably asking something similar.

Finally a voice spoke. "We can't open it."

"That's fine. I can break the lock; I just don't want to scare you." With a warning given, he twisted the latch to one side, the metal falling apart in his hands like cardboard. He pulled the door open and saw two figures huddled in the corner.

They looked up, blinking. Two young women—related, Carwyn was guessing, from the looks of them.

"I'm Carwyn." He held out his hand. "My wife and I were hired by the family of another missing girl. Her name is Summer. Are you injured?"

Both the young women crawled from the corner. One pointed toward the door. "My shoes are over there, but my feet are in pretty bad shape. They took my socks."

"Mine too," the other girl said. "But I can walk. Rachel's feet are worse."

"If you'll allow it, I can carry you to the kitchen. That's the meeting point."

"Will the guards—?"

"My wife and the others are taking care of the guards." Carwyn allowed the growl to reach his voice and saw the two girls eyes begin to tear up. "Come on." He held out his hand again. "Let's get you home."

"Oh my God, am I dreaming?" The girl called Rachel was fully crying now. "Carrie?"

"I'm here."

Carwyn lifted the girl in his arms and saw the other one take her hand.

"I'm here, Rach; you're not dreaming, okay?"

Rachel broke down, her shoulders shaking as Carwyn walked the kidnapped girls toward the kitchen. "Shhhh." He brushed a kiss over the crying girl's forehead. "There now, you're going to be all right." His rage was screaming on the inside, but he forced himself to keep alert and calm for the two traumatized girls in his care. "Try to be as quiet as you can, yes? I'm not sure where everyone is."

Carwyn saw Baojia's two soldiers escorting a pair of young men in the same direction. He flagged them down. "You there!"

"Sir?" The young soldier ran to Carwyn. "Is she injured?"

"Her feet," the girl named Carrie said. "Other than that, we're okay."

Carwyn looked at Rachel. "Will you let her carry you so I can look for others?"

Rachel nodded and wiped the tears from her eyes. "Yeah. I feel stupid not walking. I can walk if you need me to—"

"It's fine!" The female soldier was nearly as tall as Carwyn, with strong Slavic features and a slight Russian accent. "There's nothing worse than hurt feet, is there? You can't think of anything else. I've had the same."

"Really?"

Carwyn gently shifted the young woman from his arms into the soldier's, reassured that they were in good hands.

BRIGID LAY CALMLY in the water, more than slightly pissed off that she hadn't noticed the human sneaking up on her.

"So you know what I am, do you?" She focused on her amnis, felt the rush against her skin that reached the surface and sizzled as soon as it met the water. Steam rose around her.

"I know all about you fucking vampires."

Brigid finally turned and looked at him, widening her eyes, which often freaked humans out. Just a little.

It worked. The human took a step back but didn't change the angle of the weapon. It was still pointed at Brigid's spine.

Still, it wasn't against her neck anymore. That was something.

She rose slowly, her eyes locked with the human's. The water sizzling against her skin formed a cloud of steam around her, and she stared at the man with every ounce of predatory intent she could push into her expression.

She imagined his blood, hot and sweet in her mouth, his neck snapping beneath her hands, and her fangs lengthened. She curled her lip and smelled urine.

"You know about me?" She asked again. Then she dropped her voice. "Do ya really?"

"I… I know if I shoot—"

"What's your name?" She walked toward him, the water against her skin bubbling into vapor.

"J-Jess. Don't come any closer." The gun was starting to waver.

"Jessss." She hissed out his name, perfectly content to play to human fears about the big bad scary creatures of the night. "What do you think you know about vampires, Jess?" She inched closer to him.

"I know that if I shoot your neck—"

"Not my *neck*, Jess." She moved closer, and the human took a step back. "Precisely and directly through my spine, severing it completely in one shot." She widened her eyes. "Anything less than an exact shot will only piss me off, Jessy. And a pissed-off vampire—"

He shot wildly, the bullet barely grazing her neck, and Brigid leaped on him, launching herself at his retreating figure, tackling him to the ground and jerking his neck to the side.

She heard the quick snap a second before her fangs pierced his vein.

CARWYN RAN around the perimeter of the main field, checking each cabin, though most had already been opened and he saw no guards. He branched off a path that led to another clearing, another field, and another set of cabins. The first was already being opened by Baojia and Natalie.

"I promise," Natalie said. "We're here to get you guys out. We do not work for Ivan."

He could hear the furious argument between a man and a woman on the other side of the cabin doorway. He pulled Baojia away.

"Have all the guards been eliminated?"

"We've found nine, which is what Summer indicated, but there could be more. There's no guarantee that was an accurate count. Even Daxa had a hard time telling them apart from the air. I think they dressed the same to throw the prisoners off."

"Smart," Carwyn muttered. "And no other vampires?"

"None. The guards that are still alive babbled about Ivan, but no one seems to know where he runs these hunts." Baojia's expression was grim. "If I've let that man escape, Katya—"

"Katya will understand rescuing innocent people from a monster," Carwyn said.

Baojia cocked his head. "When was the last time you worked for someone who didn't fear you, Father Carwyn?"

"I don't know what that has to do with—"

"It doesn't work like that for those of us who are part of a hierarchy. Is Katya benevolent? When she can be, which is one of the reasons I work for her. But this vampire challenges her authority. Don't pretend that I made the call back in that forest. This was you and Brigid, and I backed you up because I could see the original op was blown. But if I don't get Ivan,

Katya will blame me. And a few rescued humans aren't going to make her any less angry."

Carwyn put his hand on Baojia's shoulder. "We're going to get him."

"Do you have any leads?" Baojia crossed his arms over his chest. "Because I sure as hell do not."

The sound of a human footfall made them both come to attention. Baojia's handgun seemingly appeared out of thin air, pointing in the direction of the noise, and Carwyn's head swung around to see a burly man with a silver-flecked beard poking his head from behind a tree. He was wearing the orange cap and dark clothes of all the other guards.

When he realized he'd been spotted, the guard stepped forward with both hands raised. "I'm not gonna fight. I promise."

"Do you know where Ivan is?" Carwyn asked.

Natalie was ushering two prisoners out of the cabin, soothing them, explaining what was going on, and glancing at Baojia and Carwyn as she passed. She didn't stop but hustled the humans away from the vampires and the guard as quickly as possible.

"She still passes for human so easily," Carwyn muttered.

"It's a useful tool." Baojia was glaring at the man. "You didn't answer my friend here. Where's Ivan?"

"I don't know. I swear I don't. But I'm pretty sure he'll be back tomorrow night." The guard glanced over his shoulder. "He's gonna need to pick her up."

Carwyn's felt the ice wash through his veins. "Pick who up?"

The man's face went pale. "I don't know what to do. I

just... I did what he told me, and I didn't get close. I figured maybe you two could help her, y'know? She's just a kid."

"Who's just a kid?" Baojia asked, never letting his gun waver from the man.

"The new one." He seemed to shudder a little. "Like you guys."

THE CABIN HAD BEEN BUILT in a remote clearing of the forest, at least two kilometers from the rest of the compound, but it wasn't like the others. While those had been rickety and near collapse, this one was made of sturdy blocks, a concrete floor, and a solid metal roof. The door was metal, and the locks were solid.

It still wasn't enough to hide the sobbing from the creature inside.

"Hello?" The voice was plaintive. Deceptively so. "Hey, is someone there? I hear you."

Baojia, Carwyn, and Brigid stood at a distance, knowing exactly what was inside. The smell of new amnis was everywhere, as was the smell of fresh blood.

"Ivan's?" Carwyn asked. "What was he thinking?"

"She's a human in Katya's territory," Baojia said, "who was turned—probably against her will. He has no claim on her."

"I don't know what's going on," the voice came again. "Please help me." She started to cry. "I'm so thirsty."

"She probably has no idea what's going on," Brigid whispered. "And she sounds desperate."

"Desperate doesn't mean not dangerous." Carwyn knew better than most, being the sire of many vampires, just how dangerous newborns could be. They were wildly uncontrolled, yes, but their brute strength could be shocking. Vampires as young as this one, with no mental or physical preparation, could be as dangerous as a trained warrior because they were creatures of complete and utter instinct.

Easy to kill? Sometimes. But utterly unpredictable.

Brigid walked to the door, and Carwyn tried to hold her back. "Darling girl—"

"No." She cut him off. "She's a victim, just like the others —*more* than the others, in fact. She's scared as hell, Carwyn."

Baojia held up a single finger. "Just remember, she's desperate. And if she's hungry, she will attack anything."

Brigid leaned against the door and raised her voice. "Hello? My name's Brigid, and I'm here to help you. What's your name?"

There was sniffing. "Um... it's Tiffany."

"Tiffany, do you know what happened to you?"

"I know... I mean, I don't really know. Ivan didn't tell me much. He just put me in here. And it hurt. I don't remember much." She was crying, nearly choking on her tears. "I think I... I killed someone."

"Fuck." Baojia barely mouthed the words. "When was that, Tiffany?"

Carwyn closed his eyes and said a brief prayer for the lost soul and for Tiffany's conscience. It was clear the death tormented her.

"Maybe a day ago? I can't tell. He keeps it dark in here all the time. There aren't any lights or anything."

"Okay," Brigid said. "We're going to figure out a way to get you out of there, Tiffany. None of this is your fault." Brigid turned to Carwyn. "Poor lamb. She sounds about seventeen."

"Um, Brigid? Is that the right name?"

"Yes, Tiffany. It's Brigid. I know I have an accent, so if you can't understand me, just ask again, okay?"

"I... I know this sounds crazy, but I drank his blood. I don't know what's wrong with me. Please don't come in. I mean... you can." She was crying and trying to speak through her tears. "But I don't know what I'll do. Don't come in." The girl was flat-out sobbing. "It hurts. It hurts, but don't come in."

Baojia raked a hand through his hair. "Fuck, what a mess."

"What's he doing?" Carwyn didn't understand it. Keeping a new vampire around humans was a recipe for disaster. "What the hell is Ivan doing?"

TWENTY

Summer's face was pale, her freckles dark against her skin, as she sat near the fire in the expansive living room of Katya's wine-country safe house in Ukiah, wrapped in a blanket and holding a warm mug of tea. They'd made it to the vineyard house with barely an hour of night to spare. The human victims, other than Summer, had been dropped off at the local hospital with Baojia's human employees to give statements to the sheriff's deputies.

There was no trace of Ivan, and the guards who'd tried to text him received nothing in reply.

Tiffany, the newborn vampire, appeared to be only days old. She'd been handcuffed and transported in Baojia's SUV and was currently stashed in a worker's house on the property with two of Baojia's vampire guards watching her. They'd given her fresh blood and been able to get a little more information from her, but the young woman still didn't know much and understood even less about what had happened to her.

"Was that where he was taking them?" Summer asked. "When they left the farm, he was making them vampires?"

Carwyn and Brigid exchanged a look. "We don't know, Summer."

Brigid leaned forward, certain Summer knew more than she was letting on. "One of the guards mentioned that you were 'Ivan's favorite.'" She frowned. "What did that mean?"

Summer curled her lip. "He figured out that I knew about vampires. Well, I told him. I was... I was trying to— It doesn't matter; he took us anyway. He liked..." Her hand tightened in her father's. "He liked to talk to me. Kind of... taunt me. Especially after Dani and I..." Her shoulders curled in and her face collapsed in grief. "You found Dani's body, didn't you? That's why you knew where to look."

Brigid's eyes went wide. "Summer, Daniel's not dead."

The cry that came from her mouth was nearly inhuman. *"What?"*

Jamie had a hand on his daughter's back. "Honey, I thought you knew. Daniel's in the hospital, but he's not dead. He followed the water; he got out. It must have been incredibly tough, pumpkin, but he did it."

Summer was somewhere between laughing and crying. "Where is he? Are you sure? They told me—"

"They feckin' lied to you," Brigid said. "Or they didn't know. That would explain why they didn't move the farm, actually, so that makes sense. They thought the creek had just washed his body away."

Carwyn let out a long, slow breath. "What a lad. My God. Left for dead, and he made it down to the mouth of the creek. He's still in a coma in the hospital in Santa Rosa, but he's alive. Natalie called as soon as we got signal again. She checked in with the deputy she knows."

Summer's face went blank. "He's in a coma?"

Ross and Jamie flanked her.

"He's strong," Ross said. "You know he is. He gave a message to those fishermen that found him. Helped us know where to look for you. We didn't have any other leads, Summer. We could have been looking for weeks if Daniel hadn't made it out."

She gripped her father's hand. "I want to see him. Let me see him." She stood and started for the door.

"Summer, wait." Brigid looked at Jamie. "Why don't you clean up and rest? Try to get some of your strength back before you go visit Daniel. Let your father take you tomorrow during the day. They won't let you in when it's not visitors' hours anyway. Just... take a breath, yeah?"

She sat again but looked poised to flee at the least bit of provocation. "He told me Dani was dead. I promised I'd kill him."

"Ivan?" Carwyn's arms were crossed over his chest. "Did you know about the new vampire, Summer?"

She shook her head, but then she frowned. "Maybe... I don't know if it could be why, but..."

"Tell us what you're thinking." Brigid crouched next to her, trying to coax the reluctant, angry girl. "I know it's horrible, and I know what it's like to want to forget monsters, but you said Ivan liked to talk to you. What did he say?"

"He told me about the hunts. Told me that's why they took Dani. They wanted him..." She swallowed hard. "Ivan must have wanted him for a hunt. He yelled at the guards when he found out he was dead. Told him Dani was 'valuable.' I didn't know what that meant; I thought they meant because his family is rich or something."

"But they might have wanted him for a hunt."

Baojia spoke up. "He's done this before, Summer. That's why it's so important to stop him. He abducted girls in Ensenada—waitresses at a bar he ran—and then infected them with a vampire drug that made immortals go crazy. He used those girls for hunts out in the desert."

Summer stared into the fire. "What fun is a hunt if the prey is weak?" She blinked and looked at Brigid. "That's what he told me. I asked if he was taking humans for vampires to hunt, and he said, 'What fun is a hunt if the prey is weak?' Like humans were boring or something."

"If the prey is weak…" Brigid knew in her gut what Ivan had done, but it was too horrible to say aloud.

"He said he evened the playing field." Tears came to Summer's eyes. Angry, furious tears. "That's why he turned that girl, didn't he? That's why he took us and made us work. To see who was the strongest. To see who could survive."

Ross was the one who finally said it. "That sick bastard sired newborn vampires just to let other vampires hunt them."

"ARE WE MONSTERS?" Brigid stared at the ceiling of the light-safe room that overlooked the vineyard. "Sometimes I think we're monsters."

Carwyn lay on the bed next to her and draped a brightly colored silk scarf over her eyes. "We're no more monstrous than any other creature, darling girl."

"No, lions don't hunt each other," Brigid said, pressing the silk to her eyes. "I remember when you bought this for me. It was a year after I'd turned."

"You were missing the sun," he said. "Bright things. Flowers don't look the same at night." He hooked his arm around her waist and pulled her close. "Lions do hunt each other. When a male lion battles for dominance of a pride, the first thing he does after he wins is to kill the cubs the previous male sired. It makes the females go back into heat so he can mate with them."

Brigid blinked. "That's horrible."

"That's nature." He pulled the scarf away. "We're creatures of animalistic nature, but that's not all we are. Ivan is an aberration. You know that."

"Sometimes the things our kind are capable of make me wonder."

Carwyn frowned. "What do we do that's more monstrous than what humans do to each other?"

"It doesn't matter what humans do; we should be better than that," Brigid said. "That's the point, Carwyn. Think about how many years you've lived. Think about the wisdom and experience and perspective you have. And there are vampires who are so much older than you."

"Thanks for remembering that," he muttered. "Was starting to feel like a fossil."

She smiled and turned her head. "What does it mean if we don't evolve? We should be better. We should be wiser, more patient. Kinder. We don't have the petty worries of humanity; we should be above that somehow. Keep our heads above it."

He brushed the hair back from her forehead. "Becoming

immortal doesn't make you better or worse, darling girl. It just makes you old. If anything, it makes you more of what you always were. If you were always a creature obsessed with justice" —he pinched her chin— "you become even more obsessed. And if you loved family and fun and treasured joy, you become more of that."

"So Ivan is who Ivan always was," Brigid said. "He was always going to exploit the vulnerable; becoming a vampire just made him able to exploit for more years."

"We'll stop him." He captured her mouth in a fierce kiss. "We'll end this for good."

"I think if we don't, Summer might rampage through the Pacific Northwest until she has his head on a pike."

"Now that's a picture." Carwyn narrowed his eyes. "This is the first time I've ever really spent much time with Cathy's clan in the Americas."

"It explains so much."

"So, so much." His eyes were somewhere away from her, somewhere in the distance that she couldn't reach.

Brigid kissed him softly. "I'm glad you treasure joy."

"And mayhem. Not everyone sees the connection between the two."

"Is that how you're justifying the havoc your hounds are wreaking on Deirdre's gardens in Wicklow?"

Carwyn had tended a pair of breeding wolfhounds in Wales, only to move them to Ireland after he and Brigid had married. They'd run joyfully around their estate outside Dublin, along with their expanding progeny, until Carwyn and Brigid had moved to the United States. Then they became the oversized problem of Carwyn's daughter Deirdre.

"Shhhh." He pinched her lips. "Deirdre loves the dogs.

Loves them. The angry emails are just a little game she's playing with me. I promise. Also, I miss my dogs."

"I'm sure they miss you too." Brigid grinned. "You did it again."

"What?"

She wrapped her arms around his neck. "Made me smile when I was feeling broody. Made me think about home. Made me remember some joy on a very heavy night."

"That's my superpower." He pulled her close and let his kiss spin her out and turn her around.

When Carwyn kissed her, everything else disappeared. Brigid floated in a shimmering place where their joined amnis elevated both of them, making her feel as if she'd been speeding in circles on a carnival ride.

How did he still do this to her? He made her feel like a sappy teenage girl!

Ten years together and Brigid thought she should be just a little bit used to her mate by this point. But Carwyn was a constant surprise; a glorious confusion that teased her with unerring affection only to confound her when his protective nature was riled. He was a nexus of mirth until he was utterly lethal.

It was a dichotomy that fascinated her.

Despite his size, her husband knew how to put people at ease. Unless he wanted to intimidate them. She had never met a creature more in tune with his physicality and the way others, human and vampire, perceived it.

Children and dogs adored him. Even cats had a soft spot for the giant. Insecure human men mostly avoided him, and the truly dangerous watched him warily.

And Brigid?

She played her fingers across the planes of his face. He had scars from his human years and even a little silver touched his beard and temples. His deep red hair curled in a wild explosion that reminded Brigid not just a little of a wood fire.

"Why do you love me?" she asked him again.

He turned and kissed her fingers. "I love your passion for doing the right thing even when it's the most difficult thing. I love the way you see people. You call yourself a cynic, but at your heart, you're an optimist."

"I'm an addict," she said. "I have to be an optimist in order to justify my existence."

"I love that you wear your scars like the badges of honor they are. I love that you're so damn stubborn when you know you're doing the right thing. You're this tiny immovable object in the face of doubt."

"I have to be stubborn to be married to you."

"And I'm ridiculously fond of your arse, which I know you think is on the ample side for your size, but I'm telling you, it really is perfection."

She had to bite back a smile. "No arse is perfection. They're arses."

"Clearly you do not have my perspective when we're making love and you're—"

She slapped her hand over his mouth. "Leave room for the Holy Ghost, Carwyn ap Bryn. Or your mother'll be shamed."

He grinned and bit the heel of her hand, his fangs growing long as she watched him.

I'm going to ravish you. Brigid only thought it, but she

knew Carwyn heard. He always heard her. Always saw her. He always had.

"I love you quite madly, Carwyn ap Bryn."

"That's good," Carwyn said. "Because I'm definitely going to fuck up something you've carefully planned in the next few days."

She closed her eyes. "I'd like to say you're exaggerating, but you just never are."

TWENTY-ONE

Summer sat at Dani's bedside, watching his lungs move steadily up and down while the monitors beeped on the machinery around him. His eyes moved under the lids as he dreamed, and every now and then, his face tensed in a sleepy grimace. The nurse assured Summer that he wasn't in any pain, but the bruises all over his face and arms were impossible to ignore.

The police—or sheriff's deputies, she didn't know who they were—had allowed her into his room once they recognized her from the missing-person report, but they warned her that Dani's family would be coming by and might kick her out.

This is my fault.

If she hadn't wanted to hike the Lost Coast...

If she had pushed harder to camp on the trail with other hikers...

If she hadn't convinced Dani they needed to escape...

Her father stood outside the door, speaking quietly with the officer standing guard, but Summer felt dead inside. Dani was still in a coma, and the bright, warm smile that had made her feel like the center of the universe was gone.

But he's still alive.

She sniffed and blinked back tears, imagining Dani chastising her for crying.

Summer was a realist. She saw the pins sticking out of his knee. She saw the casts and the bandages. Dani's life as he knew it was over. He would probably never play soccer again, and definitely not at the college level. He would need months of physical therapy, and it was very probable that he would blame her for it.

And Summer? She'd survived with hardly anything but a few scrapes, a twisted ankle, and badly blistered feet.

She heard the low murmur of voices outside; then the door opened. She sniffed, wiped her eyes, and turned her head to see a beautiful and elegant woman enter the fluorescent-lit hospital room. From her resemblance to Dani and the pictures Summer remembered from his phone, she knew this was Isabel Delgado, Dani's mother.

The woman examined Summer with a cool expression, her eyes taking everything in, from Summer's tangled curls pulled into a messy bun to the bloodstained hiking boots that were the only footwear she had with her.

She'd borrowed a pair of jeans from Katya, along with a T-shirt and sweater, but this was far from the graceful first impression that Summer had imagined when she'd daydreamed about meeting Dani's parents.

She stood and nearly held out her hand before she remembered she'd been wiping her tears and probably had snot on her hand. She crossed her arms and pressed her hands into fists. "You're Dani's mom, right?"

The woman lifted her chin. She wasn't tall—in fact, she might have been shorter than Summer without heels—but her presence was formidable. "I am."

"I'm Summer." Her voice broke. "We haven't met, but I'm—"

"Yes, you were Daniel's American girlfriend." Mrs. Delgado's accent was precise. "That is over, of course. As soon as he is healthy enough to transfer, Dani will be coming back to Mexico City where he can receive proper medical care and physical rehabilitation from our personal physician."

Summer felt the heat come to her cheeks. "I think whatever Dani and I *are* is up to us, Mrs. Delgado. When Dani wakes up—"

"When he wakes up" —her voice was acid— "he'll wake up to a crushed knee, a broken ankle, fractured arms and ribs, a dislocated collarbone, and a missing spleen." The corner of her eye twitched. "His football ambitions are ruined, and his long-term health has been compromised because of the criminal elements you dragged him into, Miss Mackenzie. The doctors say it's a miracle he doesn't have brain damage. Your time in Dani's company is over."

Summer's felt a chill run down her spine and recognized it for the Mackenzie rage her father warned her about. "Criminal... *elements*? You mean the ones I barely escaped from two nights ago? *Those* criminal elements?"

Mrs. Delgado narrowed her eyes. "So you say. I hear the stories about this place. About the... hippy girls who come here to make money in the drug fields."

Summer stepped toward her, her blood heating. "I'm not a drug dealer. Or a drug worker, Mrs. Delgado. I'm studying forestry at Washington State University, and I've been on the dean's list every semester since I enrolled. I'm going to get a master's degree in environmental management. My father is a high school teacher, and my mother is an award-winning musician. We might not be rich like you, but—"

"Exactly." She lifted her chin. "You are *not* wealthy. You are not particularly special or beautiful. Your father and mother are entirely ordinary, as is your whole family. Daniel..." She looked at her son, and sheer maternal fury shone through her stiff expression. "Daniel *is* extraordinary and always has been. He will be going home. Please let him recover in peace and put this painful chapter of life behind him."

Summer felt as if she'd shrunk down to nothing; she was so insignificant in this woman's eyes.

Why are you still here? She looked at Dani, then at his mother. His mother's expression echoed her own thoughts. *Who are you, Summer Mackenzie?*

You are ordinary.

Your family is ordinary.

You're nothing like Dani and you never will be.

Summer allowed her eyes to linger on Daniel for a few more minutes, knowing it would likely be the last time she ever saw him. His eyes were closed and his skin was washed out. She could see that the slight hollowing under his cheekbones that had started after they were kidnapped was still prominent. It would probably take months to fill in, months for him to regain his physical health. And his mother was right; he would never be the same.

Who are you, Summer Mackenzie? You promised to kill Ivan? Her internal voice had taken on the tone of Daniel's mother. *Foolish child. Who do you think you are?*

Summer blinked back tears. "I promise I never wanted... *this* to happen."

"I am sure you did not." Mrs. Delgado took his hand and pressed it between her own. Daniel's pulse jumped for a moment, then settled into an easy rhythm. "Just go, Summer. Let my son focus on healing. Leave him alone and go back to your life, whatever that was." She glanced over her shoulder. "Dani has had many girlfriends; I am sure he will not miss you any more than the others."

Right. Well, she couldn't have made that clearer. Dani probably had a dozen beautiful, parentally approved and proper girlfriends waiting back at home for him. Why did he need a grubby girl in bloody hiking boots hanging around?

She moved toward the door and motioned to her shoulder. "His right shoulder was wounded by the men who took us. It was a knife wound. I stitched it and used yarrow flowers to pull out the infection, but it was still looking a little red the night we tried to escape. Tell the doctors they might need to check it."

Dani's mother stared at her but didn't respond.

Summer nodded, gave one last look at Daniel, and left the room.

Her father was still waiting outside. "Hey. His mother said she wanted to thank you. Acted real polite and all." He tilted her chin up, reading her expression. "How'd that go?"

She couldn't cry anymore, especially not in front of strangers. "Can we go?" She glanced at the officer. "I don't want to give a statement right now."

Jamie Mackenzie waved a hand. "Baojia and Natalie took care of all that when they brought the other kids back. You're good, pumpkin."

"Miss Mackenzie." The officer tipped his hat. "I'm obliged to tell you that County Victim Services is available at any time, day or night."

Summer didn't want to hear it; she was seconds from exploding in tears.

The officer pulled a brochure from his pocket and handed it to Summer. "There's a phone number on there, and I wrote down my wife's phone number. She's one of the counselors over there, okay? It's not a big outfit, but she'd sure be happy to help you—"

"Thanks." She blinked rapidly and stuffed the brochure in her pocket. "Yeah. I appreciate it. Thanks."

Summer heard a door open at the end of the hall, and low Spanish voices began to echo, coming toward them. She tugged on her dad's jacket. "Can we go now?"

Jamie looked over his shoulder. "I think that's Dani's father. You sure you don't want to—"

"We need to go." Summer walked away from the voices even when one called her name. She heard her father following her, the heavy sound of his boots a soothing, familiar rhythm as he walked.

"Miss Mackenzie?" a voice called. "Summer?"

She shook her head. "Don't stop."

Her father's voice was for her ears only. "You sure?"

"Yeah."

The voice rose. "Please, Miss Mackenzie!"

She burst through the exit door and made for the truck.

Who are you, Summer Mackenzie?

What makes you think you're special?

BRIGID, Carwyn, and Baojia leaned over the map, all three staring at the circle they'd drawn that encompassed an area stretching nearly up to the California-Oregon border and as far south as Santa Rosa.

"If the farm is at the center of it, and the guy said Ivan traveled one hundred fifty miles on the truck in one night," Baojia said. "I think this is our search area. This is as the crow flies, so it's not this large in reality."

"Doesn't matter," Carwyn said. "We have days to move or Ivan will be gone. He already knows the farm is compromised and his new baby vampire is gone."

"He has a hunt planned." Brigid put a hand on his shoulder. "Or else he wouldn't have turned that girl. He's not going to abandon it now. Those things take time to set up, and he probably needs the money."

"Exactly." Baojia looked at Brigid. "What if I told you I might be able to get an invitation?"

Carwyn looked at Brigid, then at Baojia. "Are you serious?"

"There are criminal elements in San Francisco, and I have moles. Sources." Baojia shrugged. "There are always vampires looking for a thrill, and some of them have a lot of money. That's why he's doing this. But his vulnerability is advertising. Ivan is getting the word out to rich immortals somehow, and I have a feeling that I know who one of his messengers might be."

"Who?" Brigid asked.

Ever the optimist.

Carwyn put an arm around her. "Darling girl, do you think he's going to give up his source that easily?"

The corner of Baojia's mouth turned up. "I'm an ally, not a sucker. The question is, are you willing to go in?"

Carwyn's head swung around. "Say again?"

"Of course," Brigid said. "I have an identity that will work perfectly. It's already established. She's never been to the US before, but that's no great stretch. She's traveled quite widely in Asia."

Carwyn stared at his wife. "Excuse me, have I forgotten the discussion we didn't have about this?"

"Big man." She patted his chest. "Ivan knows Baojia. There's no way he can do it. He's seen you too, and everyone in Ensenada knew about the redheaded vampire priest. He'll spot you in the blink of an eye."

Baojia's face remained impassive. "Brigid is by far the easiest one to camouflage."

"Claire McKee is an established identity," Brigid said. "I've used her for multiple errands. She's in Mary Hamilton's organization in Belfast, and anyone who asks knows that Mary can be… flexible when it comes to her underlings' activities."

"She'll hold up on vetting?" Baojia asked.

"She will. Even up to Mary herself. The identity is a favor to Dublin. I'm going to need a wig though. A good-quality one."

Baojia nodded. "I can take care of that."

"We didn't agree to this!" Carwyn felt his blood begin to surge at the thought of his mate risking her safety and going into a job alone. "You know how these things can be, Brig. Claire McKee is a vapid, thrill-seeking socialite, not a killer. She's a water vampire with very little defensive reputation, and there's no guarantee you'll be able to take additional security into this job like you usually would with Claire."

"I'm fairly sure that will be *impossible*," Baojia said. "Ivan never allowed any personal security when he was running hunts in the desert. I highly doubt he's changed that."

"Being exposed to danger will be part of the thrill for her." Brigid leaned into the table where the map was spread. "Claire is vapid, but she's also bored and rich—the spoiled daughter of a powerful sire. She's *looking* for the danger, the exposure, the thrill."

"I absolutely hate this idea," Carwyn said. "I want that noted for the record."

Even if his objection was useless. He could already see Brigid's posture changing, her face settling into cynical lines. He hated to acknowledge it, but his wife was brilliant at undercover operations. She could transform her expressions, her posture, even the way she walked. He had no idea how, but over the past ten years, she had learned to become a chameleon.

He still didn't like it. "Brigid, this vampire—"

"Is lethal as all get out. I promise I know that and I'm not ignoring the risk." Brigid stood on her tiptoes and pulled Carwyn's head down for a kiss. "But I also know that Claire McKee and Brigid Connor have an advantage that Ivan will never see coming."

"The fact that you can incinerate him with a snap of your fingers?"

"We're trying to avoid that scenario, remember? Forest fires?"

Carwyn glared at Baojia, who was standing to the side, pretending as if he hadn't suggested this entire scenario.

"Hey." She pinched his ear. "Listen to me. Claire and Brigid have a husband who can track her through their mating bond. Ivan will never expect that. All you'll have to do is keep me within a reasonable distance and you, Baojia, and his people can rain down hell on any bastards taking part in this abomination."

Carwyn pretended to pout. "Raining down hell on evil vampires does sound like fun."

"See?" She looked at Baojia. "Call your source and wrangle me an invitation. Claire McKee, Belfast. I promise she'll check out."

"You got it." He started toward the door, then paused. "I'm going to mention one thing; then we're going to pretend this part of the conversation never happened."

Carwyn frowned. "What's that?"

Baojia cleared his throat. "This whole setup could happen fairly quickly. I don't know Ivan's timeline, but you're going to want to make sure that mating bond is... fresh."

Brigid pursed her lips and tried not to smile. "Right. Excellent advice. And... we never had this conversation."

Carwyn frowned. "What do you mean... Oh!" He grinned. *"Fresh."* He reached down and hoisted Brigid over his shoulder, rushing past Baojia as he headed toward their room. "So sorry. We're professionally obligated to go have lots of bitey sex the rest of the night."

"Oh no." Brigid protested with a laugh. "The sacrifices we make for the sake of justice."

"I know it's daunting." He reached their bedroom door in seconds and kicked it closed behind him before he threw her on the bed. "But we're professionals, darling. We do what we must."

TWENTY-TWO

Brigid was going to pretend she didn't hear the knock on the door at dusk the following night. They were staying in a beautiful one-bedroom suite at Katya's estate in the hills outside Ukiah, and Brigid was enjoying the seclusion of their private living room while Carwyn got ready for the night. She smelled coffee brewing somewhere, but there were far too many people wandering around the place for Brigid's liking. She couldn't believe it, but she actually missed the solitude of Carwyn's beloved van.

Not much longer, old girl.

Baojia had already reached out to the associate with criminal connections, and Brigid's wig and new, posh wardrobe were on their way from some of Katya's people in San Francisco. She could be waiting for days or hours for this hunt; she had no way of knowing.

In the meantime, the house was teeming with vampires. Human staff had been moved out since there was a newborn vampire in the vicinity. Katya was already on her way to deal with that issue and take responsibility for the young woman, who would be under her protection since her sire had abandoned her.

The knock came again, and with Carwyn taking a shower in the marble-clad bathroom, there was no one to open it but Brigid. She girded her snark and marched to the door, only to be surprised by Katya on the threshold.

"What are you doing here?"

Katya ducked under her arm and entered the room. "It's my house, remember? And I arrived before sunrise this morning. Trying to be inconspicuous."

Dressed in a pair of tailored tan pants, a cashmere knit sweater, and a trendy outdoor vest, Katya was anything but inconspicuous.

"Obviously." Brigid closed the door behind her. "How can I help you? I'm assuming Baojia briefed you about the plan."

Katya circled the living room and scanned it with a critical eye. "I don't stay at this house very often. I need to; it's beautifully isolated."

"Yeah, we like that part."

She turned her appraising gaze toward Brigid. "I have a unique problem, and I need your help."

"You have it." Brigid spread her hands. "As soon as Baojia secures an invitation, I'll be going in. I'm not sure how much contact I'll be able to maintain, but—"

"That's not my problem." Katya stared at a framed print of a redwood shrouded in fog. "Summer Mackenzie spoke to me a few minutes ago."

"She's a remarkable girl," Brigid said. "Her family raised her well. Confident. Competent. Clearly proficient in survival skills."

"She asked me to sire her."

Brigid blinked. "And wildly immature, obviously." Good Lord, what was the girl thinking?

The corner of Katya's mouth turned up. "She's older than I was."

"The world is different now."

Katya cocked her head. "Is it? I find her offer intriguing. That is how she approached it. She's a clever young woman. She listed her credentials and her future ambitions. Told me how she would be an asset to my organization and outlined why she thought it would be beneficial to both of us." Katya lifted an eyebrow. "It was persuasive."

Brigid felt her stomach drop. "You're considering it? Her father and uncle will go ballistic."

Katya raised an eyebrow. "She asked them to do it first."

"And they said no." Brigid walked to the bedroom door and closed it. "They know her best. What does that tell you?"

"That they're protective and they have their own plans for her." Katya's expression was serene but calculating. "I'm not looking to make enemies, but she's a human in my territory. She's given the first right of her blood to her clan and they refused. I am entirely within my rights."

Damn it, Katya was right. And Summer must have known enough about immortal rules to understand that. If Katya turned Summer, her family might be resentful, but no one would blame Katya.

Brigid tried another tack. "Maybe her father and uncle know she's not ready."

"Or maybe they're being overprotective." Katya turned to her. "That's the help I need from you. I turned for reasons… Well, they were my own reasons. Summer is young, but not that young. As far as her family is concerned, she had no desire to change prior to this current..." She frowned. "What did they call it? Oh yes, an 'overload of emotion.'"

"Doesn't that concern you?"

"No, I think it's fascinating." She narrowed her eyes. "What drives a human to desire immortal life, Brigid? You're young enough to remember, aren't you?"

Brigid tried not to seethe, but it was difficult. "It's not fascinating, Katya, it's tragic. The girl needs therapy."

"She doesn't have therapy." She pursed her lips. "She has you. Find out what her motives are and tell me."

"If I recommend that you do not do this, will that persuade you?"

"No. I will keep my own council on this. But I do respect your opinion."

"Does Baojia know?"

"Of course not, and I'd prefer you don't tell him. You know how he feels about humans retaining mortality. The man practically had a temper tantrum when his own wife decided to change."

"I'm not a tattletale," Brigid said. "But I'm skeptical."

"Which is why I want your opinion." Katya started for the door. "Don't take too long. That invitation call might come any minute."

BRIGID FOUND SUMMER in the library, where she was reading a book titled *Human Physiology*. The large coffee-table book was open on a low book stand, and Summer didn't look up when Brigid walked in.

"Did you know that there are roughly ten pints of blood in the average human body?"

Brigid sat across from her. "And we can only drink about four pints in one go. But when a human is turned, most of those ten pints need to be drained quickly. So what does your average vampire do?"

Summer looked up. "I don't know."

"I'll tell you. Unless they have access to surgical equipment, they exsanguinate the body as rapidly as possible, vomit it into waiting containers or on the ground if they're messy, and then they do that again." Brigid gave Summer a level stare. "Unless the human has already lost a lot of blood from an injury. It's very messy."

Brigid had the pleasure of seeing Summer's face get pale, but the young woman's gaze didn't waver.

"Of course, the human being turned doesn't know much about that, because they're already passed out from blood loss. That happens long before their blood is gone. It's a tricky process; no way of knowing for sure if you're doing it right."

"Unless you've done it before," Summer said quietly.

"Yes. Like Katya. She has one child." Brigid continued. "Then the human body goes through a fairly disgusting period as our amnis takes over where everything human about us—any remaining undigested food, urine, feces—all leaves the body as quickly as possible while we're absorbing our sire's blood and digesting what is left of our own."

Summer looked fairly disgusted but still unmoved.

"And of course, if yer very lucky." Brigid snapped her fingers, and fire erupted in her palm. "If yer angry—if your head isn't in the right place—you might be sired to fire. It's completely unpredictable. I was lucky. I only took out a house when I woke." She drifted into memories. "I didn't kill anyone, though I did injure a dog. Poor mite. He never walked properly again, and I always felt guilty about that." She looked back at Summer. "But I didn't kill myself, which lots of our kind do."

"If you're trying to scare me, you can't." Summer slowly shook her head. "I've gone over all this a dozen times in my head."

"Go over it a dozen more." Brigid leaned forward. "I promise there's something you forgot."

"I know the positives and the negatives too. I grew up around this, remember?"

"So did I. I still didn't choose it."

"But you're a vampire anyway."

"Someone made the choice for me." Was it still a sore point? Every now and then, but she'd mostly moved past it.

"Well, this is *my* choice." Summer's jaw was set. "I'm not going to miss the sun. I chose to move to Seattle, for God's sake. I don't want children; never have, even when I was younger. If I change my mind in a hundred years, I can always adopt a kid like my dad was adopted."

Dammit, those were the first two objections most humans had.

"I'm not going to have to say goodbye to my family. Some of them will die, and some of them won't. How's that different from anyone? And I won't have to hide anything from my brother, from my mom or dad, or—"

"Tell me one *positive* reason you want to do this, Summer Mackenzie. Why here? Why now? Why not wait until you're home? Wait until you've had time to process this? You've been through a horrible trauma. What you need now is—"

"I made a promise." Summer looked away, then back to Brigid. "I don't make promises lightly—Mackenzies aren't taught that way—I keep my word."

And now we're getting the real story. "A promise to who?"

"Myself."

Brigid softened her voice. "And what was that promise?"

"I promised that I would kill Ivan." She blinked, and tears fell down her cheeks. "I promised to kill the vampire who killed Dani. The monster who stole my life." She slowly shook her head. "And even though I know Dani's alive, he'll never be the same. I will never be the same."

Brigid leaned forward and took Summer's hand in her own. "When I tell you that I understand anger and hurt and trauma, I need you to believe me." She locked her eyes with Summer. "Do you believe me?"

Summer nodded.

"Revenge is not a good reason to turn. Even if feels like a good reason right now."

"It's not revenge." Summer wiped the tears that ran down her cheeks. "It's justice. For me and for every person who disappeared in those woods."

"I don't disagree with you, but yer not thinking clearly right now. How do you know—?"

"I'm not kidding myself, Miss Connor." Summer tucked a strand of hair behind her ear. "I know there are things about being human I'll miss. I know I'll never enjoy my nana's peach pie the same way. I'll miss watching the sunset. Or diving into the pond by my Grandpa Logan's place when the sun is beating down and making my skin sweat." A smile touched her lips. "I was even kind of looking forward to seeing what I'd look like with grey hair because my mama is so pretty with hers. She reminds me of Emmylou Harris, you know? She's so beautiful."

"Summer, there are other choices you can make. Ivan is not going to survive this. I promise you—"

"Changing is not what I planned." She looked down at her hand, which was still grasped in Brigid's. "That's the truth. Because in a lot of ways, vampires aren't as free as humans are. I don't like the idea of drinking blood or hurting people. And a part of me knows that I might hit a hundred and twenty and walk straight into the sun like my Great Aunt Corynne. I saw it happen; I was nine, and it was scary." Her forehead furrowed at the memory, and she looked back at Brigid. "But I made a promise to kill Ivan, and I can't do that if I'm human."

"Summer, I don't think you should do this."

"Do you think I'm bein'... overwrought?" Summer asked. "Like my daddy and uncle?"

Damn it. "No." Brigid could honestly say that Summer was looking at the situation with clear eyes. She wasn't acting rashly or out of impulse. The young woman was almost preternaturally calm. "You're not being impulsive."

Summer leaned toward Brigid and squeezed her hand. "You understand being hurt—I can see it in your eyes."

Brigid nodded.

"Did you kill him when you could?"

Brigid shook her head. "He was long dead." Her stepfather had died at Carwyn's hands when Brigid was still a child, a monster stopped in his tracks by immortal judgment.

Fire came to Summer's eyes. "Don't you wish you'd had the chance?"

Fuck yes. Brigid couldn't bring herself to say it.

"I want to kill Ivan." Summer's voice shimmered with barely suppressed rage. "I want to feel his blood running hot in my hands while I rip his throat out with my fangs."

"Does that sound rational to you, Summer?"

"Oh, it's not rational." A glint of steel in the young woman's beautiful hazel eyes. "But there is such a thing as righteous anger, Miss Connor. My grandfather taught me that."

Brigid was not going to change her mind. Maybe, in some way, she didn't want to. Summer Mackenzie was a human who saw vampires clearly, both their strengths and their weaknesses.

She'd survived. She'd earned the right to seek justice, and for Ivan, justice only existed in the immortal world.

Brigid closed her eyes and sighed. "All I can tell you is that you need to give grace to your father and uncle. They're not going to understand this, and they're allowed their feelings, just like yer allowed yours."

Summer nodded. "I know. But they'll come around. Remember, they're the ones who taught me about promises."

TWENTY-THREE

Baojia hung up the phone. "It's done."

Carwyn looked up from the cup of coffee he'd been not-drinking because it wasn't the tea he really wanted. "She's in?"

"I'm assuming that Ivan—or someone—wants to meet her to make sure, but her cover identity checked out. She's supposed to be in Eureka at a bar called the Siren's Song this Friday. She'll get more information there."

It was Wednesday; that didn't leave much time. Still, the wardrobe and wigs Brigid had ordered from San Francisco had arrived the night before, and the whole house was in a holding pattern. Far better to get the tense vampires surrounding them some action before bickering began.

"Okay." Carwyn nodded. "Have you seen my wife, by the way? She was gone when I got out of the shower."

Baojia opened a newspaper and began scanning the headlines, his eyes moving at dizzying speed. "I think she was talking to Summer in the library."

"Right." Carwyn took another drink of the coffee before

he decided it just wasn't worth it. "How's your wife, by the way?"

"She's headed back home right now. Left at nightfall." Baojia glanced up. "We try not to go more than three nights without one of us at home. It doesn't always happen, but we try."

"Excellent policy. And she's not that far if we need to interact with human law enforcement again."

Baojia looked up from the newspaper. "I *can* interact with humans, you know. I do it regularly for work."

"I know that." And likely most humans were terrified of him, just like they tended to be wary around his wife. "People are naturally disarmed by redheads; that's all I was thinking."

He arched an eyebrow. "Really? Is that why all those redheaded women in England were burned at the stake for witchcraft?"

"Don't be ridiculous. Redheads weren't burned at the stake in Britain, Baojia. They usually hung them." He tugged on his own dark red hair. "That's why I became a priest. Survival."

Baojia frowned. "I can't decide whether you're joking or not."

"God yes. I'd already been a vampire for four hundred years or so by the time that witch-hunting madness swept the country. Absolutely bizarre."

Baojia shrugged. "Life was cheap then."

"Life has never been cheap. Humanity simply thought some lives were more expendable than others." He stood and stretched his arms over his head. "We need to have a hunt of our own—the animal kind, obviously—or the aggression is going to start boiling over."

"That's a good idea." Baojia closed his paper. "The deer population in this area is some of the healthiest in the state. I'll arrange some groups. Waiting for an action is always the—"

"Carwyn ap Bryn!" Ross Mackenzie stormed into the kitchen, his usually stoic face a mask of fury. "You'll have Logan Mackenzie to answer for this betrayal."

Jamie was at his brother's side, both of them, human and vampire, reeking of challenge.

Baojia was at Carwyn's side in an instant. "What's going on?"

"My daughter has asked your boss to turn her." Jamie pointed a furious finger at Baojia. "And Carwyn's wife just gave the okay."

Baojia and Carwyn exchanged glances. "I don't know what you're talking about," Carwyn said. "Summer asked Katya to—?"

"Turn her into a bleeding vampire," Jamie said. "Some fucking nonsense about taking revenge for her boyfriend. The girl isn't thinking clearly!" He pointed at Baojia. "And your boss is taking advantage."

Baojia crossed his arms over his chest and narrowed his eyes. "Katya knows boundaries or I wouldn't work for her. That means the first thing she'd do is tell Summer to approach the clan who holds her under their aegis." He nodded at Ross. "She'd have told Summer to go to you."

Ross nearly spat the words. "We told her no! Like Katya should have." He bared his teeth. "If she wasn't lookin' to take advantage of a traumatized girl—"

Carwyn stepped toward them with his hands up. "I'm still

not clear about what is going on, but let's be clear here. Summer isn't a girl. She's a grown woman, isn't she?"

"She's my *daughter*," Jamie growled. "And she's not thinking clearly. Katya should know that."

"I agree," Baojia said. "Which is likely why she asked Brigid to consult with her. Brigid is a levelheaded woman and a neutral party with nothing to gain. She's also passionate about protecting victims of violence. You should be happy Katya asked her to speak to your daughter."

"She fucking told Katya yes!" Ross and Jamie both looked ready to fight. "She's planning on changing her tonight unless you do something about it."

Ross glared at Carwyn. "You said we were kin."

"You're part of my clan by mating and blood, Ross Mackenzie. I don't take that lightly." Carwyn dropped his hands. "I know nothing about this. Let me talk to Brigid before I say anything more."

"Fine." Ross's jaw was clenched so tightly his fangs nicked his lips and blood tinged his beard. "But you know this isn't right."

Carwyn's gut told him that this was a rash and impulsive decision made by a traumatized woman, but he wasn't idiot or disloyal enough to contradict Brigid in front of others. "Give me an hour."

HE FOUND Brigid in their room, her face pressed into a throw pillow from the plush sofa by the television. "Brigid?"

She pulled the pillow away from her face and feathers

rained down. "Sorry. Tell Katya I'll buy her a new one. You heard?"

"You're biting pillows now?" He pulled up a chair and sat across from her. "I have concerns."

"So do I."

"So Summer Mackenzie wants to be a vampire?"

"Apparently."

"And Katya asked your opinion?"

"Yes, and I gave it to her honestly."

Carwyn took a deep breath. "Brigid, I'm trying to understand why you think this is a good idea when everything about this screams rash and impulsive revenge to me."

"*Is* it impulsive?" Brigid took a breath. "A vampire had her captive for nearly three weeks, fucking with her head and telling her he'd killed the man she loved. He mentally fucked with her and took pleasure in it. She's been thinking about this for longer than a few days."

Carwyn bit his lip. "And you don't think that's even more reason that she shouldn't do this?"

"I understand what it's like to feel like yer a... thing." Brigid swallowed hard and looked over his shoulder at the wall. "That you have no agency and nothing about your fate is in your own hands. I understand that, Carwyn."

"This is her way of taking back control?"

"After talking with her, I think she wanted her uncle to say no. I think she wanted this to be her own path entirely. She met Katya and saw a potential ally, a vampire who would take her seriously."

Carwyn's stomach still churned at the idea of a young woman with her life spread out in front of her deciding to become a vampire after the most traumatic experience of her life. "If she could just wait. A year, six months even—"

"And Ivan will be dead by then," Brigid said. "If we're successful, Ivan will be dead and she won't be able to keep her promise."

A ball of dread settled in his chest. "She promised herself she'd kill Ivan?"

"After Daniel died—after she thought he was dead—yes." Brigid shook her head. "She's her father's daughter. Do you think Jamie Mackenzie would make a promise and not try his damnedest to keep it?"

He put his head in his hands and let out a long breath. "I came to our room prepared to have a raging fight with you, wife. I was already planning the makeup sex."

Brigid gave him a rueful smile. "And I walked into the library prepared to talk a woman out of turning immortal." She shook her head. "I knew five minutes in I wasn't going to be able to change her mind. Then I started to suspect I shouldn't. She knows what she's doing. She understands the risks and the rewards of this life." Brigid lifted the pillow. "As Katya's pillow can attest, I still don't like it."

"But you told Katya yes."

"She wasn't waiting for my permission. She asked me two very specific questions: Did Summer understand vampire life, the good and the bad? And did she have good reasons for wanting to turn?"

"And yes to both." He sat back and rubbed his hands over his face. "Her family is going to be furious."

"Her grandfather might be more furious that Ross and Jamie didn't agree to it." Brigid pursed her lips. "The Mackenzies are losing a huge asset by not respecting Summer's decision. Katya's not wrong in wanting the woman in her clan. She's smart, and I suspect she's going to be a hell of a fighter."

"I thought she wanted to be an environmentalist."

Brigid's eyes reflected nothing but pain. "If a storm is big enough, it can change a river's path."

He stared at her. "I'll ask you one more question."

"Aye."

"Does this decision have anything to do with not being able to kill Richard Kelly yourself?" It pained him to even say her stepfather's name, but a young woman's fate was in the balance. He had to know how neutral Brigid really was. "I know you resented me for—"

"No." She reached forward and put a finger over his lips to stop the words from coming. "The child I was *did* need to see that monster dead, to know for certain that he couldn't hurt me again. I understand that now. This isn't the same."

"Okay." He took a deep breath and squeezed her hand. "Go catch up with Baojia and stop destroying pillows. From everything you just told me, you did the right thing."

"And you'll figure out how to clean up the mess with the Mackenzies?"

His eyes brightened. "Look at that! This time I'm the one cleaning up *your* mess."

She stood and raised an eyebrow at him as she headed for the door. "Now that's a bit of fair play, isn't it?"

TWENTY-FOUR

Brigid didn't know what happened with the Mackenzies, and she didn't see Summer again that night. She had two nights to plan for her meeting with Ivan, and she had to focus. While the other vampires in the house went skulking off to hunt deer or conferenced in Katya's private living room, Brigid retreated to her suite and the dressing table that had been brought in with the wardrobe, wigs, and cosmetics.

She played around with changing the shape of her face. She'd never really had much interest in cosmetics and had her mother's brilliant skin to thank for that, but once she realized how useful they could be in transforming appearance, she made it a point to learn. On Murphy's team in Dublin, she'd often been the only woman willing to go undercover. It became a necessary tool.

She smoothed a layer of foundation over her skin with a brush, then began applying highlighter to her nose and cheekbones.

Though everyone was speaking as if Ivan's hunt was a done deal, Brigid knew the reality: jobs like this dangled on a very thin thread, and by this time, Ivan would know he was compromised.

As she blended the highlighter to soften the sharp edge of her jaw and alter the pointed tip of her nose, she tried to remember whether there were any pictures of Claire McKee online that she needed to reference. She didn't think so.

Even relatively honest and moral vampires were suspicious by nature, cautious around cameras, and wary of revealing anything that could identify them. Magnify that paranoia by a thousand when you were dealing with immortal rogues.

Brigid took nothing for granted. She started the process of lining her eyes, making them appear bigger while using the exact right colors to bring out the brown and mute the grey. The eyes she'd been born with were the color of good Irish whiskey, but they'd been shot through with a startling ash grey when she turned. It was unfortunately distinctive, and vampire eyes were far too sensitive to wear contact lenses.

If Ivan didn't like the look of Claire McKee, he could disappear into the ether and stay hidden for as long as he wanted. The farm was gone, but he had money and a network of connections from the immortal underworld. She'd formed a decent picture of the man after talking with Baojia and Natalie.

Ivan wasn't the type that needed flashy surroundings or thrived on notoriety like some criminals she'd chased. Ivan liked living in the shadows, which would make it nearly impossible to track him once he went under.

Added to that, he knew his primary operation had been breached and his newborn bait taken. *If* the hunt was continuing—and Brigid wasn't sure of that—he'd be on high alert and especially cautious. The only thing that had to be tempting him was the money. Claire had deep pockets, and Ivan likely planned to be on the run for a while.

"Brigid?" Carwyn entered the bedroom and saw her wearing a blond wig. "Oh, hello there, mysterious Miss McKee." He waggled his eyebrows. "If we have sex while you're wearing the wig, is that considered adultery? Asking for myself."

Brigid didn't fight the smile, but she did take the wig off. "I don't think I'm immortally graceful enough to have the kind of sex we have and not ruin this wig, so that'll have to be a no, darlin' man."

"Damn." He stretched out on the bed and looked at her. "How're you feeling?"

"Good." She turned and faced away from the dressing table. "I haven't done this in a while."

"You're a natural." His expression was serious. "Baojia seems confident in this connection, but I have my doubts. I don't want to be too far away from you. He's meeting you in a public location."

"Which protects us both."

"In theory. Unless he puts a knife in your throat and walks out when the humans start screaming. A cornered animal is the most dangerous kind."

The edge of her mouth turned up. "Are you worried about me, old man?"

"I want to put you on a shelf, and you know it." His voice was a soft growl. "It has nothing to do with doubting your abilities."

"I know that. To be fair, you've sent me up the wall more times than I can count chasing bear cubs."

"Why the fuck did God make them so damn adorable if they weren't meant to be kept as pets? That's all I want to know."

She stood and sat next to him on the bed. He immediately started rubbing her back.

"Carwyn, I'll be fine. I'm ready for Ivan."

"You know Baojia means to kill him, don't you?"

"As does Summer. I'll talk with him. The woman needs the kill more than he does."

"How many nights?"

"After this one? One. I meet Ivan at ten o'clock on Sunday night in Eureka."

"Which means we leave here tomorrow night to make it on time."

"Yes."

"Even farther north," he said. "Into the woods."

Brigid took a deep breath.

"Come, heart, where hill is heaped upon hill:
For there the mystical brotherhood
Of sun and moon and hollow and wood
And river and stream work out their will

And God stands winding His lonely horn,
And time and the world are ever in flight;
And love is less kind than the gray twilight,
And hope less dear than the dew of the morn."

Carwyn sat up and looked at her. "Feeling your Irish, Brigid?"

"Something about this place feels so raw. Almost primeval. What's happened in these woods where the fog hides everything? It should be comforting to be around these great massive trees, but it isn't. It feels..."

"Predatory."

She nodded. "There's this beautiful place, but this monster has made it a trap. He's used it to hide." She looked him dead in the eye. "We're going to make it stop."

SHE SAT in the corner of the booth amid the buzz of semi-intoxicated humans and put herself in the mind of Claire McKee. She wasn't acting as Claire, she *was* Claire, a vampire only a hundred years old, turned in the time before the war. Barely a woman and yearning for excitement. Spoiled and pampered by her powerful sire, she had money to burn.

She was dressed purposefully like a fish out of water, in a black designer cocktail dress, heels, and her blond wig styled into an angular bob. She was carrying a Louis Vuitton purse with roughly two hundred thousand dollars in cash, just the deposit to hold her place if Ivan approved of her.

Claire didn't feel conspicuous even if Brigid had to resist the urge to tug the edge of her dress's hemline.

She felt Ivan the moment he entered the bar. She kept her eyes on her Manhattan cocktail, playing with the maraschino cherry stem. Ivan would find her. She was the only immortal in the place.

"Claire?"

She looked up and was surprised. She'd been picturing a monster in her mind, but Ivan was surprisingly handsome, even with the scars that marked his face. He was dark haired and dark eyed with a face that blended Latin and Slavic features, which were softened by his navy-blue pants and a thick, soft brown sweater. His dark hair wasn't slicked back but fell over his forehead, a little longer than he usually wore it, if Brigid had to guess. He was starting to grow a beard to cover his scars, but of course, that took months for most vampires.

She didn't try to hide her surprise. Claire would be attracted to Ivan's type. "Are you him?"

His smile was careful. "I am." He slid into the booth across from her. "What were you expecting?"

Her lips curled a little. "I suppose I don't know." Claire dropped her voice to a conspiratorial whisper. "I don't know if Lee told you, but I've never really..."

Ivan raised an eyebrow. "Done this kind of thing before?"

"Is it obvious?" She let the excitement shine from her darkly lined eyes. Her red lips hung open, and she allowed her fangs to drop just a little. "You're discreet, right? I mean, my sire doesn't pay much attention to what I do, but I have to seem... you know, proper."

She leaned back in the booth as the server came and took Ivan's order. A locally brewed IPA. *Blending in nicely with the locals, are we?*

If Brigid didn't know what he was, he would have seemed like a well-to-do area businessman or maybe a tourist from the city who preferred to blend in. His clothing was well made and well fitted, but it wasn't flashy. His boots were worn but probably cost over five hundred dollars.

Ivan leaned toward her. "I'll let you in on a little secret, Claire. Officially, no one in authority condones... this kind of thing. But when discreet individuals such as myself organize these types of excursions, all sorts of unexpected VIPs show up." He smiled. "It makes for an interesting business."

Fuuuuck me. Brigid just realized how much blackmail material Ivan potentially carried on past hunt participants. Maybe he even took pictures, kept tabs on what the rich and immoral were doing in their spare time. Suddenly his source of income wasn't mysterious at all.

Even Claire wouldn't be naive enough not to spot the danger. "You know..." She looked at the door. "Maybe it's not a good idea for me to—"

"Hey, hey." Ivan gripped her wrist, keeping her in her seat. "I'm not after vampires looking for some fun. If you leave me alone, we'll never have a problem. I promise. I have lots of repeat clients." The smile returned to his eyes. "If they're coming back, you know they're having a good time."

"And all the... participants, we do this together? Is that safe?"

"For you? Absolutely. Trust me, Claire, you're going to have fun. A lot of fun." His eyes dropped to the designer handbag in the seat next to her. "Did you bring the deposit?"

"Yes." Her hand dropped to her bag. "It's a lot."

Ivan spread his hands. "If you want a five-star experience, you can't expect it to be cheap."

"And it is? Five-star, I mean. I don't know where—"

"You'll be sent a location and time to meet our vehicle twenty-four hours before your experience begins," Ivan said. "Be there at the exact time. Do not be late, or you forfeit your deposit and your reservation."

Twenty-four hours before the hunt? That meant he had a house or a lodge somewhere. Maybe Baojia could find the property records.

"Should I go back to the city?" she asked. "Until then? Or will it—?"

"No." Ivan shook his head. "Unless you have access to a helicopter, I'd suggest staying local. It's not going to be much longer." He looked around the bar. "I know this town doesn't have the most... ideal accommodations, but I can offer some suggestions if you like."

Claire lifted her chin. She wasn't a child. "I can manage. I'm not helpless."

Ivan smiled. "I should hope not. Maybe after this, you'll be able to tap into even more of that predatory nature."

She smiled and bit the corner of her lip, showing just a hint of fang again. "And you'll be there for the... experience?"

He looked her up and down. "I'll make a point of it. Sometimes after this type of thing, it's hard to know what to do with all your energy."

She locked her eyes with his. "I can imagine." She imagined sex with Carwyn to stimulate her body into growing aroused. Ivan had to believe her attraction or she was sunk.

There, just a hint of her amnis woke up and teased him. He caught it and a slow smile took over his face. "I do look forward to getting to know you more, Claire." He glanced at her handbag again. "But I do need that deposit."

"Of course." Keeping her eyes on Ivan, she slid her hand into her purse and took the fat envelope of cash Baojia had provided. She passed it to Ivan under the table and let his fingers brush across her knee when he took it.

She didn't gag or snarl. Success.

"I have to ask," Ivan said. "How did you hear about our little happening in the woods?"

"Oh, I was at a party and I heard a rumor from someone who worked for... I don't know who runs San Francisco, but she worked for her. I think it's a her anyway. This girl was talking about..." She dropped her voice again. "Something about a weed farm? Is that right?"

Ivan narrowed his eyes but said nothing.

Claire continued to prattle. "Anyway, this girl was just chatting up this guy and telling him about this... thing at work, but she said she wasn't supposed to say anything, which..." She rolled her eyes. "Why are you blabbing about it at a party then, you know? Anyway, that's where I heard your name, and then I asked Lee about you, because... Well, Lee knows all the fun people in the city, doesn't he? And he'd just heard rumors, but he seemed pretty excited about it, and he said he knew a few people..." She tiptoed her fingers over to Ivan's hand and teased his still fingers. "...who knew you."

Ivan made a show of smiling politely, but the smile didn't reach his eyes. Oh, he did not like people knowing about his business. Brigid had a feeling that if Ivan didn't need the exorbitant amount of money he'd demanded for the hunt, he'd never have returned Lee's call.

When Ivan remained silent, Claire started talking again. "So Lee knew a few fun people who'd gone on one of your excursions and had *really* good craic." Claire shrugged. "I told him I wanted in." She let her eyes turn predatory again. "I mean... I've been traveling, trying to get in touch with my *true* nature, you know what I mean?" Brigid tried to channel a socialite at a wellness retreat. "I mean... What does it all *mean*? I've been alive for..." She caught herself, careful not to give too much away. "A while. Shouldn't it be more exciting?" She let her eyes go a little wild. "Shouldn't it be *more*?"

She must have passed the interrogation, because the smile returned to Ivan's eyes.

"Claire," he said, "you've come to exactly the right place."

TWENTY-FIVE

Carwyn watched Brigid from a distance. They'd said their goodbyes hours before since from the time she met Ivan to the time Ivan was dead, Brigid needed to remain Claire McKee. She walked to the car and driver they'd hired from San Francisco and entered the vehicle, which backed out and departed the parking lot.

"Where did you arrange for her to stay?" Carwyn asked Baojia.

Baojia put down his binoculars. It had taken an effort to keep the vampire in the car when Ivan appeared. "There's a private lodge north of town that's vampire friendly."

"Lovely. Doesn't surprise me that our type likes this place." With the narrow streets and beautifully preserved Victorian homes that populated the old lumber town, it had a historic feel.

"She's going to email us?" Baojia asked.

"She can't use any voice command if someone might overhear. She said she'd send a message via the driver. Supposed to meet him at a gas station near Redwood Highway and West Street."

"I know where that is." He glanced at Carwyn. "You going crazy yet?"

"Are you?" Even Carwyn had to hold back from bursting out of the car when he saw Ivan, and he didn't have half the history that Baojia did. "If we kill him now—"

"Then we don't get the participants, and there will likely be newborn vampires out there, rampaging throughout the Pacific Northwest with no guidance and no idea of what they are, wreaking havoc in Katya's territory." Baojia sounded bored. "I got the memo from my boss."

"Do you ever wish you didn't have one?" Carwyn asked. "You have enough of a reputation to be independent now. Have you thought about it?"

Baojia looked amused. "You do know I'm not nearly as old as you are, right? I haven't exactly had time to accumulate a vast fortune of a thousand years or so, my wife was a newspaper reporter when she was human, and I have two kids who are probably going to want to go to college someday."

"Oh." That hadn't occurred to him. "So you're saying—"

"I need a paycheck, Carwyn. And Katya pays well for skills that don't exactly have much use outside the military."

"Well, I suppose that makes sense then."

"Yep." He tapped the driver's seat with his right hand. "Juan, let's head out to that gas station and wait for the driver." He sat back in the seat and put on his seat belt. "Plus I don't mind being part of a power structure as long as I can respect it. Katya isn't my friend or my sire, but I respect her and I like the way she runs things. Summer is a prime example."

"So she's turning her?"

"Oh, it was done last night."

Carwyn let out a long breath. "And the Mackenzies?"

"They left, and they were not happy." He glanced at Carwyn. "She'll be fine. Jamie and Ross are going to get home and Logan Mackenzie is going to smack them around for letting someone else turn his granddaughter, but Summer will be fine."

"She'll be Katya's."

Baojia shrugged. "She's a good sire. And the girl will gain some independence from her family. In a hundred years, if she wants to transfer her aegis to them, Katya won't say no. At that point, it'll be an alliance the Mackenzies will likely welcome. Good for everyone."

"Her parents are human."

"And they're welcome to visit anytime." Baojia looked at him. "I promise I'll keep an eye on her if that will ease your mind. Natalie and I both will; you know that. She's a smart young woman. She'll take a leave of absence from school, probably transfer to Humboldt after that, study forestry or whatever environmental science she was studying in Seattle, and eventually get a job with one of Katya's green-energy companies. Or she'll end up being a kick-ass soldier and train with me." He patted Carwyn's knee. "Her life isn't over. It's just beginning."

"You were manic about Natalie remaining human. Why are you so casual about this?"

Baojia frowned. "Natalie was forced to turn when we had two small children and she was diagnosed with cancer. It's nothing like Summer's situation."

"I suppose not." Something about the whole business still

bothered Carwyn. "Do you think she'll ever see her young man again?"

Baojia didn't answer directly. He stared at the lights of the highway as they drove north. "Life is long," he said. "Anything is possible."

SUMMER WOKE IN THE DARKNESS, surrounded by water, a pair of hands immediately cradling her face.

"Shhhhh." Katya, her fangs gleaming in the low light from a lamp near the doorway. "I have you. Relax." She stroked her forehead. "Relax."

Her whole body hurt except for the parts that were underwater. She flashed back to the pond behind her grandfather's house and the cool relief of plunging into the shaded depths.

"I'm a vampire now?" She knew the answer already. She could feel the pain in her jaw and taste her blood where her fangs nicked her lips.

Katya brushed her hair back from her forehead. "Are you hungry, love?"

"My throat is burning." Tears ran down her cheeks. "It hurts."

"Shhhhh." She held Summer to her chest, her cheek pressed against the vampire's cool skin. "You're young and *very* strong right now. But your control will need tempering." She snapped her fingers toward a dark corner, and another vampire appeared from the shadows. "Bring Summer her first blood."

She closed her eyes and focused on the feeling of the

water that danced along her skin. She felt high, euphoric, but still her throat burned.

The blood hunger raged when she scented the human nearby, and a high whine escaped from her throat. "Katya?" She started to panic.

"My love, you have to learn control, and I have always believed that it's best learned early and not late. I will be with you." She stroked Summer's cheek. "Do you trust me?"

"Yes." She loved Katya. Loved her with an intensity she didn't quite understand. But if Katya asked her to do anything in that moment, Summer would have said yes.

"We saved one of the guards for you," Katya said. "From the farm, remember? One of the men who hurt your Daniel. What was his name again?"

Her fangs shot down, slicing her lips. "Ricky."

"Yes. We saved Ricky for you."

"No, fuck *you*!" A voice shouted in the hallway. "Fuck all you fuckers! Let me go!"

The door opened and the man was thrown in. He was stripped down to his underwear and a white T-shirt. His long hair was a tangled mess around his face. He smelled of panic and sweat, and his blood called to her.

Katya rose and held out her hand. "Come, Summer."

She realized she was wearing a cool white shift soaked in water. As she rose out of the large bathtub, her whole body ached, but she knew the solution. She knew what would make her feel better.

Ricky scrambled to the corner of the room and held out his hands when the white apparition stood over him. "No." He sniveled. "No, please—"

He said nothing more because Summer was at his vein.

All the human's muscles were useless against her new strength. She cracked his neck with one twist and his body went limp. His blood ran down her throat, and Summer nearly wept with relief.

Katya pulled her away when the man's pulse began to flutter. "Release."

With effort, Summer pulled back. "I want to kill him."

"So kill him." Katya handed her a knife. "But do it with control."

TWENTY HOURS after Brigid checked into the house in the redwoods, she received a note slipped under her door. She opened the wax seal and read the handwritten note on vellum.

Ingomar Club, tomorrow at midnight.

TWENTY-SIX

Ingomar Club, midnight.

It wasn't much to go on and they'd have to be careful following whatever vehicle picked Brigid up. Carwyn and Baojia had switched out the SUV for an old pickup truck that could have been any one of the hundreds that populated the mountain roads. The rest of Baojia's people would have to come up when they learned where the hunt was happening.

Carwyn kept his eyes on Brigid from a hotel room across the square. "They're late."

"Maybe they had other vampires to pick up," Baojia said.

Baojia was looking at his vampire-safe tablet. "I missed a video call from Natalie."

Carwyn looked over. "Do you need to call her back?"

"I'll message. It was probably a video chat with the kids before bed." He set it to the side. "They'll be asleep now."

"Why don't you go down to the truck and start it. Or at least stand by. If we're still up here when they take off—"

"Wait." Baojia jerked forward. "They're here."

They left everything but the radios and their phones

behind them and booked it down the back stairs to where the truck was waiting.

By the time they started it and turned onto the road, the black SUV was already pulling out of the square.

"Baojia..."

"I know." The vampire punched the gas and nearly collided with a homeless man who was crossing the street. Baojia swerved and kept the SUV in sight. The vehicle entered the highway and headed north.

"Do you still see it?" Carwyn felt disconnected in the truck. He wanted to be on the ground with the wind around him and the earth under his feet. It had been two nights now since he'd taken Brigid's blood, and though their bond was ironclad, it wasn't a creature of asphalt and mirrored windows.

Baojia flipped on his radio and spoke briefly into it, using a low voice. "Misha, we're headed off the 101 North going east on the 299. Keep in range."

A voice crackled back. "Done."

Carwyn looked at the radio, which was probably more useful in some of the heavily wooded areas. "Katya's driver?"

"He's coming with the rest of them."

There weren't many vehicles on the road. It was fall on the Redwood Coast, and fog blanketed the twisting roads. Carwyn and Baojia followed Brigid in silence, trailing the black SUV at a safe distance as it steadily headed north by northeast. Every now and then Baojia would pull off the road, wait for a car to pass in front of him, then pull on again, keeping the vehicle at a distant watch. Eventually the black SUV turned off the main highway toward smaller roads that wound through ghostly timber towns, and they had to drop back even farther.

"They're heading toward the Klamath." Baojia's eyes were intent on the road. The old truck bounced and chugged along, its dashboard shorted out from vampire amnis. "I'd bet you anything. We're gonna lose cell signal pretty quick. Hey, Cara?"

The voice command turned on. "How can I help you?"

"Call Mike N."

There was a pause. "Calling Mike Nelson."

The phone rang, and Carwyn asked, "One of yours?"

"Nope. He's an accountant. He's also a liaison of Katya's. He's immortal and Hupa." Baojia nodded forward. "We're headed into Hupa land, so I call Mike."

"They're the indigenous people here?"

"Yes." Baojia pointed at a green road sign. "See that? This road is gonna end in about five miles; then we turn north or south. I'm betting it's gonna be north—it's more remote, and a fire swept through the area toward the south last year, so not much tree coverage. Going north puts us heading toward Hoopa Valley and Klamath River country."

The phone picked up. "Baojia?"

"Hey, Mike, how you doing?"

"Can't complain, my friend."

Baojia kept his voice low and even. "Letting you know we've got an issue up around your mother's place."

"Understood." The sound of papers shifting. "Any of my people affected?"

"Shouldn't be. You can call Katya, she'll give you details. I have a feeling we're headed up into the backcountry though. Nothing happening in the valley."

"Anything on the big river?"

"Not sure yet. Probably not. I'm gonna lose connection here in about five minutes, but I wanted to give you a call."

"I'll let people know you're around." The line crackled. "—long?"

"How long?" Baojia frowned. "We'll have things resolved by tomorrow night."

Or earlier if Carwyn had anything to say about it. As long as they could get reinforcements in place before dawn, there was no reason that Brigid needed to stay in Ivan's company another day.

The phone was crackling again, and Baojia hung up. "He'll call Katya if he needs more information. There are landlines."

"Is Mike under Katya's aegis?"

"Technically." Baojia nodded. "But he's a lot older than her and prefers to keep to himself. She's smart enough to let him do his thing. Mike is not Mike's original name, but that's what he goes by now. Pretty sure he's related to Katya's sire somehow, but I'm not clear on details."

"His mother's place?"

"Hoopa Valley Reservation. He maintains very close ties with his people. We're gonna drive right through it if we go north." Baojia slowed and pulled over as the SUV in the distance pulled up to an intersection. He switched the lights off, watched the black vehicle turn left, and then pulled back on the road. "If they're watching behind, they still might spot us, but hopefully we just look like an old farmer."

As they headed north, the small highway turned into an even smaller highway that twisted through pine forests, dipped into small hollows, and wound along a flowing river.

The road was smooth, and the fog dissipated as they made their way down into a narrow river valley.

"And mobile service is gone." Carwyn looked up from his phone. "There won't be any until it's finished, will there?"

"Nope." Baojia frowned, studying the road ahead of him. "At some point they're going to turn on private land and we won't be able to follow, but at least we'll know where to start searching." He glanced at Carwyn from the corner of his eye. "I'm counting on your scouting abilities to be as good as you say.

"I found Summer, didn't I?"

"We had more than a little help on that one, don't you think?"

"Still found the girl, even in those woods." Carwyn stared off into the darkness.

These woods...

He wasn't being poetic when he thought of them as haunting. These were old forests planted long before humans set foot on this continent. They held secrets Carwyn couldn't even begin to fathom.

Baojia turned on a radio in a thick plastic case and held down a button. "Daxa, you there?" he murmured into the device.

A voice came back, but it was hardly audible through the static. "Hey —oss."

"You still following that SUV?"

"—got it. It hasn't turned off the main roa— long as it stay —" The radio crackled. "—ood, I think."

"Keep on it," he said back. "I'm radioing the guys."

"Understood."

Baojia flipped to another channel and held the handset to his lips. "Misha?"

A muffled voice came back immediately. "Still on 299."

"You're going to want to head up toward Hoopa Valley. Quick as you can. I'm following this truck, and I'm guessing it's going to make for the Klamath."

"East or West?"

"Not sure yet."

"Let us know."

"I will."

BRIGID COULDN'T SEE what was happening in the darkness around her because the windows of the SUV were completely blacked out. She sat quietly, trying not to be too obvious in her examination of the other riders in the car.

There were four besides her, a couple and two individuals. The couple was a man and woman: he was Asian and she was Black. They appeared to be in their early twenties, and they were dressed impeccably in current designer jeans, fitted jackets with fancy labels, and expensive, if well-worn, hiking boots.

Brigid smiled demurely at the woman, and the stranger smiled back, showing just a hint of fang and raking her eyes over Brigid's legs, which were clad in silk stockings under a short black dress.

Interesting. It was a cheeky sexual invitation from a stranger, but then, Brigid was getting the idea that the hunt was only part of the entertainment during this "excursion."

She shifted her eyes toward the other two individuals, a

middle-aged man with Latin features and another European vampire who appeared androgynous in the distinct way of some very, very old immortals. They were very pale and had a shock of red hair.

All the vampires, save for Claire, were wearing fashionable clothing with an outdoorsy feel, but something about the red-haired vampire unsettled Brigid.

Brigid leaned toward the woman. "Are we hunting tonight? I confess, I packed the things I bought to wear outdoors." Claire wiggled her foot, which was wrapped in a slick black heel.

"It's fine." The woman's amnis felt familiar and earthy. She flashed some fang again and tossed her long braids over her shoulder. "We flew in from Paris and came ready to play, if you know what I mean."

"I do." Best not to dash the woman's hopes when she might prove useful. "I wasn't originally planning this... type of thing. I don't even have the clothes for it." Claire smiled. "I suppose if I want to really get in touch with my roots, I could always hunt naked."

The woman and her partner laughed.

"So it's your first time?" He smiled, and it was the careful smile of a politician. Water vampire? Probably.

Claire nodded, letting the excitement shine in her eyes. "Yours?"

They exchanged a glance.

"Oh no," he said. "We try to do something like this at least every six months."

The woman said, "I think it keeps you healthy. We're not supposed to be tame, you know?"

"There's nothing tame about Ivan's hunts." The androgynous vampire spoke in a soothing, low voice. The menacing immortal turned their eyes on Brigid. They were nearly black and rimmed with thick, pale lashes. "You will find out who you really are."

"Oh." Brigid only mouthed the words; she was honestly taken aback by the vampire's demeanor. They were beautiful in the way a painting was beautiful, but utterly cold. Brigid tried to get a sense of their amnis but could read nothing. They were an elemental blank.

Powerful. She knew it without a sliver of doubt. This vampire was more dangerous than the others.

"I heard this was going to be the last excursion," the middle-aged man said quietly. "At least for a while."

"Ugh," the young man said. "That means Katya must have gotten wind of it. She's such a bore."

And this was why they needed to cut Ivan off at the knees. He'd just keep moving to different places and starting the same routine, over and over. This time he'd escalated from drugged humans to newborn vampires as objects of the hunt. What barbarous twist would he think up next?

"Is it just us?" Claire asked, placing herself in the ingenue position in the group. "Are we the only ones?"

The young woman spoke again. "There are probably some people already up at the lodge."

"The lodge?"

She nodded and licked her lips. "You're in for a treat, little one."

How many vampires were they dealing with? How many newborns? According to Summer, seven humans had disappeared from the camp since she'd been kidnapped. Were they all changed into vampires? Were there more?

The SUV swerved abruptly and veered left, bouncing over a rocky patch and making the young woman across from Brigid let out a peal of laughter.

"We're almost there." She was nearly bouncing in her seat.

One of the drivers—who were both human—exited the vehicle. She heard the hard creak of a rusted gate; then the SUV pulled forward. Another creak as the gate swung closed; the second human climbed in the vehicle, and then they were bumping along a dirt road, heading deeper into the hills and the dense pine and redwood forests.

The driver rolled all the windows down, and suddenly they were enveloped in the scent of pine and damp, mossy fog. Giant trees crowded around them and ferns and vining bushes tangled in the underbrush.

They drove for what must have been another fifteen minutes before a clearing opened up in front of them and a golden-lit mansion appeared, framed by giant redwoods. Made of timber and stone, it looked like it was straight out of a magazine for luxury mountain living, save for the lack of windows on the second floor and the subtle signs of light-proofing around the house.

A fire roared in the middle of an ornate stone hearth that dominated the clearing in front of the house. Brigid counted at least a dozen isolated shadows moving at a distance in the flickering shadows.

This was not some grimy pot farm in the middle of the forest or a makeshift hunting cabin; Ivan had built an immortal fortress.

And Brigid was going to destroy it.

TWENTY-SEVEN

They sat in their truck, staring at the gate where Daxa said the SUV had disappeared. After the gate, the forest became too dense. The vampire could see no roads from the air, and she hadn't ventured far enough to see where the road might end.

"I wanted to wait for you," she said. "I'm guessing you'll want to head farther in on foot."

Baojia nodded and turned to Carwyn. "What are you feeling so far?"

Carwyn walked across the road, toed off his shoes, and sank his feet into the ground. "Nothing so far. She may still be driving or she may not be in an area where she can put her feet on the ground."

"She has to physically be touching the earth for you to feel her?"

Carwyn hated the incredulity in the vampire's voice. "At a distance? Yes. Once I get closer, I'll just... know. It's like a pull."

Baojia grunted. "Like after you sire a child?"

"A little like that, but more subtle."

"Right." He turned to Daxa. "We'll stay here and wait for Misha and the others. It's four in the morning. We have less than two hours to find the place and take cover before daylight." Baojia turned to Carwyn. "We're not getting her out tonight, my friend."

Carwyn scowled, but he'd been gradually coming to terms with that already. "She'll be fine. If she wasn't, something would already be on fire."

Baojia turned back to Daxa. "Right now, you go overhead, look for any signs of a camp or a cabin or anything like that. It'll be fairly big. Of course, if they decided to build Hupa-style, we might be screwed."

Carwyn remembered the traditional houses that Baojia had pointed out as they drove through Hupa territory. They were cedar planks built wide and low, half dug into the ground and often blending into the landscape so perfectly they might be impossible for Daxa to spot.

"I'm betting Ivan goes for big and luxurious," Carwyn said. "That fits his personality."

"You're not wrong." Baojia nodded to Daxa, who took to the air. "Why don't you go and explore while you can? We need to get our bearings and then find shelter before dawn." Baojia turned in the middle of the narrow asphalt road. "We're in a very remote area. Even leaving the vehicles here could rouse suspicion if he has human security."

"So drive back and hide the truck somewhere, but I'm going in." Carwyn walked across the road. "I'll find you before dawn."

"Good luck."

BRIGID SMILED AND exchanged cautious pleasantries with the vampires in Ivan's lodge, but she didn't feel the need to socialize too much. Claire was a young vampire, out of her element and taking a risk. She wouldn't surprise anyone if she kept to herself a little.

The room she was shown to was an object lesson in vampire paranoia. There was an extravagant outer sitting room that hid an inner sleeping chamber that looked straight out of a science fiction movie, only with no electronics. It was a vault that could only be opened from the inside, complete with steel plates that secured a door it would take an explosion to bust open. Inside the chamber were luxurious couches and a large bed with linen sheets, a fully stocked bookcase, and a refrigerator packed with snacks and blood-wine.

It was meant to be reassuring. It was also creepy.

Brigid hadn't seen anyone in the lodge drinking that night, not even blood-wine. Clearly they were all saving their appetite for something more illicit the following night.

She unpacked Claire's clothing and put it in the drawers to kill time, then surreptitiously checked her electronics. It was as she expected, there was no connection at all. No Wi-Fi, no mobile network signal.

Except...

She knew Carwyn was close. Something in her blood told her he wasn't far away and that he'd been with her the whole time. She stared at the window in the sitting room, pulling up the solid shutter that closed over the clear window so she could see the forest.

The trees had been wreathed in fog when they drove in, but as Brigid looked past the clouds, she could see the waning moon that floated over the edge of the forest. It would be closer to a crescent tomorrow, and the woods would be even darker as they hunted. Even now, there were young, frightened new vampires who were probably in pain, confused and terrified over what had happened to them.

Brigid didn't want to lose a single one of them, but she knew it might not be possible to save them all.

But she could try.

A knock came at the door. "Miss McKee?"

"Yes?"

A steward opened the door a crack. "Pardon me for intruding, but the orientation will happen in the next ten minutes. Please join the other participants in the hearth room."

Brigid blinked. Orientation?

"Of course. I'll be right down."

She'd been hoping to sneak outside and ground herself, letting her amnis touch the ground where no one could see it, but she couldn't risk suspicion.

Brigid had less than an hour before dawn. *What would Claire do?* She wasn't the type to walk downstairs fully dressed and barefoot. She wouldn't even walk around her own house barefoot.

Unless...

Oh God.

Brigid quickly stripped out of all her clothes, wrapped a woven Turkish robe around herself, and slipped out of the room.

Ten minutes until the "orientation"? Well, let it never be

said she didn't commit to a cover, because this was something only Claire would do.

She walked down the central staircase and out the front doors, spreading her arms wide and dropping her robe at the foot of the stone stairs that led to the meadow where the bonfire was burning.

Brigid strolled, as casually and as confidently as possible while wearing nothing but the blond wig that marked her as Claire McKee, across the gravel path and toward the fire, closing her eyes and spinning over the grass as she turned her face up to the moon and let the fog kiss her bare skin.

She heard the murmured reactions around her. Small bits of laughter and more than a few indications of sexual interest. Some of the older vampires were probably rolling their eyes. Nudity garnered mixed reactions in the vampire world, with older immortals generally having very loose interpretations of what was and wasn't considered "decent."

No one said anything directly, assuming—as Brigid hoped they would—that Claire was a superficial, silly vampire, looking for attention. She played with her hair and spun in the moonlight, her arms spread out to the sky.

Oh God, oh God, oh God, oh God, oh God.

She was so naked.

Jesus, Mary, Joseph, and the wee donkey—if her Aunt Sinéad ever heard about this, Brigid would die a thousand deaths.

She focused on her amnis, driving it down into the earth so Carwyn could find it and pushing the bonfire away with her mind so the flames weren't drawn to her like they naturally would be. If anyone found out she was a fire vampire, it would not be good.

She cut her foot on a stone and pressed her blood to the ground.

As if a bell had been struck, every vampire in the clearing turned their attention on her.

THERE YOU ARE.

Digging his hands into the earth, Carwyn felt Brigid's amnis threading through the ground, over rocks and around roots, searching for its mate. It was her amnis and his. Their combined essence held together by magic and mating.

Carwyn felt the instant her blood touched the living soil.

He grinned. "Gotcha."

"MADAM?" A human steward held her robe out politely, his face a mask of propriety. "Orientation will begin in a moment."

Her foot was already healed, and the vampires around the fire were drifting away, no longer amused or attracted by her nudity. There were much more exciting prospects to anticipate.

"Okay." She allowed her face to beam. "I feel so natural here. So wild. There's just something about the trees."

The steward didn't blink. "Of course, Miss McKee. Can I get you anything to eat or drink in the hearth room?"

Claire waved a careless hand. "Oh no. I'm fine." She turned to the steward and dropped her fangs, hoping to get a rise out of him. "Are you participating in the hunt tomorrow?"

He blinked rapidly, but that was his only reaction. "As advertised, Mr. Balankin's hunts feature only newly-turned-vampire prey. Much more challenging, of course, than simple human targets."

"Just checking!" She slipped on the robe to hide her expression. It was what they'd suspected, but this was confirmation: Ivan was siring vampires to use them for hunts.

She walked to the house and schooled her reaction as she took a place next to the couple she'd met on the drive.

No one used their names, but Brigid had mentally named the woman Sultry Spice and the man Smug. She called the middle-aged vampire she rode with Grouchy Spice, and the old one, of course, was Scary.

Speaking of both smug and scary, Ivan was sitting in front of the massive fireplace that dominated the hearth room, speaking quietly with Scary Spice. Ivan's scarred face and growing beard contrasted sharply with Scary's pale, poreless skin, but there was something eerily similar around their eyes.

Interesting.

They clearly had a prior relationship of some kind, and Brigid made a note to watch Scary as much as possible.

In addition to her acquaintances from the drive, there were ten other vampires at the "orientation."

"Welcome to my home." Ivan's face revealed none of the tension he must have been feeling. "All of you have paid to come and experience the thrill of a true hunt." Ivan looked from one to the next. "To be who you truly are. To experience the primal, and to do it against worthy opponents."

The company remained silent, and Ivan continued.

"Tomorrow at dusk, your prey—newly fed on fresh human blood—will be let loose from their stables. You will hear a bell on the property, and then—only then—will you be free to leave your rooms. There are ten targets." He glanced at Smug and Sultry. "As I have been informed that a number of parties would rather hunt together."

He walked around the circle of vampires.

"There is no recording equipment here. No law that binds us. We are *vampire*. You may hunt however you like, but with only yourself as a weapon." He looked at Grouchy. "No weapons. No tracking devices. Only you." He looked at Claire. "And while the feeling of freedom is greatly coveted, I do recommend you hunt wearing sturdy clothes. There are thorny plants in this area, and too many blood trails could interfere with a pleasurable hunt for your fellow guests. What you do after you finish your hunt?" Ivan grinned at her, and Brigid had to steel her stomach to keep from puking. "That is entirely optional. I'm sure everyone will have energy to spare."

A few scattered chuckles around the room.

Brigid felt her stomach churn, but on her face, she tried to only show excitement.

"Tomorrow you will hunt as you should always hunt," Ivan said. "Of course, discretion is expected. Those who violate that discretion will face the consequences."

Brigid sensed Scary's cold eyes touch her, but when she looked at them, they were already looking at someone else.

Ivan clapped his hands together. "Now for a little housekeeping: What you do here is entirely voluntary, but none of the targets will be allowed to live past tomorrow night, so do not let their pleas persuade you. If you don't kill your prey, security will as they cannot be allowed to escape the property." He spread his arms. "For our own protection, of course. Simply realize that these new ones do not belong to you."

A vampire spoke from the corner. "But we paid for them."

"You paid for a hunt, Roland, not for a slave." Ivan chuckled. "There are cheaper ways to buy humans or vampires if that's what you're looking for." He smiled as if he'd just told a funny joke. "Now, as it's almost daybreak, I suspect all of you will want to retire." His eyes came to rest on Claire. "Especially some of our younger guests."

Fuck you, Ivan.

Brigid was so ready to kill this bastard.

Tomorrow.

Tomorrow.

TWENTY-EIGHT

Carwyn left Baojia and his people to their own devices and buried himself in a cave a mile from Brigid. He settled into the earth and dreamed of her blood on his lips and her body surrounding his flesh.

It had been three nights since he held her.

Once, they had spent months, even years, on different sides of the planet, but now even a few nights without her felt like cutting off a limb.

In the tremulous space between waking and sleep, he felt her over him, straddling his hips, her body bowed over his as if in supplication. Her ear was pressed to his heart and her lips murmured something against his chest.

"Brigid?"

His eyes fluttered closed.

Brigid?

Mine. Her whisper came to his ears like a hushed prayer. *You are mine.*

BRIGID'S EYES opened in the darkness and she knew Carwyn was close. She glanced at the clock on her bedside table. Six o'clock in the evening, twenty minutes before dusk.

She only woke early when her mate was near. She felt a tug of his amnis with hers. He was close and awake, already aware that she was too.

She rose and dressed in a pair of black hiking pants with various pockets, a slim-fitting black shirt, and a windbreaker that would hide the weapon Carwyn would surely be bringing for her. She pulled on a pair of sturdy boots that were brand-new and irritatingly stiff. Claire McKee wouldn't have anything but brand-new outdoor gear, and it was annoying as shit.

When she was dressed, Brigid sat on the edge of the luxury bed and tried to imagine how many other vampires must have sat in this exact location over how many years. How many missing kids did that represent? How many needless deaths?

Her rage built to the point where it was making her shake.

Calm, Brigid. Claire doesn't care. Claire is excited to hunt and experience a little bit of real violence.

Fucking Claire.

In Brigid's experience, the only people truly turned on by violence were either sociopaths or those who had so little experience with real violence that they romanticized it in their heads.

Her husband hooted and laughed at professional wrestling. Why? Because it was entirely fake. A play of violence so obvious in its deception that it became laughable. Something he could truly enjoy.

Real violence?

No.

These amoral vampires hunting innocent, newly turned humans were playing at violence, as if it were a game or a movie. They wouldn't be the ones cleaning the blood or dragging the bodies into the sun to watch them burn. They would never face the families of their victims or watch the slow descent so many of them would make as their lives were ruined by grief.

You can't save everyone.

She couldn't save these kids. Their lives had already been stolen, just like Summer's innocence and Daniel's dreams. But she could give them a way forward if they wanted it.

She felt the sun setting. She heard distant, desperate cries in the night.

Silent minutes passed while the new vampires were fed.

She waited.

And waited.

Then, through the drifting night fog that blanketed the mountain, Brigid heard a single, tolling bell.

Bong.

She sprinted for the door, only to be elbowed in the neck by another guest as they made their way at superhuman speed down the central staircase.

Brigid took a leap over the heads of two running vampires, swinging off a pendant lamp and dropping over them. She nearly knocked her own head off running through the doors, but she made it to the outside just in time to see the last of the newborns disappearing into the forest.

She ran straight for the edge of the forest and the waiting thread of amnis that called to her. She ran past Sultry and Smug, leaping over the bonfire and making for the trees. Just as she reached the edge of the forest, she saw a flash of red in the night.

There!

She veered toward Carwyn and caught him around the neck, swinging herself into his arms and crushing her mouth to his in a fierce kiss as he ducked into the hollow of a tree.

"There you are!" He bit her lip so hard it bled. "That's my girl. My fierce, magnificent woman!"

She pulled back and cupped his rough cheeks. "Ten newborns, they released them from the stable—whatever that is—just after dusk. There are fourteen vampires hunting. We kill them all."

"And Ivan?"

"Somewhere in the house." She shook her head. "We don't have time. Some of these bastards are very dangerous." She patted his back. "My gun?"

He reached in his pocket and slapped a .45 in her hand. "I brought your Kimber. I knew you'd be missing it."

"Oh, yer lovely."

"Just remember, knives before guns." He handed her a knife sheathed in a thigh harness. "The longer we're silent, the better we can sneak up on Ivan."

She gave him one more kiss and climbed down, strapping the bowie knife to her right leg. "Where's Baojia?"

"On his way. I met up with Daxa in a clearing not too far from here. He knows where the house is now."

"Let's just pray he gets here with reinforcements in time."

CARWYN SAW the first newborn before Brigid did. It was a girl who looked barely out of school with long, tangled brown hair and a terrified expression.

She was crouched in the hollow of a fallen redwood, and the minute she spotted Carwyn, she screamed and ran.

Brigid caught her at the other end. “Calm down.” She held up her hands. “We’re not hunters.”

The girl was crying, and bloody tears ran down her mud-streaked face. “I don’t know you. I don’t know what’s going on!”

“My name is Brigid. This is my husband Carwyn. We’re like you. We’re vampires, and I know this all seems crazy, but I want you to stay with us and we’ll protect you.”

She was shaking her head, clearly confused. “What if you’re tricking me?”

“I promise we’re not.”

Carwyn knew the girl was still on the edge. He thought about his own fear when he’d first awoken, though it had been a thousand years ago. He reached into his pocket and took out a hunting knife. “Here. If I give you a weapon, will you believe us?”

He could feel Brigid’s amnis beating at him.

What are you doing?

“If we were hunting you,” he asked, “would we give you a weapon that might hurt us?”

She was still shaking her head and crying, but she wiped her cheeks. “I guess not.”

He reached out and let her hand close around the knife. “You’re just as fast as we are.” It was a lie, but one that she didn’t need to question in that moment. “Keep up with us.

Defend yourself from anyone trying to hurt you, but don't hurt any of the other newborns."

"Newborns?"

"The hikers like you," Brigid said. "The ones at the farm."

The girl's face crumbled. "You know about the farm?"

"We found it a few nights ago," Carwyn said. "There's no time to explain, just come with us."

Brigid was already heading off into the fog-laced redwoods, running between the trees, drawing her weapon twice at what ended up only being giant-sized redwood burls springing from the base of the trees.

Carwyn took the girl's hand and held it carefully as they followed Brigid. "Do you know what any of the others were doing?"

"They kept us separate," the girl said. "There are these horse stables, and they boarded up all the windows and kept us in there. They..." She paused, and Carwyn turned to see her looking ill. "They put people in our rooms this morning." She held her stomach, the hunting knife digging into her skin. "I killed him. I think. Or he was unconscious maybe." She started to shake even while they ran. "I'm a murderer."

"You're not," Carwyn said. "You're a newborn. In any right world, this wouldn't have happened to you unless you wanted it and were in the care of an older, careful sire. I'm so sorry, my girl."

Carwyn climbed up and over another fallen redwood, checking inside the base this time. He helped the girl up and over the tree.

"Beth," she said. "My name is Bethany."

"Okay, Beth." He squeezed her hand and heard Brigid in

the distance. "I want you to hide in this hollow tree for a moment, okay?"

She frowned. "Why?"

A vampire came flying from the fog, bowling into Carwyn and knocking him to the ground. "That's why!"

"No!"

Carwyn ignored the girl's screams for the moment and focused on killing the linebacker-sized immortal who'd tackled him to the ground. The man was trying to get his hands around Carwyn's neck to twist it.

"Why...?" He snarled. "You're no newborn!"

Carwyn laughed, pushed the man to the side, and rolled to his feet. He gripped the man by the ankles, spun around once, and flung him into the side of a tree. The vampire crumpled like a broken toy, and Carwyn ran over and picked him up again.

"You're right," he said. "I'm not even close to being a newborn." He was tempted to leave the man incapacitated, but there was no luxury for that. This was a battle, and the man would only try to kill another if Carwyn let him live.

He quickly twisted the man's neck, and the linebacker went limp. He held his hand out to Beth, who was frozen by the tree. "I need the knife, Bethany."

She held it to him with shaking hands.

"Vampire lesson number one." Carwyn pushed the man's head forward as he groaned and tried to protest. "A broken neck won't kill us. Nothing much will kill us but fire—which we're not doing in the middle of the forest—or a severed neck." He put the hunting knife to the vampire's neck, sliced it through the spine and the cord, and let the body drop to the ground with the neck nearly detached.

Beth promptly turned and threw up a bellyful of blood.

"Sorry about that," Carwyn said. "Most of our lives are not this violent."

"Oh my God. Oh my God. Oh my God."

He could hear Brigid struggling in the distance, so he ran, grabbing Beth's hand as they headed for a small clearing. "Survive now," he said. "Fall apart later."

BRIGID HAD JUST DISPATCHED her second vampire and caught sight of Grouchy in the distance when Baojia caught up with her.

"Ten newborns," she started. "Fourteen vampires. Three down—"

"Six down," Baojia said. "Daxa already took out two. I got another one. My people are hunting right now."

She cleaned her knife on her thigh. "Have you found any newborns yet?"

"One, but he was already dead. I killed the vampire feeding on him." Baojia's mouth was set in a grim line. "I'm sorry, Brigid."

"Don't be sorry, just keep going." She turned and saw Carwyn approaching. "Send your people out." She spread her arms. "There are woods all around that house. They could be anywhere!"

TWENTY-NINE

Summer had never been around so many vampires in her life. The woods were teeming with them—so many that her skin was crawling—and then she realized she was one of them now.

Raven, the tall, statuesque wind vampire that Baojia had insisted on being her guardian, touched her elbow. "You okay?"

Summer looked up. "I'm fine."

Raven nodded. She was Black and her skin was really dark, but Summer's new night vision meant that seeing her was as easy as spotting someone in broad daylight. Her close-cropped hair was military short, and she had the bearing and attitude of a soldier like Baojia. She was both comforting and intimidating.

"Katya wanted me to take you to Ivan," Raven said. "Are you sure?"

Summer nodded. "Yes. I need to kill him."

Her nod was terse. "Just remember, I have your back. And I promise I won't drop you." With that abrupt warning,

Raven scooped Summer up under her armpits and took to the sky.

Summer was so shocked she didn't even try to scream. She sucked in a breath that rasped across her burning throat, and swallowed hard. Raven flew them up and over the trees until Summer could see a massive house in the distance with a large fire burning in front of it.

She felt a lurch of pure anger combined with a desire to weep. He was close. The man who tried to kill Dani was so close. Was she strong enough to kill him? Was she fast enough? Did she have the guts?

Summer knew that in this fight, she could definitely be the loser.

Was it worth it?

She remembered Dani's pale face in the hospital room, the tubes and lines running out of his body to monitor him and keep him alive. The pins in his bones and the bruises on his body.

Ice-cold rage filled her chest.

I'm going to kill you, Ivan.

"We're going to drop down on the edge of the clearing," Raven said. "I can already see Daxa overhead. It doesn't look like Ivan has any air support."

"I never saw him with any other vampires," Summer said. "He hired humans to kidnap us and run the farm."

"What the hell?" Raven scoffed. "So he's an idiot."

"Maybe." Summer tried to shrug, but with Raven holding her, it wasn't very successful. "Or maybe he just doesn't have any friends."

They dropped to the ground and immediately two bullets whizzed past them. Summer dodged to the right before consciously thinking, her ultrasensitive hearing homing in on the high whine of bullets as they approached. It was as if she were listening in slow motion.

"He knows we're here," Summer said. "Has someone disabled the cars?"

"He can always run," Raven said. "We need to find this guy. Quick."

CARWYN HAD COLLECTED three baby vampires who were trailing him like ducklings as he skulked through the foggy cathedral of cedar, pine, and redwood. He'd taken his shoes off, digging his feet into the earth and drawing as much energy as he could.

"We have to leave," one of the newborns said. "Let's just get out of here!" She was a young woman named Jade with large brown eyes that constantly scanned from side to side. She jumped at everything, completely overwhelmed by her newly awakened senses. "It's too loud here. I can hear them coming."

Carwyn frowned. "Where?"

Jade turned to the right and pointed. "I hear them."

Newborn instinct tended to be supercharged, so he pushed the newborns behind his massive frame and faced the direction Jade had indicated. He whispered, "How many, Jade?"

"Two." She gripped Beth's hand while the young man behind them, a tall, wiry Latino teenager, moved to Carwyn's side.

Carwyn touched his shoulder gently. "I can take care of

the hunters."

The young man's jaw clenched.

"Trust me," Carwyn said. "Protect the girls."

That seemed to mollify the boy. He nodded and dropped back.

Carwyn could feel the hunters now. They were good. They moved silently through the trees, darting back and forth, playing with his perceptions until they...

They disappeared.

Jade whispered, "Look up."

Of course. They'd sensed Carwyn's amnis and climbed into the trees to escape detection.

"Stay behind me."

"They're right here." Jade was panicking. *"Right here!"*

Carwyn looked up just in time to see an Asian vampire holding a long spear falling toward him. He pushed the newborns back and launched his body upward, propelled by the earth beneath his feet. He met the vampire in the air, his hunting knife already drawn.

He felt the spear enter his shoulder and roared with the burning flesh wound.

Surprise was the other vampire's only advantage though. Once they reached the ground, Carwyn dug into the ground and split the earth, swallowing the other vampire up to the waist.

Carwyn pulled the spear from his body and tossed it toward the newborns, hoping one would catch it. Then he spun around, slashed the back of the vampire's neck, and pulled, detaching the head from its body. A massive spurt of blood shot up, and Carwyn heard one of the newborns retching.

"No!" A scream from behind had Carwyn spinning again.

The hunter's partner flew down from her perch in the trees and flung another spear toward the newly turned vampires with a scream. Carwyn saw it and lunged in front of the group, absorbing the impact, but not before he saw the young man protecting Jade and Beth hurl the spear toward the hunter.

His aim was true, and his new strength forced the other spear through the heart of the woman with the long braids. Her beautiful face was twisted in rage, and she looked offended that the young vampire had wounded her.

It didn't matter for long though. She broke off the spear in her chest and tossed it to the side, lunging with fangs bared as Carwyn struggled to his feet. He'd taken a spear to the shoulder and another to his gut now. He was losing blood and more than a little grumpy about it.

The hunter was at the young man's throat, holding him down as Jade and Beth tried to pull her away. They might be strong, but they had no idea how to leverage that strength.

"Beth," Carwyn yelled. "Your knife!"

The girl's eyes went wide and she pulled the knife from her pocket, where it was still sheathed in the leather case. She pulled the leather off and stabbed the hunter in the back.

That made the woman let go and snarl at Beth, who backed away as quickly as she'd struck.

Carwyn used the distraction to grab the woman around the waist and fling her into a tree. As soon as she hit the ground, the earth swallowed her, only to spit her out almost immediately.

"Silly man." The other earth vampire hissed. "Did you think that was only your little trick?"

Carwyn felt the earth beneath his feet trying to open, but he forced his amnis down and pushed out, his amnis battling with the woman's as they circled each other.

The ground beneath them bucked and rolled, one energy fighting the other until Carwyn felt for Brigid's amnis, took a chance, and *pulled.*

ON THE OTHER side of the woods, having just shot through the spine of her second hunter, Brigid felt the pull and shouted at Baojia, "Carwyn needs me!"

Without another word, she ran toward her mate.

Baojia's people had spread through the trees, some soldiers picking up newborns and whisking them away from the fight as others stalked Ivan's guests, turning the hunters into prey.

Brigid raced through the trees, ignoring the sound of vampires in the distance.

Find the man.

She veered toward his amnis, entering a small clearing where Sultry and Carwyn were circling each other.

The woman turned to her. "You?"

Carwyn used Brigid's energy and her distraction to push his elemental power at the woman. The earth rippled, then folded over the vampire's feet, dragging her toward Carwyn, who waited with a hunting knife drawn.

"How the *hell*" —the woman screamed— "are you so powerful?"

Carwyn grabbed her neck, twisted, and slashed her spine with the hunting knife before he dropped her body to the ground. Then he turned to the newborns and said, "I'm really fucking old."

All three of the newborns were looking at Carwyn as if he were a cross between Captain America and Conan the Barbarian. Their faces kept switching between admiration and revulsion. It was an interesting mix.

The thin young man looked at the bloody remains of Sultry and Smug, then at Carwyn. "Will I be able to do that?"

Carwyn and Brigid spoke at the same time.

"Yes," she said.

"Please don't."

She shot her mate side-eye. "Eventually you will be able to control your strength like Carwyn, but you'll need to learn hand-to-hand combat."

"But really, all of you should endeavor to live a peaceful life." Carwyn looked at Brigid. "But yes. Eventually you'll be able to do this." He pressed a hand to his abdomen, and Brigid saw that he was bleeding badly.

"Just your gut?" She walked over, and the hand that went to his shoulder came away sticky. "They were a pair, were they? Shoulder and gut. Anything else?"

"Is he going to be okay?" a newborn girl asked.

"He'll be fine." Brigid could already feel Carwyn drawing from the earth around him, relieved they weren't in the middle of the city. Not that there was any good place to take two penetrating wounds, but her mate would heal quickly around so much thriving, open land.

She looked at the newborns. "There will be a vampire coming this way. He's Asian, looks around thirty, and walks like a soldier. His name is Baojia, and you'll be safe with him." She put her hand on Carwyn's cheek. "I'm going to find Ivan."

He nodded. "As soon as I leave them with Baojia, I'll follow."

"Good man." She pressed a fierce kiss to his mouth and ran back toward the mansion.

She'd counted at least nine dead hunters and was hoping that the rest had been dispatched by Baojia's men. She reached the clearing and saw the bonfire burning, the pale, red-haired vampire walking around the flames.

The fire reached for them, and the void of elemental energy around the immortal gave way to sudden, blinding clarity.

Brigid was facing another fire vampire.

She bared her fangs and stood on the other side of the stone hearth, watching the vampire through the flames.

"You don't need the wig anymore." The redheaded vampire rolled their neck in a slow, lazy motion. "Are you the Irish one?"

"I'm Irish." Brigid mirrored the vampire's movements, walking slowly around the fire and trying not to think about Ivan in the house. Or in the forest. Where was he?

"I'm not." The vampire held a ball of fire in their hand, slowly turning it in their fingers. "I do get asked a lot though. Must be the hair."

"Oh aye." Brigid pulled the wig off and rubbed her nearly black pixie cut. "The hair would do it."

"I came back to the manor when I realized what was happening." They looked toward the forest where the moon was rising over the trees. "It was foolish of Ivan to take the Mackenzie girl."

How did this vampire know so much?

They shook their head. "I think she reminded him of Constantina. Do you know who that is?"

"Haven't had the pleasure of chatting with Ivan much. More's the pity."

"That woman was always his weakness." They huffed out a breath.

"It sounds like you care about Ivan."

"In a way," the vampire said. "Why do you care about him?"

"He's hunting humans and turning them into vampire prey."

"And?" The vampire tossed the fireball from one hand to another before they changed direction. "What do your modern morals mean to us?"

Damn it, she'd been trying to play it cool, but she just couldn't take it anymore. "Who are you?"

The vampire looked amused. "Who are you? I tried to introduce myself when I asked if you were the Irish one, but you ignored me." They smiled. "Rude girl."

"I'm Brigid Connor, daughter of Deirdre of Wicklow."

The vampire smiled, their fangs thin and long. "So you are the Irish one."

"Who are you?"

The vampire touched their tongue to one fang. "I'm Zasha Sokolov, of course. Ivan's grandsire." They smiled. "So delighted to finally meet you."

Shit. Brigid didn't waste her time with pleasantries. She pulled as much amnis as she could from Carwyn, spread her arms wide, and rammed the fire toward Sokolov.

THIRTY

Summer watched Raven's blood leaking out from the slashing wound to her neck as Ivan stood over her body.

"What a shame." Ivan stared at Summer. "You've gone and ruined your complexion. And gotten this very lovely soldier killed as well."

Summer was frozen between rage and fear. She thought Ivan wouldn't be able to match her strength and Raven's, but she'd miscalculated her control and Ivan's ruthlessness.

"Little Summer Mackenzie," Ivan murmured. "What a beauty you were. Is this because my men killed your Dani?" He cocked his head. "I admire your spirit. That's what reminded me of her."

"I don't know what the fuck you're talking about." Summer didn't have her knife anymore, and the gun in her waistband was useless against a vampire. Ivan had taken her knife and left her with nothing but her hands and her fangs.

Every instinct in her newly forged body was screaming at her to run. Ivan was far more powerful, and Raven was on the ground, utterly still except for the single hand that was clenching into a fist, over and over.

"Summer, run," Raven whispered. "Get out of here. Find Baojia."

Ivan was sidling toward the door. "I'm not going to kill you, Summer Mackenzie. That would be a crime." He nodded at Raven. "So you can keep chasing me, or you can save your friend. Her spine is almost severed, but not quite. Put a little blood on the wound." He winked at her. "She'll heal right up."

"I hate you," Summer said. "And I may not be able to kill you, but this place is surrounded. You're not going to get away."

Ivan clucked his tongue. "So shortsighted, Summer. You clearly underestimate me. Just like my sire did. Just like the cartel did." His scarred face twisted into a sick smile. "You've gone and wasted your mortality on a losing errand. I'm already dead, remember? Just like you."

With that, he slid out the door and down the dark hallway, leaving Summer with Raven's bleeding body.

There was no question about what she had to do. Summer would never be able to live with herself if she let Raven die to exact vengeance on Ivan.

"Summer, run." Raven was utterly still. "Go get Baojia. Get him and tell him—"

"Shhh." She grabbed the hunting knife Ivan had kicked to the corner and fought her way through the distracting smell of blood everywhere. "Tell me what to do? Is blood from my vein more healing? Is my hand enough?"

"Summer—"

"I'm not leaving you." Summer held up the knife. "Tell me how to heal you."

"The hand." Raven's eyes filled with tears. "The hand is enough."

BRIGID AND SOKOLOV were locked in a war of flames, both pushing their amnis toward the other, circling the fire that was slowly growing larger and larger, burning the grass that surrounded it, searing the bushes, and pushing toward the trees.

She was getting desperate. If no one else was able to intervene, Sokolov would burn the world around her just to win.

"It's the question every *honorable* warrior must answer, isn't it?" Sokolov said. "How do you battle an opponent who will do *anything* to win?" They glanced at the forest. "I have no problem burning this forest to the ground and killing everything in the fire's path. Vampires, humans, animals. How do you feel?"

Brigid glanced toward the trees. The fog had burned away, and there was steam rising from the ground around her. The air was damp and the forest was green, but with enough power and enough heat, any tree would burn.

Sokolov clucked their tongue. "All those *good* vampires running through the trees. The baby vampires. The humans in their homes. Once across the river, this forest is a tinderbox waiting to be lit."

Brigid felt the flames against her cheeks. "Why?"

Sokolov shrugged. "Why not?" They raked a hand over their hair. "I discovered something quite unique over the years," they pretended to whisper. "The fire doesn't burn me. Isn't that delightful? I heard you have a similar gift."

Similar, but not exact. Brigid's own fire wouldn't harm her as it always exploded outward, but another vampire's fire could kill her as sure as a blade to the neck.

Carwyn, where are you?

Brigid and Sokolov were locked in a stalemate, the growing fire harming neither of them, but both unable to best the other. If nothing intervened, the clearing wouldn't hold the flames for long.

Just as Brigid was about to scream in frustration, a low drifting fog surrounded them. The ground beneath their feet rumbled and began to shake.

Carwyn. Baojia.

The water vampire couldn't draw water this far away from the river, but he could command the fog to gather in the air. The flames Brigid and Sokolov were trading grew smaller. Brigid's amnis began to wane as Carwyn's grew stronger. The trembling beneath her feet spiked and jolted her off her feet. She fell but kept her eyes on Sokolov, who slipped between a crack in the earth and released a bloodcurdling scream.

"Brigid!" Baojia yelled from the edge of the trees. "Ivan!"

She looked where he was pointing and saw Ivan walking out to a massive truck, clearly trying to slip away while the rest of them were distracted.

"Where's Summer?"

A voice screamed from an upstairs window. "Raven is hurt! I need help!"

Brigid ignored the cry for help and focused on Ivan. She ran toward the truck, snapping her fingers, but the air was too damp with fog. She reached inside her pocket and grabbed the lighter, flicking a flame and grabbing it with one smooth movement, swirling it to grow and grow until she could fling it at Ivan's truck. She aimed it toward the gas tank and tossed another to melt the front tire.

The truck jerked to a halt, and Ivan swung the door open and leaped away just as the fuel tank exploded and the front tire burst.

He rolled across the grass, reaching out before he came to a stop and splitting the earth under her.

Brigid wrenched her ankle in the gaping hole and fell forward.

Not good.

Ivan stuck his fist in the ground and twisted, trying to roll the earth over her to smother her.

Brigid grabbed fire from the still burning truck and pulled it toward Ivan, who forced an earthen berm to rise around him.

The sky overhead grew dark as Baojia drew more and more cloud cover to dampen the flames racing around the clearing, threatening to ignite the forest. There was rumbling in the distance, and Brigid knew the air around them was being charged by all the elemental energy flying around the clearing.

She glanced over her shoulder. Carwyn was battling Sokolov, Baojia was dampening the flames, and Brigid was trying to isolate Ivan. At this point, she didn't care who killed him, she just wanted the bastard dead.

So far, battling her attacks was keeping Ivan from opening a tunnel and escaping, but she knew that would only last so long. If she let up for even a moment, he'd open the ground and escape.

"Ivan!" Another scream from the mansion, but this time Brigid didn't ignore it.

Summer Mackenzie was stalking toward them, her red hair flying in the chaotic wind. Fog swirled around her as she emerged from the darkness. She saw Ivan in his small earthen fortress and looked up.

With the fury of the darkness she'd embraced, Summer reached up and pulled the clouds down as lightning cracked beside her, scorching the ground.

The rain came with a violence Brigid had never felt. The water that had built in the air around them crashed like a wave against the rocks. There was nothing graceful about Summer's attack, but it held the raw power of her grief; it was a downpour made of blood, tears, and shattered dreams.

The water filled Ivan's berm in seconds as the earth vampire struggled to break away from the earthen shield that now threatened to trap him with water.

Summer's bloody tears mixed with rain as she ran toward Ivan, scrambled up the side of the earthen fort, and began hacking at him with the hunting knife she carried.

The blade came away bloody, and Brigid knew Summer had hit her mark.

"Summer!" Carwyn ran toward the girl, spreading his arms and pulling Ivan's earthen fortress to pieces. The ground crumbled away from Summer, but she scrambled back and kept hacking at Ivan, who was covering his face and trying to dig into the ground.

"Not so fast." Carwyn pushed up and clenched his fist. "You're finished, Ivan."

The vampire scanned the clearing with sheer panic in his eyes.

Brigid looked for Sokolov, but they were nowhere to be found. Ivan's grandsire had fled, leaving the immortal to face his victims.

Brigid heard sobbing in the distance and three newborns were there, holding each other as Ivan fought off Summer's knife.

Their fight wasn't elegant or masterful, but Summer had pure rage and newborn strength on her side. Ivan's face was a mass of bleeding cuts when Carwyn finally pulled him into the middle of the clearing.

He looked up at Brigid's mate in panic. "Three against one, Carwyn? I thought you believed in fair fights."

Carwyn spread his arms, and the ground gripped Ivan up to the waist. Brigid felt the enormous draw of energy as Carwyn's amnis battled Ivan's.

"Summer, now!" Brigid pointed at Ivan. "Do it now! Carwyn can't hold him forever."

The newborn raced over, hunting knife held in an icepick grip. She crouched down, grabbed Ivan by the hair, and slashed the back of his spine with deadly efficiency.

Ivan blinked rapidly; then his head fell forward, and the pouring rain turned the ground around him to bloody sludge.

Summer fell to her knees next to the body of her enemy, then lifted her head to the sky and screamed.

THIRTY-ONE

Carwyn sat in Katya's house in Ukiah, his arm around Brigid as he drank a potent combination of bloodwine and donated human blood, complete with delicious, delicious thinners to keep it from coagulating.

Brigid saw him making a face. "Drink it. All of it. You still have two fairly large hollow spots in your person, and I'm not talking about the permanent one in your head."

"I'm drinking it." He wrinkled his nose. "But I don't have to like it." The chemical taint was why he normally never drank donated blood, but he needed to heal the stab wounds, and he didn't want to leave Brigid's side.

Carwyn and Brigid had bathed and changed out of their bloody clothes, Carwyn donning one of his most cheerful Hawaiian shirts to comfort himself, along with a pair of grey sweatpants and a pair of Bigfoot slippers he'd found at a gas station on the highway.

They were currently resting in their private sitting room with Baojia while the other soldiers in the house tended to the newborns and tried to explain what on earth had happened to them and why they couldn't just go home.

"So no one has any idea where Zasha Sokolov went?" Brigid asked, sipping her own glass of blood-wine.

Baojia shook his head. "It all happened so fast. By the time I finished dampening all the fire you two had stoked, Sokolov was gone. Carwyn had split his attention between fighting the Russian and you while you were fighting Ivan, trying to hold off Sokolov and still help you."

Brigid glared at him. "Did you think I wouldn't be able to handle Ivan on my own?"

"Don't ask me to ignore it when someone is trying to kill you, wife." He growled. "Being reasonable only stretches so far."

"It doesn't matter," Baojia said. "Sokolov slipped away in the confusion, and probably that's for the best. The last thing we needed in the middle of all that was a forest fire. My tracker found their scent, but that was it. They reached the river and that was the end."

"So the Sokolovs definitely know who we are," Carwyn said. "That's not great, but it's not unexpected."

"Why do the Sokolovs know you?" Baojia said.

Brigid wrinkled her nose. "We maybe interrupted their trafficking pipeline on the East Coast a few years ago?"

"Oh yeah. That would piss them off. Drugs or people?"

"People of course."

"Yeah, that'd piss them off." Baojia crossed his arms. "I had no idea Ivan was related to that gang. How the hell did I not know that connection? Completely explains why he always had access to money when he needed to start over."

"We'll deal with Zasha Sokolov in due time," Carwyn said. "There are other things to focus on right now."

"How's Summer?" Brigid asked.

Baojia shrugged. "She watched Ivan almost kill Raven—who's going to be fine; Summer did an amazing job with the triage—then she killed him using one of the most astonishing displays of raw power I've ever seen." The vampire frowned. "I don't know what to do with the kid. She's got the brains of a doctor, the skills of a soldier, and a hell of a lot of raw power."

"Some of that is probably purely related to grief," Brigid said. "The same way I brought down an entire house minutes after I woke up."

Baojia's eyebrows went up. "Exciting."

Carwyn squeezed her shoulders. "She always liked to make an entrance."

Brigid shook her head. "No. No, I did not."

"Oh right," he muttered. "That's me."

"I'm just saying," Brigid said, "that Summer's big explosion of power may not happen again for a long time. You might need to prepare her for that so she doesn't think there's something wrong with her."

"Good point." Baojia took a deep breath and let it out slowly. "It's not going to be easy for her."

"It's never easy," Carwyn said. "But she's under Katya's aegis now. That means you and Lucien are both nearby."

"Hopefully Katya will be a good sire." Brigid squeezed Carwyn's hand.

"Don't worry," Baojia mumbled. "I'll keep an eye on her."

"And I'll take that back to the Mackenzies," Carwyn said. "Thank you, my friend."

"Thank *you*," Baojia said. "You helped Katya get rid of a very nasty problem in her territory. She'll owe you a favor."

"The house," Carwyn blurted.

Brigid turned to him with a frown. "What?"

Carwyn looked at her, then at Baojia. "Ivan's house. It belongs to Katya now. If she wants to repay the favor, we want the house."

Brigid's eyebrows rose. "We do?"

"It'll give us a base here," Carwyn said. "It's isolated and self-contained. The forest around there is coastal, so the humidity is better for you. And it has lots of room if the family wants to visit."

Brigid's smile was slow and sweet. "Our own Cochamó home."

"And we'll put a memorial there," Carwyn said. "For all the lost ones we weren't able to save." Carwyn looked at Baojia. "It's just an idea."

Three of the ten newborns Ivan had brought to the hunt were killed in the fighting before Baojia's people could save them. Their families, tragically, could never bury them or know what had happened to their lost children. The weight of that knowledge tore at Carwyn's heart.

Baojia looked at Carwyn with narrowed eyes. "It's a good idea. You realize, of course, that you'd be asking for free passage in her territory?"

"Do you think that will be a problem?"

"Depends on how well the Mackenzies take Summer's decision to choose Katya's aegis. You have prior allegiance through your daughter-in-law."

And he also knew Logan Mackenzie well. "I'll have a talk with the girl's grandfather if it becomes an issue."

Baojia smiled. "I'll let you know what she says."

"Good." Carwyn had essentially agreed to be an intermediary between the two clans if it came to that. He didn't think it would.

Baojia stood. "I'm going to take off. My boss has sudden custody of nine baby vampires, and I have a feeling this is going to make my life interesting for a while."

"We'll make sure to stop by the house before we leave," Brigid said. "Say hello to Natalie for us."

"Will do."

They waited for Baojia to walk out of their quarters and shut the door.

"Katya will agree," Brigid said. "Because you've basically guaranteed that the Mackenzies won't try to start an argument over Summer's turning."

He scoffed. "Logan Mackenzie isn't the type to start pissing matches. I already told Baojia the same."

"But you'll use the promise of your peaceful intervention as a bargaining chip to get a grand house?"

Carwyn shrugged. "We have the van, but we're practically living on the West Coast now. It's better that we have our own place."

Brigid smiled. "I thought you loved the van."

"Oh, I do." He picked her up and walked toward the bedroom. "But I confess, my blushing bride, that I also love having a king-size bed."

"Is that so?" She toyed with the collar of his flowered shirt. "You know, I hadn't thought about that."

"That's because yer a wee fae sprite I can fit in my pocket, Brigid Connor." He tossed her on the massive four-poster bed and lifted an eyebrow. "Want to see if we can break this one too?"

"You're still healing, Carwyn."

He leaned over her and took her mouth in a long, luscious kiss. "I do love a challenge."

EPILOGUE

The red-haired woman stood in an observation room, watching the young man on the other side of the glass take tentative steps in the walker with the help of a broad-shouldered therapist. The patient walked toward a short woman in an immaculately styled red dress. Her chin, like his, was set at a stubborn angle.

He finished five steps and was breathing heavily with the effort. "I feel like a fucking old man."

"Language, *nene*. Just a few more please," the mother said. "A few more steps, and then we'll stretch."

The physical therapist was standing by the young man and adjusting his grip. "Let's go, Dani. You want to get back on that soccer field or what?"

"Fuck you, Greg." The young man huffed out as he took another step. "I told you it's called football."

"Dani, language!"

The physical therapist laughed. "It's cool, Miss Isabel. You know I like that attitude."

The young man's skin was still wan and he'd lost weight,

but Daniel Uriarte was clearly a fighter. She could smell the chemicals around her, the scents of chemical cleaners, the pervasive smell of sickness.

"He's working very hard." The man next to the red-haired woman spoke. "We expect a full recovery."

Natalie turned to Daniel's father. "That's wonderful to hear. When do you leave for Mexico City?"

"Next week," he said. "The doctors say he's stable enough for air travel. He hasn't needed oxygen for over a week now, and his ribs are completely healed."

"I'm so glad."

"Miss Ellis—"

"Call me Natalie."

"I spoke to my wife after your cousin came to visit." Pablo Uriarte was clearly conflicted. "Please know that Isabel was not her usual self after Daniel went missing. She wasn't thinking clearly, and she needed a target for that anger."

Natalie's eyebrows went up. "So she decided the right target for that anger was a traumatized young woman who'd escaped from her captors less than twenty-four hours before and had been tricked into thinking her boyfriend was dead?"

He looked suitably ashamed. "How is your cousin?"

Natalie took her time to respond because there was no easy answer. "Being kidnapped was..." She pressed her lips together. "Let's just say she'll never be the same. Like Dani."

"I am thinking about my son. I know this young woman risked her life to get them away from that farm, that she is the only reason he's still alive, according to the doctors who examined his shoulder. He asks about her all the time. If you could just give me a contact number for Summer—"

"That's really not a good idea right now." She softened her

voice. "You're thinking about your son, but I have to think about my cousin."

Pablo Uriarte clearly wasn't a man accustomed to hearing the word no. "All I'm asking for is a number. Surely she doesn't blame Daniel for his mother's—"

"It has nothing to do with Dani. Please know that. Summer loves him..." Natalie took a deep breath. "Summer loves him very much. But she's going through a lot right now. Her life has completely changed, and she's had to drop out of school. She needs time to heal."

Pablo nodded. "I do understand, but Miss Ellis—"

"Please call me Natalie."

"Dani has tried to call her so many times, but it only goes to voice mail. I think it would be good for them to talk, don't you? For both of them?"

Natalie looked at the young man who was barely recognizable from the pictures Summer had shown her. Daniel was intent on his feet, taking one step in front of the other, probably weaker than he'd ever felt in his life.

There was no way of knowing how he would react to Summer's choice.

"Maybe after a while." She held out her hand. "Thank you for letting me see him. Summer wanted to be sure he was recovering before she left."

"We'd like the same assurances for Daniel. He would like to speak to her, even if it's just on the phone."

"I'm sorry; as I said, it's not a good idea right now." She glanced at Daniel one more time. "Maybe after she's had some time."

"If you won't give me Summer's number, will you at least

give me yours? That way we have a way to contact you when we're back home."

Natalie offered the man a smile as she walked toward the door. "You don't know much about Summer's family, do you?" She paused at the door. "Don't worry. When she's ready, Summer will find you."

"Do I have your word on that, Miss Ellis?"

Natalie took a deep breath. "No. If you knew Summer, you'd know that no one makes her decisions for her. If and when she's ready, she'll call you."

NATALIE OPENED the door behind the driver and slid inside the sedan. Summer and Raven were waiting for her.

"How is he?"

"Walking now," Natalie said. "According to the nurses, he's making slow but very steady progress."

"But did you see him?"

"Yes. He's clearly still weak and he has to use a walker, but I can tell he's getting better. They're going back to Mexico City next week."

Summer stared straight ahead and nodded woodenly. "You talked to his parents?"

"His father." Natalie tapped on the driver's window, and the car started slowly inching its way through the hospital parking lot. "I think Dani's father knows that his mom was out of line, but I don't think he knows exactly what she said."

"You didn't tell him, did you?"

"Of course not, Summer." Natalie reached for her hand.

"He asked to see you, but I told him you needed time to heal too."

Summer tried not to think about the year ahead. She'd be going to one of Katya's homes in the Cascades, completely isolated from humans. Even their driver that day was a vampire, which was why none of the electric locks or windows worked. Raven had offered to come with her for moral support and also to keep her from breaking out of the car if they passed a particularly tasty-smelling human while they were stopped at a red light.

This was her life now.

The wound around Raven's neck was only a thin, wine-colored line now, and seeing it was one of the few things that kept Summer from walking straight into the sun most mornings.

She could still do something with her life. She could still have a purpose.

And eventually her father would start speaking to her again.

Eventually.

"Did you talk to your grandpa last night?"

"Yeah. Mom too." Summer blinked hard. "They're cool. It was good to see them. Mom was kind of emotional."

"Not your grandfather?"

Summer shook her head. "He was really… I don't know. Just kind of matter-of-fact. Like he wanted to say stuff, but he didn't want to start a fight or anything, you know?"

"Yeah, I know that kind." Natalie winked at her. "I'm married to that kind."

"Right." Summer was drawn to Baojia, and maybe that

was why. His personality did remind her of her steady grandfather, not her hot-blooded father.

"Your dad will get over it." Raven reached over and patted Summer's hand. "And hey. Remember, you have your family. Some new vampires aren't so lucky."

"Yeah." She squeezed Raven's hand. "I know. Thanks for the reminder though. Keep reminding me when I'm being an asshole, okay?"

Raven smiled. "Done."

Summer kept her eyes on the hospital as the driver pulled away, feeling as if her heart were stretching thinner and thinner every second they drove away.

Her skin ached. Her body ached. Her throat ached.

She wanted Dani, and she couldn't have him. Maybe she never would again.

"He asks about you every day," Natalie said softly. "That's what his dad said. He asks about you every day."

Summer blinked hard, but she couldn't speak past the pain in her throat.

"I'm just saying," Natalie said, "when you fall in love with someone, sometimes it doesn't matter much if they have fangs."

Maybe someday…?

Someday.

I promise…

I'll see you again, Dani. I promise.

Summer made up her mind then and there. Her life was going to be long, and she was going to live it to the fullest. After all, that was what Ivan had tried to steal from her: her life, her future, and her joy.

Forget that, Summer decided. And forget them. She was going to learn to love her life and her future again. She was going to love again, if for no other reason than out of pure spite.

She'd survive. She'd thrive. And somehow she'd be happy.

It was another promise, but this one was to herself.

The next Elemental Covenant book will be PALADIN'S KISS, coming Summer 2022.

Read more about Carwyn, Brigid, Natalie, and Baojia in the Elemental World series.

ElizabethHunterWrites.com.

FIRST LOOK: PALADIN'S KISS

Brigid saw the flashing blue lights in the side mirror, and her fangs dropped. She turned to her partner, who was driving the van. "I told ya it was a speed trap."

Carwyn glanced to the side, then the rearview mirror. "I was barely over the limit." He pulled over onto the rough gravel shoulder. "I'll do the talking, wife. You have a habit of rankling law enforcement."

Brigid glanced at the three unconscious humans in the back of their converted Volkswagen van. "Can't imagine why."

The back of her throat burned when she smelled the humans behind their vehicle. The men behind her stunk of alcohol, methamphetamines, and sour sweat. It was easy to ignore their scent, but the officers behind them?

They smelled like dinner.

"He's sitting on the hood of his car," Carwyn muttered. "No respect for the schedule of others."

"It's a tactic to make us nervous." Brigid narrowed her eyes as she watched her side mirror. "They definitely think we're carrying drugs. Second one out of the car."

"A camper van with California plates driving through rural Louisiana in the middle of the night?" Carwyn smiled as the man who'd been perched on the hood of the cruiser started to walk toward them. "I can't imagine why they'd think drugs were an issue."

She cranked down the van window and saw the outline of a second officer on the other side of the police cruiser, eyeing her window with interest in the flashing lights.

"Tá dhá cheann acu." *There are two of them.* She spoke in Irish, unwilling to give any information to the humans. "Second one is staying back"

Carwyn glanced in the mirror. "Noted."

"Má chuardaíonn said an carr..." *If they search the car...*

"They won't." He was wearing a black button down shirt dotted with blood stains. He carefully buttoned it up to the neck.

Brigid frowned. "What are you doing?"

He quickly folded a receipt stuck in a cupholder and fiddled with his collar. "Keeping us from having to incapacitate any more humans tonight."

She rolled her eyes and sat back, her eyes continuing to flick to the side mirror where it looked like the second officer had lit a cigarette.

Gimme.

Brigid stared at the glowing tip of the cigarette, the fire that lived under her skin pricking her to act; she pushed it back with practiced resolve.

Not tonight. Not here.

The human officer approached Carwyn's window, and the scent of his blood made Brigid's mouth water. She needed to feed, and not from blood in the drug-laced veins of the humans in the back of the van. This one smelled like he believed in clean living, mother's cooking, and wild game.

Delicious.

The police officer finally sauntered to the window. He was a human in his early forties, if Brigid was guessing correctly. He looked tired and a little worn out.

Putting in the hours, Brigid recognized the expression. Punching the clock. This officer was sick of night shifts and bored to tears.

He cleared his throat and spoke in a broad Southern accent. "Evening, sir. Do you happen to know how fast you were going?"

It was as if her husband turned to a pile of friendly jello instead of the mountain of muscle he was. "Oh, I'm so sorry, officer!" The Welsh vampire laid on a thick Irish accent.

Brigid snorted and covered her mouth, turning it into a cough.

Carwyn continued, "I do believe I was going eighty kilometers an hour, was I not?"

The officer frowned. "'Scuse me? Where y'all from?"

"Oh shur we're from a humble Catholic mission in Ireland. I'm Father Cormac and this is Sister Mary Clarence from the Sisterhood of the First Miracle in Kerry." He motioned toward her. "Sister Mary Clarence, wave hello to the nice Gardaí." Carwyn turned back to the officer. "She can't speak, sir, as she's recently taken a vow of *complete silence.*"

Jesus, Mary, Joseph and the wee donkey, she was going to kill him when this was over. Brigid leaned forward and waved.

The human frowned. "From... Did you say Ireland?"

"We're borrowing a vehicle from the parish in Los *Angeleez*, where we flew in from our last mission in…" He glanced at Brigid.

She smiled and pointed to her mouth.

"Fiji," Carwyn blurted. "We were on a mission to Fiji."

The police officer was already turned in circles from the accent. "I… I don't know where that is."

"Beautiful place." Carwyn nodded solemnly, his accent growing broader by the moment. "A beautiful part of the Lord's creation full of heathen…cats."

She snorted again, and covered it with a cough.

"Cats?" The officer asked.

"Yes, that's where we work, you see. In animal evangelism." A beatific smile spread over his face. "Working among the world's most vulnerable creatures to show the love of God to the voiceless." He nodded toward Brigid. "That's why my dear sister doesn't speak."

"Because of the cats?"

"Exactly. You don't eat the flesh of God's created animals, do you, young man? Ours is a strictly vegetarian mission."

The officer rallied. "Sir, can I see your drivers' license? You were speeding."

"Was I? Surely not." Carwyn fumbled for his wallet. "The sign said fifty-five miles an hour there, and that's nearly ninety kilometers and I was doing only eighty."

The officer frowned. "Right. You were doing eighty in a fifty-five."

"But eighty is below ninety, so I don't see how I could be speeding."

Brigid could see the police officer doing the math in his head. "I don't… I'm not sure what you're used to—"

"I'm a law abiding man, sir. A servant of God and the church."

Brigid's skin prickled when one of the humans in the back shifted his arm. The windows may have been curtained, but all the officer would have to do is look back and the three bloody and crumbled men would be visible.

Carwyn said, "We're trying to reach our new mission in New Orleans, you see. There's a pack of feral dogs roaming the city that needs to know the Lord. Are you a Christian man, officer?"

The man stammered. "Of course I am. I mean... I guess it's been a while—"

"Perhaps the Lord brought you to me and my dear Sister Mary Clarence tonight. Do you need to unburden your heart? Perhaps call your mother or grandmother? I have a mobile phone here and we can do that. Can I pray for you Officer... I'm sorry, what is your name sir? We could say a prayer right now. Together."

"Okay, just slow down." The police officer let out a nervous laugh and patted the side of the vehicle. "There's your... blessing. Okay?" He stepped away. "Y'all keep it nice and below fifty-five, you'll make it to New Orleans nice and safe. Take the warning; keep it slow."

Go. Just go now. Brigid braced for another round of blarney from her mate. Carwyn had a tendency to push a bit too far, which often caused more problems than it solved.

"Oh bless you, young man." Carwyn made his voice creak, just a little, even though the officer looked older than the vampire did. "Bless you and your cats, sir."

"Right. Y'all have a good night and keep it slow."

Carwyn started the van and pulled into the road, leaving the still-flashing blue lights in the distance behind them.

"Can we turn back to the interstate now?" Brigid asked.

"As soon as we drop off our young friends here." Carwyn glanced across to her. "I see that you've chosen to break your vow of silence."

"Mary Clarence? We're making Sister Act jokes to the humans now?"

"Sister Mary Clarence had the voice of an angel; it was a compliment."

"Evangelizing feral cats in Fiji," she muttered. "I can't believe that worked."

"It wasn't the feral cats, darling girl. I threatened to call his mother and pray with him. I could see the Catholic guilt radiating from him as soon as I called myself Father Cormac."

"Never underestimate Catholic guilt." She saw a sign flash by. "Take the next right." She glanced at the human who'd moved before. "They're starting to wake up."

ALL VAMPIRES HAD an element given to them by their amnis, the immortal energy that lived within them like a current beneath their skin. Her husband was animated by the earth, the foundation of his energy, his immortality, and his massive strength. He stood over six feet with shoulders the size of a minor mountain range, a shock of dark red hair on his head, and a short beard he'd been growing for over a year.

So it came as no surprise to her that in addition to the handcuffs she'd used to secure the men to the railing,

Carwyn had also buried them up to their waists in front of the sheriff's substation in Lafayette Parish.

They were definitely not wiggling out of that restraint.

The men all had signs around their necks that advertised their crimes. One read: Ask me about the stolen property in my garage! Another read: I stole the Bensons' car and beat up an old man. And the last one had a sign that read: I deal drugs to high school students.

Carwyn clapped his hands together. "And that's what happens when you try to carjack a couple of vampires."

Brigid saw the moment the humans began to wake.

They were bruised and had to be aching, but she didn't have any sympathy. They'd attempted to disarm her husband with friendly banter and false welcome at their local pub before sticking a gun to his back in the hallway, forcing him to their van, and trying to rob them.

"Hello boys." Brigid crouched down in front of the three men. "Remember what happened?"

What happened had been Brigid. The men didn't know that she'd followed them out and saw them pull the firearm. Unlike most vampires, Brigid knew what kind of damage a gun could cause on their kind if used in the right way.

No gun was going to end a vampire's life unless it completely severed their spine at the base of their neck, but a bullet wound anywhere along their nervous system could be catastrophic, if not life threatening. As best as Brigid could figure, amnis worked with the nervous system, so any major damage to the spine or a primary nerve could produce severe consequences.

She looked at the men. "You put a gun to my husband; that wasn't wise."

The ringleader of the group blinked slowly. "You have fangs."

"I do, but don't flatter yourself. I'd sooner drink from a sewer than your neck. I understand addiction—heroine was my candy—but that doesn't excuse the violence. Get help before you end up dead." She stuffed the number of a local rehab place in their pocket. "You don't want to meet me again."

He was still staring. "You have fangs."

"Jaysus." She stood and sighed. "What else should we do? Just leave them here?"

Carwyn was squinting at the darkness. "I think that's our only option. Do you think the alligators leave the bayou and go roaming?"

"Carwyn, if I have to deal with you chasing any more wildlife—"

"They wouldn't come and take a bite out of one of these two, would they?"

Brigid started to protest the men were fine, but she had to admit Carwyn might have a point. She crouched down in front of another one of the men. "Wake up." She patted his cheek, giving him a slight shock from her amnis when he was slow to rouse.

"Fuck." The man jerked awake. "Where the hell am I?"

"How far can an alligator travel from water?" Brigid asked. "We're not from around here, so I don't know."

The man looked around himself in a panic. "George? Buddy?"

"Answer the question." She patted his cheek. "Alligators. Are you in danger from them if we leave you here?"

The man they called Buddy appeared to still be sleeping,

but he spoke slowly, and in an accent that Brigid barely understood.

"Yeah, gators gonna be a problem all right," he muttered quietly.

Did she care?

Not really, but Carwyn might.

Brigid stood and walked back to the van. "He said the alligators wouldn't be a problem."

Her husband frowned. "Are you sure?"

"Very sure. Come on now; we need to get to New Orleans before sunrise." She walked quickly to the van.

Carwyn started to follow her. "We'll call and report them from the highway."

"Excellent idea." That should get the men arrested before the creatures ate them.

The last thing Brigid needed was another red mark against her soul. She may have been immortal, but eventually, she'd be judged.

And if it wasn't Saint Peter, she'd have to face Carwyn.

They were heading back toward the highway within minutes, and Brigid sighed in relief. No more local police officers. No more shady characters at darkened petrol stations. They were back in the world of the American Interstate system, replete with garish neon signs, brightly lit parking lots the size of football fields, and plastic-packaged food that smelled of chemicals.

"I need to feed," she said. She'd been half hoping the police officer wouldn't fall for Carwyn's friendly Irish priest bit and cause them problems.

No.

He hadn't agreed to be her dinner.

"We'll be at a safe club in two and a half hours. Can you make it that long?"

She cracked open a bottle of blood wine and drank. "This should keep me from any road rage incidents."

"Good, but crawl in back to drink that unless you want another encounter with law enforcement."

"Fine." She crawled in the back of the van and kicked her feet up on the bench. "Onward then."

"To the wedding!" Carwyn grinned as he took the on-ramp.

"To the wedding." Brigid took an extra gulp of blood wine.

To the wedding.

The *wedding*.

On second thought, maybe she should have stayed behind with the alligators.

PALADIN'S KISS is now available for preorder
at all major retailers!
Available August 23, 2022.

Looking for more to read in the Elemental Universe?

Elemental Mysteries

The four books that started it all!

The explosive international bestseller where history, romance, and the paranormal collide.

A phone call from an old friend sets Giovanni Vecchio back on the path of a mysterious manuscript he's hunted for over five hundred years. He never expected a young student librarian could be the key to unlock its secrets, nor could he have predicted the danger she would attract.

A Hidden Fire
This Same Earth
The Force of Wind
A Fall of Water

Elemental World

Romance, intrigue, and political suspense set in the Elemental Universe.

Follow your favorite characters from the Elemental Mysteries as they hunt down a deadly vampire drug that threatens the Elemental World.

Building From Ashes

Waterlocked
Blood and Sand
The Bronze Blade
The Scarlet Deep
A Very Proper Monster
A Stone-Kissed Sea
Valley of the Shadow

Elemental Legacy
The continuing adventures of Ben Vecchio and Tenzin

What happens when a human raised by vampires teams up with an ancient vampire of impossible power, zero social skills, and an endless fascination with bright, shiny things?

It's very hard to predict.

Prequel novellas:
Shadows and Gold
Imitation and Alchemy
Omens and Artifacts
Novels:
Midnight Labyrinth
Blood Apprentice
Night's Reckoning
Dawn Caravan
The Bone Scroll

LOOKING FOR MORE?

Whether you're a fan of contemporary fantasy, fantasy romance, or paranormal women's fiction, Elizabeth Hunter has a series for you!

THE ELEMENTAL MYSTERIES

Discover the series that has millions of vampire fans raving! Immortal book dealer Giovanni Vecchio thought he'd left the bloody world of vampire politics behind when he retired as an assassin, but a chance meeting at a university pulls student librarian Beatrice De Novo into his orbit. Now temptation lurks behind every dark corner as Vecchio's growing attachment to Beatrice competes with a series of clues that could lead to a library lost in time, and a powerful secret that could reshape the immortal world.

Ebook/Audiobook/Paperback

THE CAMBIO SPRINGS MYSTERIES

Welcome to the desert town of Cambio Springs where the water is cool, the summers sizzle, and all the residents wear fur, feathers, or snakeskin on full moon nights. In a world of cookie-cutter shifter romance, discover a series that has reviewers raving. Five friends find themselves at a crossroads in life; will the tangled ties of community and shared secrets be their salvation or their end?

Ebook/Audiobook/Paperback

THE IRIN CHRONICLES

"A brilliant and addictive romantic fantasy series." Hidden at the crossroads of the world, an ancient race battles to protect humanity, even as it dies from within. A photojournalist tumbles into a world of supernatural guardians protecting humanity from the predatory sons of fallen angels, but will Ava and Malachi's attraction to each other be their salvation or their undoing?

Ebook/Audiobook/Paperback

GLIMMER LAKE

Delightfully different paranormal women's fiction! Robin, Val, and Monica were average forty-something moms when a sudden accident leaves all three of them with psychic abilities they never could have predicted! Now all three are seeing things that belong in a fantasy novel, not their small mountain town. Ghosts, visions, omens of doom. These friends need to stick together if they're going to solve the mystery at the heart of Glimmer Lake.

Ebook/Audiobook/Paperback

And there's more! Please visit ElizabethHunterWrites.com to sign up for her newsletter or read more about her work.

ACKNOWLEDGMENTS

I'm so grateful that I'm able to live in a state that has such diversity of people, landscape, languages, and origins. I would not be the writer I am if I had not been born in California, and I remain grateful to the people of my home state for their character, vision, and ambition.

The forests of Northern California are a place where I grew up wandering in the woods, watching my grandfather fish, and picking blackberries on the side of the road. It's a complex, mysterious, vividly alive place and I was so fortunate to visit the Lost Coast during the research for this book.

I want to say thank you to the quirky and wonderful community of people who make this part of the world their home. This is not a community that asks to be in the spotlight, so I'm grateful for your welcome and openness. This book is richer for your insight and suggestions. Thank you for sharing your world.

Many thanks to my sister Gen, who bravely threw her clothes into a bag, grabbed the dog, and jumped in the car with me for a very last minute road trip. You're a champion and I love you.

And to Chidi, the adventure doggo. We couldn't have done it without you.

ABOUT THE AUTHOR

ELIZABETH HUNTER is a nine-time *USA Today* and international best-selling author of romance, contemporary fantasy, and paranormal mystery. Based in Central California and Addis Ababa, she travels extensively to write fantasy fiction exploring world mythologies, history, and the universal bonds of love, friendship, and family. She has published over forty works of fiction and sold over a million books worldwide. She is the author of the Glimmer Lake series, Love Stories on 7th and Main, the Elemental Legacy series, the Irin Chronicles, the Cambio Springs Mysteries, and other works of fiction.

ElizabethHunterWrites.com

ALSO BY ELIZABETH HUNTER

The Elemental Mysteries

A Hidden Fire

This Same Earth

The Force of Wind

A Fall of Water

The Stars Afire

The Elemental World

Building From Ashes

Waterlocked

Blood and Sand

The Bronze Blade

The Scarlet Deep

A Very Proper Monster

A Stone-Kissed Sea

Valley of the Shadow

The Elemental Legacy

Shadows and Gold

Imitation and Alchemy

Omens and Artifacts

Obsidian's Edge (anthology)

Midnight Labyrinth

Blood Apprentice

The Devil and the Dancer

Night's Reckoning

Dawn Caravan

The Bone Scroll

Pearl Sky (December 2022)

The Elemental Covenant

Saint's Passage

Martyr's Promise

Paladin's Kiss

The Irin Chronicles

The Scribe

The Singer

The Secret

The Staff and the Blade

The Silent

The Storm

The Seeker

Glimmer Lake

Suddenly Psychic

Semi-Psychic Life

Psychic Dreams

Moonstone Cove

Runaway Fate

Fate Actually

Fate Interrupted

Vista de Lirio

Double Vision

Mirror Obscure

Trouble Play

The Cambio Springs Series

Long Ride Home

Shifting Dreams

Five Mornings

Desert Bound

Waking Hearts

Linx & Bogie Mysteries

A Ghost in the Glamour

A Bogie in the Boat

Contemporary Romance

The Genius and the Muse

7th and Main

INK

HOOKED

GRIT